back in time, many centuries ago, Ten...
the wilderness to sell his soul to Sata...
...me the first of the Ice People. At that ti...
with Satan. In return for worldly gain,
...child from each generation of his descen...
...Devil and perform his evil deeds. Those
...gnised by their amber cat-like eyes and
...ers of witchcraft and wizardry. In time, ...
...supernatural powers, the like of whi...
...r seen.
...h a kettle, Tengel the Evil had stirred a s...
...ilingly summoned the Prince of Darkn...
...ed in a secret place. Until the kettle w...
...e would continue to torment his descen...
...his then is the Legend of the Ice Peopl...
...ther or not it is true. However, sometin...
...ury, a 'chosen one' of the Ice People wa...
...eadly curse and tried to use his power...
...s instead of evil. He became known a...
...this is the story of his descendants – b...
...t is about the women in his family.

and histor...
C. St Jean...

Far
into
beca
pact
one
the
reco
pow
with
neve

I
unfa
buri
curs

T
whe
cent
the
deed
and
all,

The Legend of the Ice People

Book 5

Mortal Sin

MARGIT SANDEMO

Translated from the Swedish
by Gregory Herring and Angela Cook

Tagman

The Legend of the Ice People

Mortal Sin

The original Norwegian version was published in 1982 under the title
Sagan om Isfolket 5: Dødssynden by Bladkompaniet, Oslo, Norway

First published in Great Britain in paperback in November 2008
by Tagman Worldwide Ltd in The Tagman Press imprint.

Tagman Worldwide Ltd
Media House
Burrel Road, St Ives, Huntingdon,
Cambridgeshire, PE27 3LE
Tel: 0845 644 4186
Fax: 0845 644 4187
www.tagmanpress.co.uk
email: editorial@tagmanpre

Published by agreement witl Schibsted Forlag ... copyright to the ...ks
shall be and remain the prop ...tor's subject only to the ... granted.

Copyright © by Margit Sand ...mo 1982.
English translation © Greg ...ing 2008.

The right of Margit Sandem ...to be identified as the a ...s work has been
asserted by her in accordanc ...th the Copyright, Design & Patents Act 1999.

ISBN: Paperback 978-1-903571-85-9
A CIP catalogue record for this book is available from the British Library

Text & Cover Design: Richard Legg
Translation: Gregory Herring and Angela Cook

Printed by CLE Print Ltd, St Ives, Cambs, PE27 3LE, UK

Tagman www.tagmanpress.co.uk

This first English translation of *The Legend of the Ice People*
is dedicated with love and gratitude to the memory
of my dear late husband Asbjorn Sandemo,
who made my life a fairy tale

THE ICE PEOPLE - Descendants of Tengel the Evil

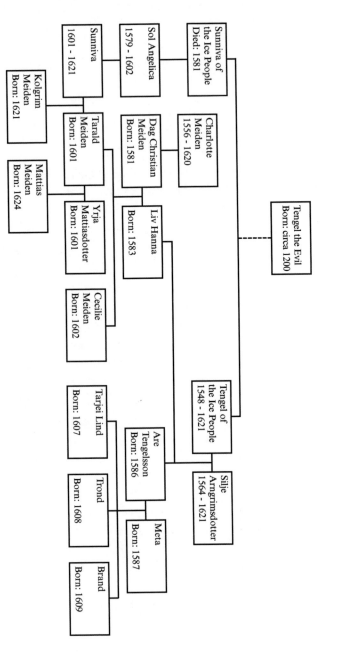

Chapter 1

In the deep mid-winter of 1625, Cecilie Meiden stood in the bows of a ship as it moved smoothly towards the entrance of the harbour at Copenhagen. Since leaving Norway, the vessel had sailed through much bad weather and was now long overdue. The early darkness of that February evening was already settling over the sea and the city and, despite wearing thick fur mittens, Cecilie was blowing instinctively on her fingers from time to time to keep them warm in the raw winter chill.

Not wanting to touch the tar-blackened timbers of the hull, she stood freely on the deck, shifting and adjusting her stance to the roll of the ship with the ease of an experienced sailor. It was wonderful to feel the fresh sea air on her face and standing there alone, as far forward in the ship as she could, made her feel as though the whole world belonged to her.

As she gazed towards the harbour, however, she found herself thinking back over the past few months and years, and some pangs of unease crept into her thoughts. How could she have made such a mess of her life? Surely it had not all been her fault?

For what must have been the hundredth time she told herself she could not bear to see Alexander Paladin ever again.

She knew it would be impossible for her to look him in the eye without revealing what she knew of his unspoken vice. In fact it had come as a big surprise to her that knowing his secret could cause her so much anguish. This was perhaps because she had never fully admitted to herself just how much Alexander meant to her.

As the ship began to slow and to manoeuvre towards its moorings, she found herself recalling their first fateful meeting. At the time she had been frightened, unsure of herself and saddened by the news that had just arrived from home about the effects on her family of the recent plague. She had recently arrived as a total stranger at the Court in faraway Denmark. Then, by mistake, Alexander Paladin had entered her room and in that short meeting he had seemed to give her back the strength and courage to go on. She had liked him very much from the first moment and he had continued to support her in that small and difficult world that was always filled with intrigue and envy. Whenever he was near, her whole being seemed to fill with happiness.

One of the King's cavaliers, he was an unusually handsome man with obvious strength of character and an air of quiet authority about him; dark-haired, manly and with aristocratic features, he had a distinctive yet melancholy smile. And without her realising it, that unforgettable smile was to have lead so bizarrely to her downfall.

Alexander Paladin had always been reticent and reserved. He had made it very clear that he liked her – but nothing more. He had conveyed unmistakeably that he was a man she could trust, a true friend who cared for her. Why then should it hurt so to discover his secret? Shouldn't she of all people, a daughter of the Ice People and the equally broad-minded Meidens, be able to accept and understand it? Why should she be so disturbed?

2

It was during her home visit to Norway that she had learnt the painful truth about the enigmatic Alexander. The explanation had come from cousin Tarjei, a grandson of Tengel the Good and a young man already possessed of great knowledge and an uncanny understanding of human nature. And how had she reacted? She had been shocked and saddened. Perhaps that was only natural. But had she really needed to throw herself into the arms of young Pastor Martinius simply because his sad smile reminded her of Alexander? It had been uncanny how alike those two men were in so many ways.

Never before had Cecilie regretted anything as much or so fiercely as she did that short passionate encounter with Martin. How horrid, how repulsive it had been, in retrospect. Two people: both bitter, disappointed and alone; both desperately needing at that time to be loved or – to be more brutal – needing to be physically intimate with somebody.

In effect she had willingly allowed herself to be violated. Were she ever to marry, she would have to stand before her husband and confess that she was not a virgin. How would that unknown man react? Would he turn away from her because of her rash actions? Or would he understand?

Through the turmoil of her thoughts she realised the ship had come alongside and mooring lines were being thrown ashore. Although people at Court knew when she was due to arrive, she could see that there was nobody on the quayside to meet her. Even though they had been delayed by the stormy weather, from the vantage point of the castle it would not have been difficult to see that the ship had arrived. Now she would have to make her way there alone – through unlit streets, where all manner of riff-raff might be skulking in the shadows waiting to creep up on her. She looked around for someone on the ship who might accompany her, but in vain. So, grasping

3

her travelling case firmly in one hand, she took a deep breath, summoned up her courage and went ashore.

Beyond the bustle of the well-lit port area there were few signs of life in the narrow empty streets of the town, now that the day's trade was over. As she hurried onward towards the castle, Cecilie Meiden realised that she was afraid. Sol of the Ice People, whom Cecilie resembled in so many ways, would have looked on this as a challenge. Sol had loved darkness and turmoil. She would probably have liked nothing better than to meet some gang of ruffians intent on robbing her; they would have given her the opportunity to exercise her extraordinary talents to defend herself. Despite being a descendant of the Ice People herself, Cecilie had not been endowed with any of their mysterious powers. She had only her wits to depend upon.

But as she walked on, inside her mind she was still trying distractedly to justify her past actions to herself. She knew how a lady must conduct herself and her demeanour at Court had always been in every way perfectly ladylike. It seemed it was only when she was at home with her warm-hearted, loving family that she allowed herself to relax a little. But what had possessed her to hurl herself headlong into the Pastor's embrace? She shook her head, shuddering afresh at the memory and lowered her eyes, like a schoolgirl brought in shame before her teacher.

She was utterly mortified now over her uncharacteristic behaviour in the tool shed at the churchyard. Her only consolation was that it had been Pastor Martinius who had taken the initiative. If he had not put his hands upon her and whispered enticing words of loneliness and desire in her ear, then it would never have happened.

But she could not console herself that easily: she knew she had been very willing, so very willing.

During the first stretch of her journey through the narrow

4

streets that led up from the harbour, Cecilie suffered nothing worse than some crude insults from a pair of street whores warning her to stay away from their patch. She pointedly ignored their shouts and hurried on, but unbeknown to her, a greater danger was lurking at the end of the last street before Copenhagen Castle. She had to pass through an alley that seemed to her to be packed with a noisy crowd of wretches – vagabonds, drunkards, whores and criminals of every hue. In the middle of the alley they had built a fire of straw to warm themselves, and were busy cursing and blaspheming loudly over how unfairly life had treated them.

Cecilie hesitated, but she knew she had to get past – there was no other way. With her heart in her mouth, she hoped she would be invisible and walked on as fast as she could. Far up ahead she glimpsed the open square in front of the castle. Fires were burning up there as well, and she could see the silhouettes of horses and riders – life of a completely different kind. Although it was not far to the square, to Cecilie the narrow alley suddenly seemed like an endless road filled with anxiety and danger.

She almost managed to get past the fire and the raucous crowd without being seen, but just as she was about to heave a sigh of relief, she heard a lisping, fawning voice close behind her. Her back stiffened at the sound and her blood ran cold.

'Well, well! Look what we 'ave 'ere!' murmured the voice and Cecilie felt someone grab hold of her cape.

Turning quickly, she found herself staring into the insolent face of a man who was leering toothlessly at her. She realised at once that this was not a situation where the protests of a refined, self-confident young noblewoman would do any good. It was clear she faced two stark choices: to stand and fight – or turn and run. Quickly choosing the latter, she tore herself free and began running. Another man joined the leering individual and they began together to chase after her.

'We'll let you keep your virtue, gracious lady, just you let us take care of that case o' your'n,' yelled one of them, making a grab for her travelling bag.

Cecilie's instinctive reaction was perhaps characteristic in some ways of her more robust Ice People ancestors. Not bothering to point out that they were already too late to take her virtue, she swung the case at them with all her might. Made of wood, it struck the leering man with some considerable force and he tumbled backwards. Another man immediately joined the chase and Cecilie stumbled on ahead of them as fast as her skirts would allow, but she was no match for them and they caught up with her at the very moment she reached the edge of the wide, open square.

In the flickering light of the fires, Cecilie saw a group of soldiers on horseback approaching, but before she could cry out, one of ruffians grabbed her, putting his hand over her mouth, and tried to drag her back towards the alleyway once more. As he did so, his companion tugged violently at her travelling case.

Cecilie twisted her head free for a few seconds and managed a short muffled scream before the hand silenced her again. Hearing her cry and seeing her distress, several of the soldiers rode quickly towards her and when Cecilie's assailants saw the mounted men approaching, they immediately released their grip on her and melted away into the shadows of the dark alley.

'Are you all right, Mistress?' asked a bearded officer.

'Yes, thank you!' panted Cecilie. 'A thousand thanks to all of you!'

She was gasping for breath and her legs were shaking so violently that she was barely able to stand up. At that moment another rider reined in his mount beside her.

'Cecilie, heavens above, it's you!' said a voice she knew very well. 'My dear child!'

She lifted her eyes, and in the light from the fires she saw that the proud figure astride the horse was Alexander Paladin. She could not begin to describe the joy she felt at seeing him there. Gone instantly were all thoughts of his irredeemable secret; instead she saw only a dear friend, looking noble and larger than life, clad in shining breastplate, black cape, big knee-boots and sporting a large feather in his hat.

Her face lit up. 'Alexander!' she cried, smiling in delight.

He bent down and took her outstretched hands. 'Have you just arrived from Norway?'

'Yes. The ship was delayed and nobody came to meet me.'

'I did not know you were coming,' he told her, shaking his head. 'People at Court can sometimes be so inconsiderate.' Turning, Alexander instantly handed over command to one of his men. 'I must go with Mistress Meiden and see that she arrives safely inside the castle.' Dismounting quickly he handed his horse to the rider next to him.

'It's wonderful to see you again, Cecilie,' he said pleasantly as they walked towards the castle gates. 'Copenhagen has been empty without you. But how have things been for you?'

'Oh, Alexander! It was lovely to be back home for a while!' She then described in vivid detail what life was like at Gråstensholm.

When she had finished, Alexander Paladin put his arm around her shoulders and said: 'It's good to see that you are so happy, my little one.'

She smiled gladly back at him – then suddenly remembered again the terrible truth she knew about him. Sadly, she realised once more, his commanding manliness could not be hers. Without meaning to, she moved away from him very slightly and, perhaps sensing her thoughts, Alexander dropped his arm from her shoulders. In a strained silence, they walked past the guards and entered the domestic wing of the castle. When they reached the door to her room, he turned to face her and said very quietly: 'I believe you know?'

Cecilie nodded. In the glow from the lamps hanging from the walls his eyes looked black and filled with infinite sorrow.

'Who told you the truth?'

'My cousin, Tarjei. He is the one with knowledge of medicine – and is also very worldly wise. I have sometimes spoken to you about him.'

Alexander nodded. 'Of course, yes, I remember.' He hesitated, looking uncomfortable. 'And how did you take it?'

Cecilie found it very difficult to speak. She wanted only to rush into her room and close the door. But she knew he did not deserve to be treated in that way.

'At first I didn't really understand it. Your … situation I mean. I had never heard of anything like it before. Then I became … troubled and …' She fell silent, biting her lip and on the verge of tears.

'And?' he encouraged her softly.

'And very sad,' she whispered.

Alexander stood quietly for a long time. Cecilie looked down at the floor. Her heart was hammering.

'Yet just now, when we met out there,' he said gently. 'You were happy then, weren't you? Glad to see me?'

'Yes, I was. Just for that moment I had forgotten.'

'And now?'

'What do you mean?'

'Now that I want so badly to retain your friendship, Cecilie.'

She hesitated before replying. Could she cope with such a friendship? Was she strong enough to hide her distaste? How humiliating would it be for him to sense her contempt and her unspoken criticism? Suddenly she remembered her own experience with Martinius and a tide of her own shame washed over her. What did she have to be proud of?

'You have my friendship, Alexander,' she answered softly. 'You know you do. It is important to me.'

'Thank you, Cecilie,' he said, breathing a sigh of relief. 'I am very glad.'

She smiled at him uncertainly and placed her hand tentatively on the door handle. Realising it was time for him to go, he took her hand and kissed it. 'When will you be leaving the city?' he asked quietly.

'To travel to Dalum Abbey, do you mean?'

'No. The royal children are now at Frederiksborg. They are staying there for a time.'

'Oh, are they? I did not know that. Tomorrow I must find out what is happening.'

'Yes, do that! And please tell me too. Goodnight, my dear friend.'

Cecilie's gaze followed his tall confident figure as he walked off down the corridor. He moved gracefully, she thought, like a Knight of the Holy Grail and, as she continued to watch him, she reflected that Paladin was another name by which the Knights of the Grail were known. So he truly did bear his name with dignity – and yet there was that other ugly incomprehensible flaw that took the shine off this otherwise perfect nobleman. How strange life could be, she reflected sadly as she closed the door behind her. It was only later when she was settled in her room that she realised she had forgotten to ask him why there were so many troops mustering outside the castle.

The very next day she heard the rumours about Alexander. His position, she discovered, was very uncertain, and it was only the support of the King and his excellent ability as an officer that had saved him from terrible disgrace. There was talk of a court-martial or trial, but she could not find out any details. She was now deeply concerned for his sake because, in spite of everything, she realised that she shared a very deep and heartfelt affinity with him.

* * * *

Cecilie had not been back in Copenhagen for more than a few days before she suffered an even worse shock. This time, she discovered that she was going to have to face up to an even more earth-shattering dilemma of her own – the consequences of her fleeting ill-considered encounter with Pastor Martinius.

The day of the discovery was the worst of Cecilie's young life. At first she was petrified; then she reeled quickly back and forth between panic and hope. She felt all the wrenching emotions and upset that every young woman since the dawn of time has ever felt after an impulsive act of love. She wrung her hands so hard and so frequently that her arms ached; then she laughed nervously and hysterically over and over again, telling herself it wasn't possible – and anyway she could not be sure for several weeks yet at least.

Then, next came the fury: for a long time she cursed the young priest from the depths of the ocean to the heights of heaven, calling him by all the worst, most insulting names she could think of. Eventually when exhausted, she admitted to herself reluctantly that she too had been equally at fault. She hadn't exactly tried to resist his advances.

But to whom could she turn for good advice? Luckily not much time had passed. It was in fact only fourteen days earlier that she had met Martin in the potting shed in the churchyard, so she could be absolutely certain of the time. Although she could not be completely sure of her condition, Cecilie had enough intuition to suspect that this was very serious.

While waiting to leave Copenhagen, she had been asked to finish embroidering a dress for Anna Catherine, the King's daughter by Kirsten Munk. But she did not manage to sew on many beads. The patterns floated together in a muddle before her eyes and all the while she imagined fearful pictures from the future, seeing herself with a child nobody would accept, cast out and condemned, punished in some way she could not presently imagine. Sighing repeatedly, she tried again and again without much success to concentrate her attention on the beaded embroidery.

In three days time, she knew a carriage would be taking her to Frederiksborg. What should she do until then? There would be no compassion shown to her if her condition became known. The best she could hope for would be expulsion from Court. But should fate be really unkind, she knew the pillory could await her – and after that nothing but a life of shame.

Cecilie had become aware of her condition that morning. On rising she had felt suddenly light-headed and had vomited. But it was not only that which had disturbed her. A week earlier she had expected her monthly menstruation to begin but it still had not happened – and this was otherwise always on time, without any exception. As a result, every single minute of that day her mind had been in turmoil.

She had considered and then rejected many harebrained ideas. Of course she knew there were several different ways to drive out an unborn infant from the womb: you could work like a woman possessed, dance a jig until you were almost dead from fatigue, lift heavy loads until your spine was fit to break, go to see a wise crone or take different potions. The list was endless, but Cecilie knew in her heart she had not been brought up to take life.

By evening she had made her decision, although it hardly helped calm her fears. If only she had more time to prepare, she thought. If only time had not been so important. She really could not afford to waste one day. Having made up her mind, although she was still almost scared out of her wits, she made her way discreetly to Alexander Paladin's quarters.

'His Grace is not at home,' said his servant, and Cecilie's courage began to ebb. 'He is in the barrack wing.'

'Ah, so when will I be able to see him?'

'I do not know, Baroness. He has so much to attend to at present. His Majesty, our King, is arming for war against the Catholics. A great many troops are assembling.'

At that moment Cecilie had no interest at all in the wars of nations. She knew nothing about the press-gangs rampaging through Norway, for she had already left Gråstensholm before they arrived, and was therefore unaware of the fate of her own cousins. She was merely thinking about her immediate problem. Only a short time ago she had been dreading this visit, but now she was very anxious to meet Alexander and the delay irritated her.

'Oh, what am I to do?' she half whispered, her face pale and drawn. 'It is a matter of haste! Time is so short!'

The servant wavered, then said: 'If you would care to enter, I shall try to send a message to His Lordship.'

Cecilie considered the alternative: the pillory, perhaps? This was not a proposition she relished. 'Yes, please do send a message,' she told him and stepped through the doorway. As she followed the servant, she put her hand on his arm and he stopped instantly. 'Tell me,' she said tentatively, 'I have heard some fearful rumours. Is our good friend, the Marquis, in trouble?'

The servant's expression hardened, but because he was aware of Cecilie's closeness to Alexander, he understood her kindliness and saw the warmth and worry in her eyes.

'Indeed he is, Baroness. In truth his situation is extremely serious – a matter of only a few days at most. Then it will be the end.'

Cecilie nodded. 'A court-martial?'

'Yes.'

No more needed to be said and a moment later the servant showed her into the elegant drawing room and disappeared. Although what he had told her had made her undertaking easier, Cecilie felt no sense of triumph. Her wait was a long one and did nothing to calm her nerves. Her hands felt cold and clammy, and she paced the floor continually, examining every last detail of the room.

It was so exquisitely furnished. Here were heirlooms of the highest quality, including decorated Renaissance chairs, a map of the world that she could not really understand and beautifully bound books. Alexander Paladin must be very prosperous, she thought. But could his great wealth help him now?

Cecilie had been standing looking at a portrait that hung on the wall and was startled when at last she heard his hurried steps in the hallway. The blood rushed to her cheeks and, clenching her hands tightly, she turned to face the door. Her eyes were wide with apprehension; this was the moment and she knew she had to choose her words carefully.

Pulling the door open without ceremony, Alexander entered the room with a rush, his expression grim. 'What is it, Cecilie? The messenger said it was a very urgent matter – I was in a meeting of the King's Council.'

The apprehension she was feeling had made her even more tense. 'And you must hurry back?'

'Yes, indeed I must.'

'Can you spare me half an hour?'

He hesitated. 'Less, if at all possible. The Council does not suffer interruptions gladly.'

'Forgive me,' she said, her eyes downcast. 'I shall make

this as brief as I can, but it is not something I can explain in a few minutes. I really need several days!'

'Sit down,' he said. His tone was gentler now. He sat down facing her. 'You are clearly in distress. What has happened?'

How handsome he was, she thought, with his fine aristocratic features and eyes that always seemed to be beckoning her. All these things had no meaning now, she reminded herself – it was time for other things to be said. But although she had carefully rehearsed everything she was about to say, suddenly she found words were failing her.

'Alexander,' she began haltingly then stopped again. 'Alexander – if I were to propose something, I would not want you to think that I sought to hurt you or offend you …'

He raised his eyebrows in puzzlement, but said nothing.

'Please do not think … I am intending … blackmail!' she stammered. 'Or anything like that – I know that you are in trouble, but I will support you. You must not forget that.'

He waited, still saying nothing and she sensed she could feel the distance growing between them. She stared at him helplessly for another long moment, then blurted out: 'I need your help, Alexander. Most desperately!'

He looked at her warily, 'Is it money?'

'No! No! But I believe I can help you too – I believe we can both help each other!'

Cecilie realised this was not going at all well. She had seen his shoulders stiffen at her last outburst and she sat twisting her fingers nervously, squeezing them so tightly that they hurt. All the time her heart was pounding loudly inside her chest and she felt sure he must be able to hear it.

'I know that you are in trouble, but I know nothing of the particulars. Yet …' She broke off again, realising that in her desperation she was repeating herself. 'Please excuse me, I know I have already said that.'

14

'Go on,' Alexander said tightly. 'You need my help. In what way?'

Cecilie gulped. 'There is no other way to say this. Whilst I was at home this Yuletide past I did something terrible and foolhardy – an unforgivable act of stupidity for which I cannot forgive myself nor yet explain away. This morning I discovered that I am with child!'

Alexander gave an astonished gasp and stared at her speechless.

'It has not been long,' she assured him quickly, 'not more than two weeks. But I have also discovered that you risk losing your commission – and maybe your head too – because of your ... weakness. Something has happened while I have been away, hasn't it?'

Alexander said nothing for a long moment. 'Yes,' he replied at last in a strangled voice, getting to his feet. It was obvious that he could not bear to look her straight in the eye and he turned away before continuing. 'Do you remember young Hans?'

'Yes.'

'He … he left me for another.'

It was so strange to hear him speak like that, she thought, exactly the same as describing any normal tale of heartbreak between man and woman. She struggled to understand, images whirling in her mind, until Alexander's voice interrupted her thoughts.

'They were both discovered *in flagrante*, and the new companion of Hans has also named me. He has spoken on oath at his trial saying that Hans had told him about me.'

Cecilie could feel his pain. 'And what of Hans?'

'He is very loyal and denies it, for which I owe him my gratitude. But no one believes him. It puts me in a horrifying position, Cecilie.'

He had turned to face her again while he was speaking.

15

Sitting down once more, he felt able to look at her now that he had told her almost everything.

'The case will be heard in a few days, and I shall be called to explain myself there. I shall have to swear an oath on the Bible. I am a devout man, Cecilie. I cannot perjure myself. It would be unthinkable.'

'So the King himself cannot save you?'

'He has taken me at my word – for the time being. Should he discover that I have lied to him, then I am finished.'

Cecilie nodded, feeling lost for words. She knew precisely what such disgrace and humiliation would mean to a nobleman like Alexander. He would be left to the mercy of the seething crowds, threatened with flogging in the streets, abandoned by his peers.

'Who was he?' he asked softly.

Suddenly Alexander had made her predicament the focus of attention. It startled her a little, because she had briefly forgotten all about it. Nonetheless, his glimmer of interest warmed her heart.

She averted her eyes, disgusted with herself and what she had done. 'A good friend of the family,' she replied, 'a priest in a fearfully unhappy marriage – starved of human kindness. The whole episode was so shabby! So unnecessary!'

'But why, Cecilie?'

'If I did but know! At the time I felt compelled.'

Alexander smiled, thin-lipped but still amused. 'You have a strange way of expressing yourself, dear Cecilie, but I understand what you mean. Sometimes such things are so very compelling.' He looked at her inquisitively for some time before adding: 'You will understand that I wish to know more about this man's character. Is he intelligent?'

'Oh, yes! And he has a fine and noble manner. He was the victim of impossible circumstances, with a wife who refused him his conjugal rights. I, on the contrary, can blame no one but myself.'

'Is he very different from me?'

'No! Oh no, not at all. Quite the opposite,' she said fervently. 'There would be no questions about that ...' Cecilie stopped speaking suddenly in confusion, the colour mounting rapidly to her cheeks.

Alexander bit on his knuckles. 'I think I am beginning to see what you are considering, but are you certain that this is what you want?'

'I should not have come here otherwise. It was not an easy decision, you must believe me!'

'I do believe you. But you have only been thinking about it since this morning, is that not so?'

'Time is very important, you must see that.'

'Of course I do. There is however one thing that worries me.'

'And that is…?'

'What made you give yourself to *him*?'

'Why does that worry you?'

'Do you not see it, Cecilie? Think about it!'

He had understood – he had recognised the similarities between himself and Martin!

She sat up straight. 'I will admit there was a time when your indifference both confused and saddened me. But you must understand that all feelings and desires I may have had for you were swiftly quashed – left cold as the grave – when Tarjei told me about your ... predilection.'

'And still, you gave yourself to a man who reminded you of me?'

'Let us say it was the last flickering of the flame, a flame extinguished forever by that perverse act. I am healed and inured, Alexander, and I am strong. I will not be a burden to you. You can live your life, and I mine.'

'That would not do you justice. You are young … and …'

His obvious reticence became too much for Cecilie. Fear and shame were tearing at her very soul and she stood up abruptly.

'Forgive me,' she muttered. 'Please overlook my lack of forethought!' She hurried towards the door, but he was ahead of her. His hands grasped her arms in a vice-like grip and his fiery eyes stared into hers.

'Please, Cecilie, you must not feel humiliated! Never – not you! You are so dear to me! I welcome your offer with open arms. Can't you see how I must clutch at any straw? Your words have aroused such hopes in me in my hour of desperation. But it is you I am concerned for, my dearest friend. You cannot know what it is you are asking of yourself.'

'What other choice do I have?'

'None, that's true. Please forgive my hesitation just now. I know it must have been demeaning for you. Let me spare you the further indignity of begging for my help by saying something you have not, but which must be said. You have to know that you will never have my love … not ever. A marriage between us will never be consummated.'

'I know that. I can live without it.'

He looked at her thoughtfully. 'Can you? It is a great sacrifice. Greater than you might think.'

'My aversion to all things erotic started fourteen days ago and, believe me, I think it will remain with me for many more years to come!'

Alexander was nodding absent-mindedly and although he was watching her, his thoughts were obviously far away. Realising this, Cecilie stood in silence, running her long thin fingers to and fro along the backs of her gloved hands. She wondered what she would do if Alexander *refused* to take pity on her.

18

Naturally she could return home. But she would bring shame upon her kind warm-hearted parents. She was, after all was said and done, the notary's daughter. Yes, they would be sure to forgive her and accept the child, just as they had once taken back Sol and her little daughter, Sunniva. But could the family name withstand any more scandals?

Grandmama Charlotte had been the first to come home with a 'stray' in her arms. That had been Cecilie's own father, Dag. Later Sol had brought Sunniva to them. Now it might be Cecilie with her bundle of misfortune. But even though it might have become something of a family tradition, it seemed hardly right for her to place another heavy burden on her parents, however broad-minded they might be.

Yet far worse than anything else was the thought of returning to the parish of Gråstensholm, to where the married pastor, Master Martinius, lived. She never wanted to lay eyes on him again. He was a kind and friendly person in every way, but the sin they had committed together, devoid of all feelings except loneliness, now forced them apart. Like drops of water on a red-hot iron, they skimmed in every possible direction, always away from each other. And besides, if Martin's adultery became known, she would certainly lose her head on the block – and so might he. Her bleak reflections were taking her spirits spiralling downwards towards new depths of despair, but she was jerked back to the present by the sudden sound of Alexander's voice.

'Before anything is agreed, dear Cecilie, how had you thought to arrange this – between you and me?'

'The practical details? Is that what you mean?'

'Yes.'

'I have given it some thought,' she said hurriedly. 'If it is at all possible, I had thought we should each have our own bedchamber – next to one another so that no suspicions could arise. But the rooms would remain private, each to his own. There is nothing out of the ordinary in that, is there?'

'No, not at all,' he replied, waiting for her to continue.

'There is just one thing I beg of you. I understand that you cannot change the nature of your being, but will you show me the courtesy of not taking your friends to your bedchamber? Maybe another room – further away – could be … used?'

How did she dare speak so freely? Cecilie had surprised herself, but she had to set down clear boundaries and that meant trying to hide her reluctance to talk about the subject. Alexander frowned, obviously giving deep thought to what she had said.

'These are reasonable terms,' he agreed, nodding slowly. 'Except that you demand I exercise greater discretion than before. And yet I must indeed be more careful for my own sake, even though it was Hans who was the wayward one in this instance. He paid no heed to whether anyone saw him or not.'

As he finished speaking, a pained expression returned to Alexander's face, and once again the bond he had with the other man took her aback. For Alexander it seemed so filled with – *love*! There was no other word. Despite herself she could not help but feel a little moved.

'However, we cannot begin to live as you suggest in my rooms here. My family has a manor, Gabrielshus, some distance from Copenhagen – not far from Frederiksborg, as it happens. We shall move there.'

'But will that not be too much trouble for you?' she interrupted.

'No! No, not at all – I shall be pleased and delighted. Besides, you know how I have always found pleasure simply in looking at you. Your beauty is rare, with a mystical quality – your dreamy almond-shaped eyes, skin so pure and auburn hair. Everything about you fascinates me.' There was a considered pause, then. 'Now – you are giving me the freedom to meet other … friends. But how shall it be with you?'

'Do you mean you are asking for *my* discretion, should I decide to entertain other men behind your back? Or are you demanding my absolute fidelity?'

'I have no right to ask you to remain celibate when you have shown me such ... largess.'

'So you are asking that I be discreet and that I am judicious in my choice of friends?'

He nodded, his face tense.

Cecilie smiled. 'I have already told you! I shall not step over the line. But *should* such a thing ever occur, and I become attracted to another man, let us discuss it then. I believe we owe each other that much honesty. All I will say is that, for now, I have had enough of men and their affections.'

Alexander took a deep breath. He seemed quite touched by it all. 'Oh, well! Tell me, Cecilie Meiden, small tough unusual girl that you are … Do you really want to marry me, in spite of all the difficulties?'

Her lips trembled slightly. 'Yes, Alexander, I do – so very much! This will be a marriage of reason. There are a good many such marriages and many of them are very happy. Thank you.'

Alexander took her hands in his. 'Considering the hopelessness of our dilemmas and the conditions we have set for ourselves, I think you and I have every probability of becoming truly happy. And of course I shall probably be off to war very soon.'

'Oh, no!' Cecilie exclaimed loudly. 'Surely not!'

'Your eyes are lovely when you're startled, Cecilie. Yet you must appreciate that for me to fall in battle would be the perfect outcome for you.'

Her gaze hardened. She was glaring at him. 'That was the

meanest thing you have ever said to me! I never thought you could be so unkind.'

'Don't take on so, my little powder keg! I was not mocking you. It was simply an observation.'

'My affection for you as my friend is beyond measure, as well you know. I cannot have that friend taken from me.'

It seemed as though her words had raised his spirits. 'I had planned to return,' he replied with a certain irony.

She smiled with relief. Suddenly she remembered the time. 'But Alexander! Your meeting! You could spare only half an hour!'

'Oh, forget about the King's Council – this is far more important! However, you are right; I should leave now, but I will see you later on.'

Cecilie, her eyes closed, stood alone for a while. She breathed a long slow sigh before whispering very quietly to herself, 'Thank you, Lord.'

She was still not sure that this marriage was a good solution to her problems. It was not perfect in any way. But considering the muddle she had got herself into, and the problems Alexander was facing, nothing could be perfect.

Chapter 2

Shortly after leaving Cecilie, Alexander Paladin rejoined the gentlemen of the King's Council and did not fail to notice the many glances of displeasure at his long absence. While he been away, the King himself, Christian IV, had arrived in the chamber and on seeing this, Alexander decided to take the bull by the horns and turned directly to address the King.

'May I humbly request an audience with Your Majesty when we have adjourned this Council?' he asked, making a formal bow.

'Granted,' answered the King, inclining his head slightly and giving his troubled cavalier an inquisitive glance.

The Council of War resumed its deliberations and the King listened patiently to all the varying shades of opinion that were expressed by its members. He was very keen to intervene in the growing war between Catholics and Protestants in Germany and made no secret of the fact that he was looking for supporters in this intention. There was something approaching a consensus for this policy, but the meeting stopped short of outright final approval of the move. The King, however, clearly felt he had almost achieved the objective he sought and had gained sufficient support for interim measures he wished to take and, as soon as the discussions had finished, he beckoned Alexander Paladin to join him in an anteroom.

'So tell me Marquis Alexander, what is on your mind?'

They were both fully aware that Alexander's life depended on the outcome of the trial four days hence and the king clearly understood that the request for an audience was directly linked to this matter.

'If it please Your Majesty,' Alexander said awkwardly. 'I am to begin a preparatory march with my troops to Holstein within the week. With so little time in hand, I am asking Your Majesty's consent to marry at once. Tomorrow perhaps … if arrangements can be made.'

The King's eyebrows had risen skyward and for a fleeting moment his expression was one of utter astonishment. Then, with a visible effort, His Majesty regained his composure. 'And whom have you chosen?' he asked slowly.

'The Baroness Cecilie Meiden.'

A flicker of amusement appeared in the King's eyes. 'Of course! My good lady's Norwegian maid-in-waiting, or I should say, our children's governess. It has not gone without notice that she is a delightful girl – and talented! Her maternal grandfather was none other than the legendary Tengel, whose hands possessed the power to heal. We never met him, but our people in Norway could not praise him more highly. But what is the noble rank of this family? Meidens – ah yes! There have been several marriages in that family of social expediency. You have enjoyed the company of the Mistress Meiden for some time, have you not?'

'Since first she came to Court, Majesty. Yes, it has been four or five years now.'

'Indeed!' exclaimed King Christian, who was standing at the window of the anteroom, looking out through the small glass panes at nothing in particular. His expression had suddenly become one of triumph, which he did not trouble to conceal – and nobody else but Alexander knew the reason for this.

As usual, the King was locked in a quarrel with his morganatic wife, Kirsten Munk, and again, as usual, the root cause lay in her less than discreet flirtations with other men. At one time she had even tried to win over Alexander Paladin – who was widely acknowledged to be an extremely attractive man – but that was before she had heard the rumours whispered about him. When approached, Alexander had rebuffed her in no uncertain terms and reminded her that she was married to Christian IV, their King.

Quite fortuitously the King had overheard this conversation and when, like Potiphar's wife in the Biblical story of Joseph and his coat of many colours, Kirsten Munk became angry at being slighted, she came to her husband to accuse Alexander of trying to seduce her. In the event however, Christian himself was able to refute the accusation by telling her he had overheard everything Alexander had said to her.

Kirsten Munk was able to extricate herself from this awkward situation only by arguing that she had in reality been testing the strength of Paladin's loyalty to his liege lord. But from that moment on, she became Alexander's sworn enemy. Indeed, the reason for much of her hateful animosity towards Cecilie was because Alexander was so often to be found in the company of the young Norwegian noblewoman, apparently preferring her companionship to that of Kirsten. This was something the beautiful Royal found intolerable, and she was determined to prove that Alexander cared nothing for women. These were the complex thoughts and reasons that lay behind King Christian's smile.

Still smiling mischievously, he turned affably to his cavalier. 'We gladly grant your request, Marquis Alexander. But we insist that you be wed in our newly decorated chapel at Frederiksborg with all pomp and ceremony!'

'And what a magnificent victory over Kirsten that will be!' the King thought to himself.

'Heaven save us!' thought Alexander, on the other hand. This was all rather sudden and everything would have to be managed at very short notice.

'Will there be time?' Alexander asked aloud in a hesitant tone. 'We decided to wed because I shall shortly be saying farewell to Cecilie. It is unfortunate that Baroness Meiden's family will not have the opportunity to attend.'

'There will be time a-plenty!' roared the King. 'In any case, your betrothed is bound for Frederiksborg, is she not? My dear Paladin, allow us to arrange everything with our Chamberlain.'

Had it not been for the need to observe etiquette and decorum, King Christian at that moment would have been rubbing his hands with glee. His affection for Kirsten Munk was nowadays only superficial. She was a very elegant attractive woman – something of which she was well aware – and it was her beauty alone that still captivated the King. The deeper conjugal bonds of companionship, however, had long since been broken.

One courtier indeed had described Kirsten Munk in the following terms: 'She is a delightful, beautiful woman with a robust figure, rounded, sensual features and fair hair. She perhaps risks becoming very large, however, with the advancing years. Full of vitality and eager to flatter, she partakes in entertainment, play and dance with great passion. Impetuous, whimsical and uncontrolled, she is also intensely erotic. And miserly and avaricious! Far from being a caring mother, she makes much of the differences between her children. But she has surprised everyone by announcing that it is her intention to join her husband when he marches against Germany, if this war comes to anything …'

This was probably a very apt description of a highly

unusual woman. She had many admirers, but her fiery ways also meant that she had equally many critics and enemies. However, most people suspected that, despite their acrimonious marital differences, King Christian continued to retain a bitter, yet faithful, devotion to his unusual spouse.

'Yes indeed, we *shall* do it!' shouted the King, consolidating his intentions aloud. 'We shall arrange a glorious, great wedding for you in the chapel, Marquis!'

Although somewhat taken aback by the King's sudden decision, Alexander smiled with genuine gratitude and bowed deeply to thank him for his consideration and generosity.

* * * *

A few days later, Cecilie was sitting beside a splendid formal secretaire in her bedchamber at Gabrielshus, the Paladin family manor near Frederiksborg. She was still wearing her elaborate antique wedding gown as she wrote a letter home to Mama Liv, at Gråstensholm. Her hand was shaking slightly as she wrote and this broke the flow of the words from time to time.

'Dearest Mother and Father,' she wrote, 'I have so much to tell you that I am at a loss to know where to begin! I am so sad that you, all my most beloved family, are not here today – but time has been so short. Alexander is off to war and it is so awful for men to fight and perhaps even die so unnecessarily …'

She broke off and read what she had written. 'Oh, dear!' she thought, 'how disjointed this letter is. What will they think of me at home?' However, with a flourish she finished the muddled sentence quickly and continued in a more controlled hand, determined to convey what she had to say more clearly: 'Dear Mama, only two days have passed since Alexander

Paladin asked for my hand! I accepted with all my heart, because he is a very fine man and a good friend. But the ceremony had to take place at once, before he leaves for war, and there has been no time to get a message to you, even less to hold the wedding at Gråstensholm – which would have been the right thing to do.

'Ah, if only you could have been here! My dear Mother and Father, Tarald and Yrja, we were wed this very day and His Majesty the King insisted that we hold the service in his chapel at Frederiksborg, his favourite castle. How very grand it was! The King and his Court were in attendance, with all the little royal children – except for Elisabeth Augusta, the youngest one. They looked so sweet and earnest. My two charges, whom I cherish the most – the unhappy Anna Catherine and the self-reliant Leonora Christine – were allowed to join us in the chancel …'

Still feeling breathless and overwhelmed by the speed of events, Cecilie stopped again and put down her quill to look back over the day. She could still see Alexander's warm calm eyes watching her as she stood shyly at his side before the altar. His barely perceptible smile, she knew, was an indication of his awareness of the pretence and charade in which they were taking part. Yet he looked so handsome, dressed in his colourful uniform.

Anxious and overcome with emotion, she had begun to shake as they knelt side by side, in front of such a distinguished congregation. But as soon as he had taken her hand in his firm grip, her trembling ceased. She was unable to hide her astonishment as the priest read aloud Alexander's list of titles. There were names and references to Schwarzburg, Lüneburg, Göttingen, Gottorp, mentions of Marquis, Count, Duke and other lesser titles and many other distinguished associations. In comparison Cecilie felt so insignificant. Who was this man she was about to marry? Her own minor title 'Baroness Cecilie Meiden of the Ice People' seemed pitifully short by comparison.

A little later, after the ceremony was over, came the most unexpected moment of all. Whilst they were enjoying a magnificent banquet at a table at which the King was also seated, Alexander's colleagues began to call jocularly for him to kiss his new bride. As she recalled the fury she had seen in Alexander's dark eyes at that instant, Cecilie did not notice that her pen had made a blot on the leather top of the secretaire. His eyes in fact had become almost jet black with exasperation, but his anger had subsided when he noticed how disappointed she looked. His expression had quickly softened and he had reached out his hand to her and lifted her gently to her feet. He had then placed his arms around her, kissing her gently and sensuously to roars of approval. But they both knew that it was merely for show. In that instant she had told herself: 'Now he really does detest me,' and she had stood rooted to the spot for a long moment, scarcely able to move.

If only it had been a few months earlier, she thought yearningly – before she had found out about his secret predilections. Then she would probably have felt joyously weak and ecstatically happy at being kissed by him. Now there was only a sense of despair and discomfort. Still, the whole Court had cheered and applauded wildly for along time, except for Kirsten Munk, whose down-turned mouth had portrayed her acid contempt. In that instant, a fleeting malicious thought came to Cecilie: 'If you bite into an old crab-apple often enough, you soon start to look like one.'

Alexander had explained the reason why Kirsten Munk disliked her with such intensity and the story had amused Cecilie. Even though she knew she would never have Alexander to herself, it was quite certain that they understood each other very well and realised how important they were to each other in their different ways. This meant they would always have good reason to stand together – just so long as they were not forced to extremes in circumstances like that public wedding kiss. It was easy for Cecilie to imagine the wilful Mistress Kirsten's rage when Alexander snubbed her, and just as easy to understand why she looked for every possible opportunity to draw attention to his perverse weakness. Any success in that direction would always be solace to her pride and revenge for her 'defeat'.

Shaking her head suddenly, Cecilie roused herself from her daydreaming, looked down at the half-finished letter, and began a spirited description of the beautiful royal gown she had borrowed, all the glittering finery of the Court and the adornment and decoration of the chapel.

On hearing the heavy oaken door being opened, she turned to find Alexander standing there. This was something she had not expected, because he had given over the bridal chamber to her and chosen an adjoining room for himself.

The immense four-poster bed had been decorated and made ready for the wedding night with the finest embroidered linen, a heavy silk eiderdown, and a beautifully embroidered lustrous bedspread made especially for a bride's bed. There were freshly cut flowers filling the room with their perfumes and a table laid out with wine and every possible delicacy for the newlyweds to enjoy.

In the midst of this great display of sumptuousness, Cecilie stared at Alexander. He was wearing a striking nightgown and in the warm glow of candlelight he looked almost irresistible.

'I realised,' he said with an apologetic grin, 'that it would not give the right impression if the bed in the next room had been slept in on our wedding night.'

'No – no, of course not,' stammered Cecilie. 'You are right. But what had you thought …'

'I was thinking I might sleep on the large chaise in here,' he said lightly, 'so long as you have no objection.'

'You mean right now? Are you tired?'

'Not at all – I am wide awake.'

'As am I – then let us sit and pass the time together.'

'A good idea,' he grinned again. 'But …' he hesitated, 'but we ought to make use of the bed in some fashion or other.'

'Yes,' she agreed. 'Perhaps we could play a game?'

Alexander pulled a face. 'The only game I approve of is chess – and that is not a game for women.'

'Why not? I know all the moves!'

'Thank you for that,' he retorted. 'That is about the worst thing you can say to a passionate chess player. Besides, the few women I know of who have tried to play have lacked the patience to think through their moves properly. They want to be done – finished as quickly as possible. Then they badger us all the time with questions like: "Will you soon be finished?" and play heedlessly.' He paused smiling ironically. 'So who, may I ask, has taught you the moves?'

'My father – there was no one else for him to play against at home at one time, so it fell to me to entertain him.'

'Oh, well, I suppose we can suffer the misery of one game.'

He knew at once where to find the chess board and men, and set them out with fastidious precision. The exquisite pieces and inlaid board were made of decorated ivory and mother of pearl. 'This all comes from the East Indies,' he explained, 'the Danish company out there. Now I warn you, Cecilie! I shall not play "nicely" just to let you be the victor.'

'Nor would I expect you to show any such mercy.'

'Excellent,' he said appreciatively, but he pulled a wry face, indicating that he knew the game would be nothing more than a quick bloodbath.

While Cecilie was examining the pieces, admiring them

one by one, he glanced over at the secretaire. 'You were writing a letter. To home?'

'Yes,' she replied and quickly went and turned the paper face down. 'Although we now are man and wife, the time is not yet right for us to share too many confidences.'

'I had not thought to read it,' he said abruptly, sounding slightly aggrieved.

Cecilie cursed her clumsiness. 'Please forgive me,' she said with frank honesty. 'I will get better at this, I promise.'

He gave her a brief, faintly sad smile and turned his attention to the game. The board was positioned in the centre of the enormous bed between them and they lay comfortably, facing one another across the chessmen.

'Ought you not to take that off, now the ceremony is long over?' Alexander gestured with one hand towards extravagant antique gown.

'Of course, how thoughtless of me.'

He waited while Cecilie went into her boudoir and changed into her lace-trimmed nightgown. Anxiously she pulled the ribbon around the collar a little tighter in order to show less *décolletage* before she returned to the bridal chamber.

Alexander's eyes were very expressive as he watched her approach the bed. They seemed to say: 'You look beautiful – very pretty and attractive – but you need not have tightened that ribbon quite so prudishly. I would not have been tempted.' She was not absolutely certain that those were the sentiments behind his gaze, but that was how she chose to interpret his expression.

Without either of them passing any comment on their curious wedding-night situation, they began to play. Cecilie quickly understood what Alexander was trying to achieve after just a few moves, from the way he had positioned his queen and one bishop. It was an attempt at what was known as 'fool's mate' – the swift and merciless defeat of a beginner. But being well versed in that stratagem, she avoided the trap silently and with ease. Alexander's own expression gave nothing away. He probably thought that she was too ignorant to notice his intentions and that she had managed to move the correct piece to parry him purely by luck.

When his first strike proved unsuccessful, Alexander followed the usual tactic of putting his queen in a new, equally perilous position. But Cecilie recognised this gambit as well. She had tried to trick her father with it on many occasions, and Alexander's strategy caused her no difficulty.

He continued to press home his attack, trying to beat her down quickly and decisively. Consequently Cecilie found herself busy parrying and countering, and had no chance to move her pieces into attacking positions as she would have liked. Whilst he was contemplating his next move Alexander, in an attempt to distract her, said, 'His Majesty in a conversation with me mentioned your maternal grandfather, Master Tengel. You have spoken of him to me before. He must have been a singularly special person?'

Cecilie did not reply immediately. By his conversational interjection Alexander had unwittingly given her just the short breathing space she needed. In a trice she was able to work out a fresh ploy in her mind.

'Indeed Master Tengel was very special,' she replied at last, moving out her second knight to a new position. 'I worshipped him. Sadly he died whilst I was here in Denmark. I believe he took his own life – and Grandmama Silje's.'

'What do you mean?'

'I just think he did, but I don't know for certain. Perhaps it was the grief he suffered because of my nephew, Kolgrim. He is a child of our kin seemingly burdened with the family's evil curse … '

As she thought and spoke of Kolgrim for the first time in

some weeks, a sudden disturbing notion occurred to her. 'With that in mind, Alexander, I suppose there is a small possibility – a tiny possibility – that the child that I am carrying may also be cursed.'

Caught unawares by this disturbing statement, Alexander moved a pawn that he should have left alone.

'Check,' said Cecilie calmly.

He swore softly and retrieved the situation.

'Can you tell me more about this evil inheritance? I have heard it spoken of, but I do not know enough.'

'Yes, you will have heard of our evil forefather, who cast a spell over all his kin. Ever since then, almost every generation has had a child that has inherited the curse. There was a witch named Hanna, whom mother and father knew when they were children, and an uncle, Grimar. My own mother's father was of the next generation.'

'So he was one of the accursed?'

'Oh, yes! But with great determination he resisted the curse and turned his powers to doing good. He used his extraordinary skills to help people. He was an outstanding man.'

'And then? Who followed him?'

'In my parents' generation? It was the infamous Sol, my mother's cousin.'

Alexander smiled. 'Ah, yes! We've heard of Sol. But what of your family now?'

'Among the *grandchildren* of Tengel?' Cecilie paused, thinking, and forgot about the chess game. 'It is strange – but there is nobody. My favourite little rogue Kolgrim, the scoundrel, belongs to the latest generation. And because there is already one born. I do not think that the child I am carrying will be tainted … But in my generation? Sometimes I think it could be me, but I have not discovered that I have any special talents.'

'But you do,' was Alexander's dry response. 'You play chess like a man. And that is a compliment.'

'Perhaps a dubious one,' she replied lightly. Cecilie firmly believed that women were every bit the equal of men and although she had rarely made this view known publicly, she nevertheless held it with great conviction privately. 'If only you knew how many times I have held back from shouting: "Will you soon be finished?"' she said with a mischievous grin.

Alexander smiled spontaneously at her wit and nodded towards the board. 'I think it is your move …'

'Yes, I know … Anyway, let me just finish. What I was going to say was that the "chosen ones" among the Ice People are able to foretell things – or they have other supernatural powers. Or sometimes they are just plain evil … Also – and this is very important – the chosen ones always have cat-like eyes: amber and green, almost glowing. I do not have such eyes myself.'

Alexander reached over and lifted her face towards him. Looking directly into her eyes with genuine curiosity, he said: 'No, these are much too dark – nor have I noticed anything cat-like about you!'

'I know, but my reason for thinking as I do is because everybody tells me that I look so much like the witch, Sol. Except that she was a thousand times more beautiful.'

'Now *that* I don't believe,' said Alexander gallantly.

'Thank you,' she smiled. 'Yet some of the "chosen ones" are anything but beautiful! They are almost deformed! Now Hanna and Grimar … they were said to be monsters. And as for Kolgrim – when he was born, it was said that he was an appalling sight to see! When I first met him, he was a charming young mischief-maker with a strange influence over the women of the household. Despite being a horrible child to deal with, the housemaids forgave him everything and anything! Grandfather Tengel was also malformed at birth. Each of them took their mother's life in childbirth.'

'That will not happen to you!' exclaimed Alexander with surprising passion.

'As I said, I do not believe there to be any danger. But I do wonder over one thing.'

'Which is?'

'Something that Grandmama Silje once said when we, her grandchildren, were all with her. I heard her whisper to herself: "No, he must be wrong. I see no yellow eyes in any of them." She was unaware that she had spoken out loud and did not mean for me to hear her.'

'So you believe that your grandfather had discovered the evil strain in one of you?'

'That was indeed what I thought her to mean. But maybe she just noticed something in their eyes. Now I don't know.'

'How many grandchildren did he have?'

'Six in all. Poor Sunniva died giving birth to Kolgrim. But she was not his real granddaughter. She was Sol's child and my second cousin, so I do not think I should count her. That leaves my brother Tarald and me. Then there are my cousins, the three brothers, Tarjei, Trond and Brand.'

'Tarjei is the clever one, is he not? The healer? Could he be the one?'

'Well, it's possible. But he was always grandfather's great hope. And Grandmama Silje was so obviously worried when she muttered those words – I find it hard to believe that Tarjei was the one she meant, even though he seems the most likely.'

'Check!' said Alexander.

'You snake! All this time you were talking just to distract me!'

She turned all her attention back to the board to get herself out of the tight spot and when she had managed to redress the balance, she said: 'For us to have saved each other from a cruel fate by our marriage is all very well. But in my anxiety I had quite forgotten that I might be forcing an unwanted child upon you.'

'On the contrary, my young Cecilie! It has been my greatest sadness that I would not be able to continue the family line. This pastor would seem to have my looks, as well as being a good and intelligent man. You are also a fine and clever woman, so I think everything will be all right.'

'It is kind of you to say so, Alexander. Thank you. You ought to know that I believe that daughters are to be valued just as much as sons. However, because your distinguished family name will otherwise die with you – and this is the only chance to save it – I earnestly hope I will bear you a son.'

Alexander bit his lip. He did not answer for fear of hurting her feelings about having a girl. But he could see she understood that his chief wish was the same as hers. 'My sister will never believe her ears when she hears about this,' he said, changing the subject slightly.

'You have a sister? I didn't know!'

'She lives far from here, on Jutland. She only comes to visit Gabrielshus very occasionally.'

Cecilie was somewhat surprised that Alexander had a relative whom she had never heard of. 'Are there any more?' she asked inquisitively.

'No, only Ursula. Though you must not let the thought frighten you. Despite renouncing me, she has a good heart.'

'I see. No, I am not afraid; I'm simply mulling it over. You say very little about your family, whereas I babble on about mine all the time.'

'That's because they are such a joy to you, dear friend. I only wish I was part of such a large family.'

Instead of replying, Cecilie relieved him of one of his pawns. He retaliated by putting her in check. She quickly undid the damage without too much effort, but realised that she could not concentrate on both the conversation and the game at the same time.

'Do you want to tell me anything more about *yourself*?' she probed, gently.

Alexander knew precisely what she meant, but he shook his head firmly. 'No, I don't! Not at present.'

They both turned their minds exclusively to the game. Alexander poured them some wine and they drank each other's health, hardly taking their eyes off the pieces in front of them as they did so. Somewhere in the house a clock struck the hour. It was two o'clock. This night will soon be gone, Cecilie thought solemnly. But for some strange reason she was quite enjoying herself and she told Alexander so.

His broad grin in response revealed his perfect white teeth. 'Yes, so am I. Would you care for something to eat?'

'Afterwards – I shall put you in checkmate first.'

'Really? Then you ought not to leave your queen exposed in that way! For now she is mine. No mercy!'

She had meant to sacrifice her queen, but she wasn't going to tell him that. With a deceptive shrug, she brought her castle out of the shadows. She was a 'tower player' and had been waiting for the way to be free for them. Alexander had fallen straight into her trap; blind to the consequences, he gaily took her second knight.

'Dear me, that was careless of you, Cecilie. Are you getting tired?'

'No, I'm not. Are you?' she said and moved her castle again with mock casualness. 'That's check.'

He stared at the board dumbstruck. 'Damnation!' was all he could say – and all he could do was to move his king. He had no other choice.

Cecilie's hand was hovering over her castle, ready to

deliver the *coup de grace*, but suddenly she wavered. She had no desire for victory over Alexander on this night in particular. Not him of all people – so she rather feebly moved an irrelevant pawn forward.

Alexander's eyes widened theatrically. 'Cecilie! What I said about showing no mercy goes for me too! I should never forgive you if you let me win out of kindness.'

'Not kindness, Alexander, just female strategy. But have it your way. May I withdraw that last move?'

'You *have* to!' he said menacingly. 'Not even a five-year-old would have done something so foolish as to move that pawn when I can be trounced in three moves!'

Obligingly she returned her pawn to its former position and brought out her castle.

'Check again,' she murmured.

Alexander thought for a long time; a very long time. Cecilie studied in great detail his attractive well-formed hands and the pattern of the brocade on his nightshirt. Absent-mindedly she noted that the candles in the candelabra had burned rather low.

His position was desperate, but he was not going to surrender. After much consideration he believed he had found a way out – by a daring tactic!

'Aha!' said Cecilie. 'How clever you prove yourself to be, Alexander!'

'Don't start being spiteful,' he admonished her, although he was clearly proud of his move. Not only had it provided some respite, it had also given him the opportunity to develop an attacking strategy later on – if he managed his game properly. If he lost a number of important pieces – well, that couldn't be helped.

She had carried out something of a massacre, but now it was Cecilie's turn to stop and think. Their positions were absolutely locked.

To move the game forward she took a pawn. It was a mistake, but she did it because she was worried that Alexander would become impatient with her for taking so long. And now she had put her beloved castle in danger. But by manoeuvring swiftly she succeeded in saving her favourite piece. Thirty minutes later they each had only a few pieces left in play and they were at stalemate.

With a loud yawn, Cecilie stretched out lazily on the bed. 'I'm sorry Alexander but long drawn-out endings always bore me. Shall we call it a draw?'

'Yes, as you say,' he agreed. 'Thank you for an excellent match, Cecilie! For a while I was seriously afraid I should lose, and I couldn't have endured that – not after my arrogant outburst at the start!'

Cecilie smiled inwardly. Although she could have made it checkmate a couple of times, she had never really wanted to defeat him. On each occasion she had stopped herself in time. It was good to be sharp-witted, but one shouldn't go too far – well, not always! Instead of revealing these facts, she said simply: 'It did take a long time though, didn't it? I'm really hungry now! And it's the middle of the night. This is positively indecent!'

'But most sensible,' Alexander replied, smiling warmly. He put away the chess pieces and then brought some food over to the bed.

He is evidently considerate and reliable, she thought.

For a while they said nothing, as they ate and drank, savouring the bonds of friendship, understanding and purpose that were growing ever more powerful between them.

Cecilie could sense that Alexander had been mulling something over quietly inside his head during the long silence, but she was taken aback when, without any warning, he declared vehemently: 'My life has been hell, Cecilie!'

'Oh,' she thought to herself, 'he's going to tell me! He *wants* to tell me. Just *me*. I hope I shall be worthy of his trust.' She could feel her heart beating hard inside her chest. As she waited for him to speak further, she felt very anxious – but excited too.

Chapter 3

Alexander, a man who had always guarded his privacy and his past with total dedication, was now, to her amazement, telling her very frankly that his life had been hell. In that first instant Cecilie was uncertain as to what her best reaction should be to this startling revelation. She cudgelled her brain desperately for an understanding and sympathetic reaction, but in the end could only respond lamely by nodding her head.

'I think I understand why that could be,' she said at last. 'But there is so much I do *not* understand.'

'It is the same for me.'

'Have you always been … as you are?'

He made a face. 'I cannot say. In truth, I am not sure about that. Why do you ask?'

'Because Tarald went on to explain some other things to me. He said that those who are born so, are never likely to be otherwise. However, those who have *become* like that …' She broke off in embarrassment for a moment, struggling to find the right words. 'Shall we just say that those who have become "perverse" through the influence of others might possibly change their character again.'

'I hardly think so,' sighed Alexander resignedly. 'Had it

been that simple, the battle would be half won! Some of what he says may perhaps be true, but the problem is for me far more complicated. I know one or two men who enjoy the company of women *and* men. One is married and has children. Yet his secret affection for men is completely unknown to his wife and everyone else at Court.'

Cecilie, of course, was extremely curious, but dared not ask who it was. She knew everybody at Court so well and hardly dared start wondering who it might be. After a few moments she decided to stop thinking about it and looked enquiringly at Alexander again.

'And you,' she asked softly. 'How do you fit into the whole picture?'

'I cannot lie with a woman – I cannot!'

'Have you tried?'

He did not answer.

'Please tell me.'

She whispered her words encouragingly, although almost inaudibly, trying above all else to convey patience and understanding. When he still didn't respond, she moved closer to him and looked directly into his face.

'Do you despise yourself, Alexander?' she asked quietly. 'If you do, that can be dangerous.'

'No, it is not,' he said quickly. 'For me, to like men is natural. It is the reaction of others that makes me ashamed.'

'That's understandable. May I be quite candid?'

'Yes.'

'Do you lust after them? People that you meet and suchlike?'

'No, Cecilie, that is quite wrong. How do you feel when you are in love? Do you always crave a man straight away?'

'No. First I might start to like someone – feel an affinity with them.'

He nodded in agreement. 'Precisely! That is how it is between me and another man when a deep closeness begins to grow between us. Then slowly, infinitely slowly, a lasting friendship and comradeship is formed and finally … we might want to live with one another.'

'But that is exactly how it is between a man and a woman!' she exclaimed.

'Of course it is! But that is what other people cannot see. The love, the intimacy, the intuitive understanding between two people, one for the other.'

'When did you discover that you were like this?'

Although it felt feeble to say 'like this', she could not think of another way to put the question. She had asked the question in the hope that Tarjei may have been right and that Alexander had been affected by some event in his past. But was it a vain hope? It was certainly a hope that showed that she still harboured impossible dreams about their marriage. Alexander, however, had lapsed into a reflective silence again and it was a long time before he said anything at all.

'I cannot remember anything particular in my childhood,' he began reluctantly, making himself comfortable on the bed with a mound of pillows at his back. 'No matter how I try, I simply can't. I had many siblings and we lived here, at Gabrielshus. They all perished in the plague of 1601. Only my sister Ursula and I were spared.'

'You could not have been very old, then?'

He grinned. 'No, I was six years when it happened.'

So now she had learned something else about him! He was approximately thirty-one years old.

'Your poor parents,' she said sympathetically, almost whispering, 'to lose almost all their children.'

'Yes, ten children taken from them all at once. Afterwards our mother became quite fearful of what might happen to

Ursula and me – especially me. I was the only one who could pass on the family name, you see. We were not allowed to go anywhere – or do *anything*! It was all quite unbearable.'

Cecilie thought she might have found a reason for his predilection in what he had said, but decided there was none. There were over-protected boys in vast numbers, yet they mostly grew up to be perfectly normal men.

'What about your father?'

Furrows appeared on Alexander's brow. 'I have no clear memory of him. A large and heavy man who … Oh, I don't know. My mother used to cry a lot when he was alive. I remember that he had many paintings and pictures in his room. I never liked going in there.'

'What sort of paintings?'

Alexander just pulled a face and shrugged his shoulders. Either he could not remember or he didn't want to answer.

'So your father died young?'

'Yes. It was the year after my brothers and sisters.'

'What happened then?'

'Well … nothing happened really until I was a few years older.'

'And were you drawn to other boys or young maidens?'

'That is the thing I cannot remember. It was my mother's wish that I join the military, as an officer, as is customary in our circles. It was then that I heard my comrades talking about womenfolk and the escapades they had enjoyed with them. I would listen, thinking I too would have my opportunities.' Alexander paused, looking distressed and swallowing hard. 'I don't know that I can carry on.'

'I beg you, try,' Cecilie said gently. 'I want so much to know more about the man I have wed. I want to understand – and help if I can.'

He bowed his head. His face seemed very pale in the glow

of the candles, which were now burning very low. Cecilie reached over and pinched out the flame of the candle nearest to her. Alexander then snuffed out the others, gradually leaving the room in total darkness. It evidently suited his mood better.

'There was a young man there, one of my fellows,' he said, the strain showing in his voice. 'We became friends straightaway. We were always together, come rain, come shine. He was forever meeting different girls and he insisted always that I join him. I think he attributed my reluctance to being shy in front of women. But you see, Cecilie, I had no great desire to meet them. Quite simply I cared nothing for their looks or their manner. More and more I found myself wanting to touch my friend. My hand longed to caress the curls that fell around his neck and I wanted to *show* him my friendship, by embracing him when he was happy and consoling him when he was miserable. Yet I still did not understand my feelings. Then finally he managed to persuade me to join him when he went with some girls and arranged it so that I found myself alone on a garden seat with one of them. She was very pretty and attractive in every way, Cecilie, but I was terrified! I knew what was expected of me, and in a half-hearted manner, I did my duty – but only with chivalrous words, nothing more.'

'As you did when we first met,' Cecilie pointed out. 'You were very amiable, but reserved then.'

'Probably, but with one difference.' She could almost hear him smiling as he spoke, but he waited a little while before continuing. 'I was not frightened witless when I spoke to you. However, the girl I was speaking of had apparently taken a liking to me, because she moved close to me and placed her hand on my knee. Quite intimately! Such a feeling of distaste welled up inside me. It was so strong that I could not force myself to remain still. I had to feign a bad headache and take

46

my leave at once. I as near as ran all the way back to the barracks.'

Just then Cecilie's hand brushed inadvertently against his on the bed. She could feel that it was damp with sweat. It had clearly taken a lot for him to share his confidences and she felt very touched and filled with gratitude. In that instant she realised that she would never forget this night; the darkness surrounding them like a protective mantel; the curious atmosphere; the intimacy. She found it difficult to control her emotions, feeling overwhelmed suddenly by a sense of regret and loss. She also felt deeply downhearted and saddened by the way things were. Yet she had no desire to dwell on the precise reasons for her sudden emotional upheaval – it would have been too unpleasant.

While she had been lost in thought, Alexander had also been silent, biding his time until he felt able to continue. She heard him shift on the pillows in the darkness beside her and this time he cleared his throat anxiously before he spoke.

'At that point I began to wonder about myself more critically. My friend's tales about girls had been troubling me for some time. But now, to my bewilderment, I realised that I was jealous! And so, one evening in our barracks when a group of us were playing cards – drinking wine, laughing and making merry – in my cheerful mood I put my arm across his shoulder. I felt a strong desire to draw him close to me. Although I took my arm away at once, all through the card game I could feel his presence. I kept glancing at him, and became increasingly desperate because he was so unbelievably attractive. I was joyously aroused just thinking about him, and suddenly realised that I wanted him. I made my excuses, saying I had some work unfinished, and left.

'Walking out into the winter chill, I went down to the shoreline where I found a frost-covered old tree stump and sat down. I wished myself dead, Cecilie! My heart was filled with love for that young man. Can you imagine how I felt? Yes, I had heard stories that such perversions existed, but I had always thought of them as foul jests. Now I would be the butt of such jokes – one of those unfortunates whom my comrades sneered at and made fun of. I was enraged. I cried and cursed myself. I remember I was so disgusted that I bit my knuckles until they bled. I prayed to God to make me normal again, but still my desire for the young man would not leave me. It was with me that day and every day until I requested a posting elsewhere and it was approved. He was interested only in women and regarded me as nothing more than a friend and fellow officer. For my part, I would have died rather than reveal my true feelings.'

Slowly Cecilie began to feel both sympathy and despair for Alexander. She also realised how little she knew about people and their suffering.

'And after that?' she asked softly. 'What happened then?'

'At first I tried everything to rid myself of these inclinations. The hours spent in prayer, in my room and in church, were without number. Yet for many years I loved that young man, although I never saw him again. Eventually I resigned myself to my fate and tried to accept that I was different. Everything calmed down after that. But, as God is my witness, I never dared reveal myself with so much as a smile.'

Cecilie found she had become agitated, impatient and concerned all at the same time and she sat up straight on the bed. 'But how could you live like that,' she railed at him. 'How could you live as a … a *celibate*?'

He shrugged and moved uncomfortably in the darkness. 'I told myself that if monks could remain celibate then so could I. But then I met Hans …'

Again Cecilie waited for him to go on. But this was something he was clearly not happy to be drawn into and she had to be patient for a minute or more.

'It was Hans who took the first step,' declared Alexander at last with another deeper sigh. 'He was an experienced young man and he took a liking to me. The way he looked at me, so languidly, so invitingly was unforgettable – I could hardly believe my eyes! He was extremely lovely to look at … Well, you've met him so you know … and I could not help myself falling for him. I saw my hope in him because he was a pleasant young man in every way. But even then, I still continued to struggle against these tendencies within me.'

Once Alexander had begun to tell his story, the words tumbled out of him in a torrent. Some sentences lacked context, and he gabbled sometimes, almost as if he was determined to get everything said regardless of the exact way the words came out.

'I am amazed that you were able to keep your nerve through it all,' said Cecilie encouragingly. 'It must have been very difficult indeed.'

'It was often extremely troubling, yes,' he conceded. 'I know that I must have acted like a fool at times. I walked great distances along the castle passageways and corridors, just hoping I would catch a glimpse of him. Yet I also avoided places where I *knew* I would meet him. I forced myself to make conversation with many women just to prove I don't know what to God knows who … Oh, Cecilie, I was so afraid! Terrified! And so one day Hans asked me if I should like to join him on a visit to some friends. With great trepidation I said I would go.'

Cecilie wished that the candles had still been burning. She wanted to look into his eyes and wanted him to see the sympathy in hers. She sensed that he needed her, and moved her hand across the bed until it touched his. She gave it a quick, gentle squeeze before letting go and moving her hand away. She guessed he would not appreciate too much intimacy just at this point.

'I was so relieved,' he continued after another long pause. 'Hans had obviously understood! He had seen through me, but I did not know how. Perhaps my horrified glances, curiously seeking his, had told him too much. Eventually I met his friends. They were like me, Cecilie, and they were many. I could tell you names that would take your breath away. I was embarrassed beyond measure at first, but they were most welcoming and spoke of their own lives, which were startlingly like my own.

'But above all else they taught me to finally accept that which cannot be explained. Never to feel shame, but likewise never disclose oneself to others and never, *never,* expose them, my brothers. From them I learnt that it is the judgement of the world outside that is the hardest thing to accept. They had found that inner happiness was possible once they had overcome their own despair.' He paused again, drew a very deep breath and pulled his knees up tight to his chest. 'Hans accompanied me home that evening,' he whispered. 'I will not say any more than that.'

'Nor do you need to,' replied Cecilie, her eyes brimming with tears and her voice quivering. 'So the only proper relationship you have had has been with Hans?'

'Yes. All went well for two years. Towards the end we were nearly found out, as you know. Hans was so careless, as though he took pleasure in watching me worry. Maybe he thought he was invincible or immortal or some such thing. Then he left me for another fellow, newly arrived in the city. Knowing no better, this man had no hesitation in divulging that I had been Hans' friend before him. You know how it is; people always wish to pull others down into the mire with them.'

Cecilie nodded. 'I expect that tendency is in most of us.'

'Indeed. And today I must return to Copenhagen to attend the trial.'

Hearing the word 'today', Cecilie felt a sudden stab of alarm. Yes, the night was almost past and dawn would soon be breaking. Her wedding night would soon be well and truly over.

'I shall come with you,' she told him decisively. 'You should not go alone.'

'Please, no, Cecilie. It could all become somewhat unpleasant.'

'But I shall be able to support your testimony. You say you will not perjure yourself. Well, I have no such sensitivities. We Ice People have always had our own form of religion, which is more down to earth than traditional Christianity. Besides, is a trial really warranted? Is this marriage not evidence in itself?'

'Perhaps it is. In any event it ought to be a weighty argument. I do not believe it is commonly known that there are men who can "befriend" both women and men. If it is, then this feigned marriage will help but little. Otherwise ...' He stopped speaking suddenly and shot off the bed. 'Dear God!' he cried in a frantic voice. 'There is something important we have forgotten. Your honour also must be protected, dearest friend.'

Cecilie watched in puzzlement as he lit one of the candles. It felt strange to see him again – they had been no more than voices in the privacy of darkness for so long – and it seemed to her incredible that this was the powerful virile stranger who had confided in her so many astonishing details of his life. Yes, for despite everything, he was still virtually a stranger, this Alexander Paladin. And that thought sent a new surge of excitement coursing through her. This is the man I am to share my whole life with, she reminded herself, and the very thought of it made her head spin.

Alexander had taken a sharp knife from the fruit bowl on the table. He made a small cut along the tip of one of his fingers and squeezed out the blood. It looked almost black in the candlelight.

'Move over,' he ordered. 'Quickly.'

Confused, she did as she was told. Without looking at her, Alexander let a few drops of blood fall onto the bedclothes, somewhere near the middle of the mattress. He watched as they soaked into the sheet, then wiped the knife clean and returned it to the fruit bowl.

'Now that's done,' he said with satisfaction in his voice, 'the gossip tomorrow will be that the marriage between Alexander Paladin and his virgin bride, Cecilie, has been consummated.'

She let out a sigh of surprise and relief. 'Thank you, Alexander, that was very sweet and considerate of you.'

'It will be helpful to both of us,' he replied with a friendly smile.

A moment later Cecilie started to laugh. 'I'm sure there have been far more boring wedding nights!'

He joined quickly in her laughter. 'Yes, and more embarrassing ones too, I expect! Thank you for your fine friendship, young Cecilie, and for your understanding.'

'Did it help to talk about it? Make it a little easier, I mean?'

'If you did but know how much! Somehow everything feels more innocent.'

'It is the same for me. I understand so much more now. A little while ago I felt a tiny pang of anxiety because I didn't know you at all – I am wedded to a stranger and we shall live together in a very unconventional marriage. But it is the same for you! Do those same thoughts not frighten you?'

He had left the candle burning and he glanced at her briefly as he considered his reply.

'I did think so yesterday, just for a short time. Then I reconciled myself to the thought that a marriage such as ours can perhaps be easier to conduct than conventional marriages. Ours is founded on respect and consideration, isn't it? We are avoiding the emotional turmoil that can arise from living intimately together – like envy or the fear of being unloved or simply lacking the opportunity to live one's own life. I'm sure you agree, Cecilie, that everyone has the right to a small private corner of his or her soul, into which no other person may intrude. That is why so many marriages collapse – because one person desires to own and control the other totally, unable to tolerate them having interests of their own, no matter how innocent.'

She nodded her agreement. 'I believe our friendship will be worth a great deal to us, Alexander. Thank you for the things you have told me – I feel more relaxed now. I am so afraid you see, that I shall be in the way!'

He smiled at her and she noticed, not for the first time, that his eyes always had such warmth in them whenever he smiled. 'You need never worry about that, Cecilie. And the very same goes for me – I do not want to stand in your way.'

'You'd never do that,' she laughed. 'Alexander, I'm just beginning to feel how weary I am.'

'And I – this has been a very tiring night! We should try to sleep a little.'

They each lay down on their own side of the bed with a good space between them and Cecilie fell asleep almost at once. Now that he had unburdened himself to her, an unfettered and relaxed Alexander also followed suit shortly after.

* * * *

The following morning, those whose duty it was to confirm that the union had been satisfactorily consummated during the night, filed very quietly into the room. They saw the sleeping couple lying very close together, and during the night they had unknowingly clasped each other's hands.

A procession such as this was unavoidable according to the traditions of the times. Because Alexander Paladin belonged to a princely line, wedding custom required that a deputation of the kingdom's good men and women bear witness to the consummation of a marriage. In days gone by, it had been customary for the worthy male and female observers to remain in the nuptial chamber all through the wedding night, but that was now seen as an intrusion and the practice had changed. It was a concession that the two sleeping 'miscreants' could be truly grateful for.

Now the procession tiptoed silently across the floor and stood round the great canopied bed. Not a word was spoken, for fear of disturbing the apparently exhausted pair. The admirable men and women merely nodded their silent approval. Everything appeared to be in order, they agreed without resort to words. As they turned to file out, not one of them paused to wonder why all the candles in the chamber had burned so low.

Chapter 4

Despite Alexander's protestations, Cecilie did travel to Copenhagen with him. No one, she argued, could help him better than she could. But although he knew she was right, he was still opposed to the idea and did his best to dissuade her from her plans.

'I do not want you to lie for my sake,' he told her forcefully. 'It makes me feel very uncomfortable.'

'For the sake of those very dear to me I can lie until I'm blue in the face,' rejoined Cecilie firmly. 'And it will not offend my conscience in the least. It is something I have inherited from my ancestor, Sol, and I feel no shame in that. But she went even further, so they say. She gladly took the lives of everyone who harmed her kin.'

'Thank you,' he said with a shudder, 'but I don't believe you will need to go that far.'

In the end Alexander realised that his resistance was futile and he even gave way to Cecilie's insistence that she should be allowed to attend the trial. When they reached the city they found the judges had convened in one of the halls at Copenhagen Castle. A lot of people had already arrived and, this being both a sensitive and notorious matter, Cecilie could see any number of officers and gentry among them. More and more, she was discovering what an important man of state Alexander Paladin was.

King Christian was not present, nor Kirsten Munk. Nonetheless she recognised many distinguished gentlemen and ladies of his Court and knew that among them would be spies reporting to both. In the distance she caught sight of Hans; she hadn't seen him for a long time. He was indeed beautiful, almost too beautiful for her liking. He was foppishly dressed, weighed down with glistening adornments of gold and his wavy hair was perfectly coiffed. But his manner was a little too feminine, she thought while there was nothing remotely feminine about Alexander – he was agonisingly virile!

The other man in the case was older, his skin darkened by the sun, as though he had lived in more southerly climes. His hair formed a wreath around his ears and neck and, like so many middle-aged men, his life-long ale-swilling had left him with a large pot-belly. A chamois leather coat hung like a bell-tent from his stomach, and his legs looked ridiculously skinny in their tight leggings. The sight of his huge collar worried Cecilie. He looked as though the weight of it would topple him over at any second; but she reminded herself that it was the fashion of the time, which many men chose to follow.

The pot-bellied man's fate was sadly already sealed. He had been caught *in flagrante* so there would be no saving him. Cecilie's heart went out to him, but she could not resist asking Alexander one question.

'How could Hans leave you for *him*?' she murmured quietly though clenched teeth.

'Money,' her new husband answered just as discreetly. 'And a castle as a gift.'

So he was a wealthy man, thought Cecilie, looking again at the pot-bellied figure. Rich people, she decided, deserved but little sympathy. It was an illogical thought, because Alexander was also very prosperous, but she resented this stranger who had denounced him in such an unwarranted fashion.

The case involving Hans and the stranger had been heard by the judges at an earlier sitting. The matter now before the court related to Alexander Paladin, whom the stranger was trying to drag down with him. Alexander had told Cecilie that Hans had built his defence around the fact of his youth, claiming that he had been enticed and seduced by the older man. Although unpleasant, it was perhaps the most natural course to have taken.

'Alexander,' said Cecilie in a whisper, moving closer to her husband, 'do you want to save Hans?'

'I can do nothing for him except try to see that he does not lose his head on the scaffold,' he replied, anguish showing in his face. 'Hans has shown loyalty to me by saying that he only boasted about me to impress this other man.'

More likely, he was trying his best to save his own skin, thought Cecilie. She was terrified that Alexander would be interrogated before she was, and had begged the court notary to allow her to give evidence first, saying she had important things to disclose. She was only able to do this because the notary knew her father, Public Notary Dag Meiden of Norway, very well. But while Cecilie had not been shy about using her family connections, she did not know if her request would be granted.

She was sure that if Alexander gave testimony first, he would trip over his own two feet. He would never commit perjury – and he would most certainly take the blame for dragging Hans into this shambles. And that, she had promised herself, must be prevented at all costs.

Cecilie listened attentively as one witness after another made their statements. Some of them spoke out unequivocally in support of Alexander Paladin; he was a real man, said one and a great war strategist, as though that had any bearing on the matter at hand. Others – a few only – believed he had often behaved suspiciously. Several had noticed Hans Barth's early morning departures from Alexander's house, and Cecilie found herself inwardly cursing the young man's arrogance.

Then a lady-in-waiting, of whom Cecilie had not taken much notice until now, drew the court's attention to Alexander's affectionate friendship with Cecilie, which had lasted for several years. Cecilie felt like jumping up and embracing this unassuming woman and promised herself that from then on she would always be grateful to her. Alexander's manservant also spoke warmly of his master and vehemently denied that he might have any deviant tendencies. He is lying under oath, thought Cecilie, a manservant above all others *must* be aware. The servant, in his turn, also emphasised the long friendship between his master and his new bride.

Another courtier told how he and others had processed to the bridal chamber at Gabrielshus early the previous morning and he could bear witness to the fact that Mistress Cecilie had been a virgin when she arrived and that the marriage had been consummated on the wedding night. These words were seemingly accepted by the court as being of profound significance.

Then suddenly Cecilie's name was called and her spirits leapt. She was to speak ahead of Alexander at least. 'Dear God, thank you,' she mumbled under her breath as she made her way to the witness stand with a faint feeling of bewilderment. What she should perhaps have said, she realised later, was: 'Thank you, dear notary!'

In a steady voice, she told the court who she was and, with her hand resting naturally on the Bible, she swore her oath without the slightest trace of a blush on her cheeks. The judge then began the questioning by asking her how long she had known Alexander Paladin.

'Four and a half years, Your Excellency,' she replied, hoping that she had chosen his preferred form of address.

'And for how long has he courted you?'

'We have been very good friends for four and a half years. He has courted me for nearly as long, although I cannot give an exact date when it began. These things so often grow a little at a time.'

'So why has he not asked for your hand in marriage before now?'

'We have often spoken of marriage,' she lied, without any faltering, 'but I wanted to return home first to inform my parents and ask if they would give their consent – should Alexander seek my father's approval for my hand. This is as it should be. I have now returned from visiting my family for the first time in all these years, and they were happy for the Marquis Paladin to be courting me. My parents would be pleased to receive him when he called as my suitor. Unfortunately time was not with us. War is in the offing.'

'God in Heaven, how she can lie!' thought Alexander, his admiration tinged with fear. 'She is fighting for me like a tigress defending her young!'

'And was it because of the war that you chose to marry at this time?' asked the senior judge.

'Yes, of course! My husband leaves for Holstein within the week and no one can say when he will return.'

'So your decision to wed had nothing to do with these proceedings?'

'Excellency, this trial is beyond my comprehension,' Cecilie answered passionately. 'I can no more understand these allegations against Alexander, than I can the rumours about him that I have heard circulating for quite some time. They can only have been started by someone who seeks his downfall – a slighted woman seeking revenge perhaps?'

The sound of muffled giggling was heard from the ladies-in-waiting. Kirsten Munk's attempt to seduce the Marquis was obviously common knowledge. Not everyone was so fond of Mistress Kirsten – in fact her arrogance and petulance had won her very few friends at Court.

At that moment, although she did not know it, by fighting for someone dear to her, Cecilie had in a strange way become Sol. She had in her far more of Sol's qualities than she had ever realised, and Alexander watched his new wife with amazement. How she had changed in that instant; proud and defiant, she stood before the judge, her head held high and eyes blazing. Never had he seen her looking more beautiful than she did now. Her dark auburn hair shone in the light from the windows – its shimmering tones were exquisite – her skin seemed as soft as a petal and her teeth flashed brilliantly from time to time when she drew back her lips like a hissing cat about to strike. Yes, in fact she is *just like a cat*, he thought to himself, suddenly astounded. She almost seemed to be fulfilling the description she had given him of her family's 'chosen ones' on their wedding night. But alas, while every other person in that hall, like Alexander, was also admiring the beauty standing in their midst, Sol's more vulgar attributes were somehow also starting to affect Cecilie's personality.

Cecilie herself was faintly horrified by her sudden desire to humiliate those around her with well-chosen and unpleasant words, and she had to struggle to prevent herself uttering all her thoughts aloud. First and foremost, she felt an intense hatred for Hans and found she wanted to get back at him in some way. This, she found nearly impossible to understand, but the same feeling also welled up in her for all the self-righteous onlookers, engrossed in the scandal, who were obviously hoping for Alexander's downfall. Luckily at that moment the notary took over the questioning and changed the emphasis of what was being asked.

'You are acquainted, are you not,' he asked mildly, 'with Hans Barth?'

'Naturally!' said Cecilie briskly. 'He is a good friend to both of us.'

'And are you also acquainted with the fact that this man, Hans Barth, has sometimes spent the night in the home of the Marquis?'

'But of course! And I have done likewise!'

A collective gasp of surprise reverberated through the hall. In his seat, Alexander was immediately alarmed. What, he wondered, was she thinking of? What might she say next?

The judge pounded the floor impatiently with the tip of his mace and addressed the hall. 'Might I remind this assembly of Marquis Alexander's unimpeachable honour – a matter upon which we have recently heard testimony.' He turned and faced Cecilie. 'Perhaps you would enlighten us as to what occurred during these nightly sojourns?'

'Gladly, Your Excellency. My husband is a passionate player of chess and, as you probably know, a game can often take several hours. When playing, Alexander loses all sense of time. It is neither Hans' duty nor mine to remind him of the lateness of the hour, his need for sleep or his honour.'

She sincerely hoped that Hans was a chess player – she had forgotten to ask!

'And you, My Lady, also play chess?' the notary asked with some surprise.

'Yes.'

The notary looked over to where Alexander was sitting. 'Is this true?'

The Marquis stood up. 'My wife has a brilliant clarity of mind, Your Excellency. She is a far more challenging opponent than Hans Barth, who it can be said is competent – but nothing more.'

Cecilie stared blankly at Alexander trying to decide if this statement was his way of taking some petty revenge on Hans or whether he was lying. When she saw how calmly Alexander looked directly at the notary she knew it was the truth. After all Alexander had told her he could never lie to the court.

In any event she knew now that Hans played chess. Glancing across at him, she saw from his expression that he resented being displaced as a chess player by a mere woman. The emotion in his eyes was unmistakeable.

'Oh, hurrah! Hurrah!' she thought wickedly.

The notary muttered: 'Very sensible I'd say; teaching one's wife the rules of chess!'

'She already knew how to play, Excellency. Her father had taught her.'

The notary's face lit up. ' Ah – my friend Dag Meiden! Yes! And there is nothing wrong with the clarity of his mind either!'

We won that skirmish, Cecilie thought as she looked back at Alexander, who was in the process of sitting down again. He too seemed satisfied with the outcome of the exchange and the chess interlude was clearly over.

'Marchioness Paladin, what I wish to ask you now is very personal,' said the judge evenly. 'Have you ever noticed your husband to harbour any deviant tendencies in his personality?'

'No – never!'

'Can you be certain?'

Cecilie looked back at him with a shy smile. 'I am positive, Your Excellency. On the contrary – indeed I can say that Alexander has often and in many ways shown his impatience to be married to me.'

'Where in the world did you find such indiscretion?' she asked herself as soon as the words were out. She was aghast at what she had said and dared not look at Alexander. Nevertheless, the effectiveness of her words was confirmed in the sound of gentle but knowing laughter that could clearly be heard coming from all around the public gallery.

'And Hans Barth,' continued the notary when the laughter subsided, 'what about him? Have you noticed him to have any unnatural affinities?'

More than you know, Cecilie thought, but her serene expression betrayed nothing of her silent inner reflections. 'Well, I cannot say that I am *that* well acquainted with him – but, no. We would often share conversation, the three of us. And sometimes we indulged in heated discussions. But never have I seen or even suspected the sort of indecencies that have been rumoured.'

The notary declared at that point that he had nothing more to ask and the judge dismissed Cecilie as he announced an adjournment for deliberations. She was not allowed to talk to Alexander during the break in proceedings, but she caught his eye across the hall and returned his flickering smile of encouragement. She realised she was petrified of the moment when he would face interrogation. Everything would be lost. Why couldn't the stubborn fool just tell a few untruths? But she knew Alexander was incapable of doing so. His soul was far too pure for him to lie on oath.

Much earlier than had been expected, the judges and officials returned to their places in the hall. They all sat down, except the senior judge, who remained on his feet. 'It's all over,' Cecilie said to herself. 'I pray that it is all over.'

'After listening to the Marchioness, Lady Cecilie Paladin's testimony before this court,' said the senior judge gravely, 'we have come to the conclusion that there are no grounds on which to continue this farcical hearing. Furthermore, we find this to be an insidious and underhand attack on one of Denmark's most honourable noblemen, Alexander Paladin.' Turning to address Alexander directly, the judge cleared his throat and said: 'You are now free to leave this place, My Lord, by the grace of many who have testified to your innocence, and most of all by the words of your wife, Lady Cecilie.'

The hearing had taken place before laws were introduced forbidding any wife to bear witness either for or against her husband and at this point Hans may well have wanted to protest wildly against the verdict of the judges. But to Cecilie's relief, his face remained expressionless and he did and said nothing. She concluded that he had probably realised that any such protest would have only made his situation worse.

'Pursuant to matters relating to Hans Barth,' continued the senior judge in the same sonorous tone, 'this court …'

Hans Barth's fate was of no interest whatsoever to Cecilie. She was already on her way out of the hall, jostling forward to meet Alexander outside. But it was some time before he emerged and she felt a little put out, because he had obviously wanted to remain behind to hear the verdict handed down on Hans. But eventually he pushed his way out through the throng and came and joined her.

'Thank you, Cecilie! I don't know how I shall ever be able to thank you enough!' he whispered closer to her ear. 'And Hans' death sentence has also been overturned, thanks to you. He will suffer the birch and then some hard labour, but you saved his life. I am so happy!'

Cecilie stifled a long string of vile oaths that were struggling for expression on behalf of Sol and herself. She had been fighting solely to save Alexander – that was all. But she had been left with little choice other than to speak well of Hans. All these things were probably inevitable, she admitted inwardly. But had it really been so essential for Alexander to show her how happy he was about the revised outcome of the case against Hans? That rankled with her and she found it difficult to put it from her mind.

As soon as the trial was over, Cecilie had to return to her duties at Frederiksborg, as she was still a lady-in-waiting. But now a carriage collected her at the end of the day and took her to Gabrielshus. She and Alexander passed the next few evenings happy in one another's company, talking or playing a game, but never again did they share a bed. Then one evening Cecilie asked him if he had seen Hans since the trial.

'No, of course not!' he replied hotly. 'Have you taken leave of your senses? Firstly, he is locked well away, imprisoned in some unknown castle, fortress or penal colony. Secondly, he abused and ended our friendship. Lastly, it would be ridiculous of me to visit him and give rise to new rumours and suspicions.'

'But you would like to see him?'

'Not in the least. Why, only last night I lay thinking just how little he means to me now. At the trial, when I hadn't seen him for a while, I thought him to be almost repellent. Like an over-decorated mannequin!'

Cecilie nodded. 'I felt just the same. In fact on seeing him again I was bewildered by your association with him. I had not expected you to have a preference for his sort.'

'He was far more reserved, discreet and dependable when I knew him,' answered Alexander almost at once. 'Clearly now he goes wherever the wind blows him. He's seemingly become most unreliable.'

'I think you're right,' replied Cecilie. 'Absolutely right.'

* * * *

After the high drama of the wedding, the trial and all that had gone on in the days leading up to them, Cecilie found it a struggle to bring her focus back to the more mundane nature of her work in the King's household. Her charges, the royal children of the King and Kirsten Munk, were all growing bigger and stronger and it was four-year-old Leonora Christine who was temperamentally the strongest of them all.

The unhappiest was Anna Catherine. Her mother hated her because of her resemblance to her royal father. The remaining girls and the only boy were exceptionally arrogant and unpleasant to their subordinates, a practice in which they had been well tutored by their mother and their grandmother, Ellen Marsvin, who was nominally the children's guardian until they came of age.

The worst behaved of the siblings was six-year-old Sophie Elisabeth. She was uncontrollable, with a jealous nature, and frequently indulged herself in outbursts of childish violence. She was endowed with every conceivable objectionable trait and brought misery to the lives of every royal nursery maid, in the same way that later in her life, she would inflict misery on Christian von Pentz, her husband.

Cecilie rarely, if ever, saw the bona fide royal children, those in line to the throne from Christian IV's marriage to Anna Kathrine of Brandenburg. They almost never stayed in the same part of the kingdom as Mistress Kirsten's offspring, not least perhaps because there were many who questioned the very validity of the King's marriage to Kirsten Munk. No formal ceremony had ever taken place, yet he referred to her always as 'my dear wife' and declared that she was his legitimate spouse. She, however, referred to all her children very disparagingly as 'whore's brats'.

Cecilie herself had a soft spot for King Christian. Much could be said of him, but it could not be denied that he cared deeply for his nearest and dearest, and most of all for his children. He showed them all the greatest consideration, gave them the best of everything and looked after them well. His loyalty to Kirsten Munk also never wavered and despite everything, he was probably quite fond of her, although she had been unable to accept that he had christened their first daughter Anna Catherine in memory of his deceased wife. Much of her hatred of the child had probably stemmed from that, thought Cecilie.

The unkind housekeeper had not changed either. Many were the times Cecilie had to console her two favourite charges after they had been scolded or beaten by her or their mother. Leonora Christine would suffer because she most often asserted her strong personality, whereas Anna Catherine was picked on simply because she became the irrational object of their ill temper.

Only infrequently did they receive visits from Kirsten Munk, though more out of duty than motherly love for her children. On one such visit the sight of Cecilie, victorious in court on Alexander's behalf, made her disappointment and hurt pride flare up more fiercely than ever. Kirsten immediately vented her anger on her blameless children, lashing out uncontrollably at anything and anyone, before finally storming out of the room leaving a chorus of frightened children's screams behind her. All this tension and friction made Cecilie's daily tasks more onerous and because she was expecting Alexander to depart any day with his troops, she remained on edge and ill at ease.

Then without any warning it was announced that more time would be required to draw up and conclude detailed plans for the conduct of the war. In truth a lot of statesmen and councillors were still dubious about giving their full support to King Christian's ardent desire for battle, so among other preliminary arrangements already agreed, Alexander's departure for Holstein was postponed indefinitely. This news came as a great relief to both Cecilie and Alexander, but they had scarcely had a chance to adjust to the situation and settle into a quieter domestic routine when another small bombshell dropped into their lives.

One evening as she returned from her royal duties, Alexander met Cecilie in the entrance hall at Gabrielshus and greeted her, not with his customary warm smile, but with a worried frown.

'What is it, Alexander?' she asked in a concerned voice. 'You are looking very anxious.'

'My sister arrived today,' he said shortly. 'She says that above all else she wants to see *you*.'

She studied his face but his expression told her very little – and yet that in itself said a lot.

'Heaven help us!' she muttered. 'Give me strength, Alexander.'

He smiled bitterly. 'Do not concern yourself. I am the one she dislikes.'

But Cecilie could not help worrying that her sister-in-law's attitude to Alexander might also spread to her. She touched her hair subconsciously, trusting that it was still tidy, but her knees were trembling as she stepped reluctantly into the house and walked towards the drawing room where their recently arrived visitor was waiting.

Countess Ursula Horn, Cecilie could see at first sight, was older than her brother. Her general bearing was austere, almost grim and while her hair was dark, like her brother's, she wore it pulled severely back from her face. There was an icy chill too, in the bright blue-grey eyes that scrutinised Cecilie critically as she entered the room. Whereas Alexander's nose was straight, Ursula's was hawk-like and typically aristocratic and her thin, well-defined lips were painted a vivid red.

From the outset, Cecilie was more than a little frightened of this daunting woman. She knew only that Ursula Horn was the widow of a German sailor who had died a hero, and that the servants at Gabrielshus had a restrained look about them whenever her name was mentioned. So Cecilie bowed her head deferentially towards her older and higher-ranked sister-in-law, who responded with an abrupt and unfriendly nod of her head. Alexander had quietly followed Cecilie into the room and now he stopped behind her and laid his hands gently on her shoulders. Cecilie relaxed briefly at his pleasurable gesture; they very seldom ever touched each other in the normal course of events.

'Ursula, this is Cecilie,' said Alexander with a forced smile. 'She has just arrived back from the royal apartments at the castle.'

His sister pretended not to have heard him. 'What exactly are your reasons for marrying this bastard?' she snapped harshly. 'Money? Or a title?'

'Love,' replied Cecilie, feeling rage rapidly replacing the apprehension she had been experiencing earlier. But her voice remained steady and she repeated her answer calmly. 'Yes, love! What other reason could there have been?'

'Don't imagine you can fool me! Oh, no! I shall soon find you out …' She looked around the room and moved quickly towards a tasselled bell-pull used for summoning the domestic servants. She tugged it violently and shouted at the same time at the top of her voice: 'Magdelone!' the name of a chambermaid, who appeared almost instantly at a run, 'has this fraudulent young woman started running the estate yet?'

Catching her breath, Magdelone curtsied formally. 'No, Milady – and we all of us here already have great affection for Mistress Cecilie.'

'Hmm,' mused Ursula ambiguously. 'All right, that will be sufficient.'

Very slowly she turned to inspect Cecilie more carefully, but did not speak until the footsteps of the maid had died away along the corridor.

'You are, so I have heard, governess to His Majesty's children by that impostor … Kirsten Munk?'

Ursula almost spat out the name of the King's mistress and the look of distaste on her face was unmistakeable. At least we have something in common there, thought Cecilie. We are not entirely at odds with one another.

'I am indeed governess to the royal children,' she replied briskly. 'That is correct.'

'Well, I suppose that's particularly appropriate – you can hardly expect to have children of your own.'

'We hope that we shall,' interjected Alexander pointedly, at the same time pressing lightly on Cecilie's shoulders.

'Don't be ridiculous!' Ursula hissed without so much as a glance in his direction. 'I will not speak to one who has so dishonoured the name of our family with such sickening conduct. You will never have children – and that is something you both know!'

Sol's spirit stirred within Cecilie once more and the harsh and brutal nature of the Ice People could be heard unmistakeably in her voice. 'We shall try our very best, Ursula,' she retorted with icy defiance. 'Don't make hasty judgements about us.'

Her sister-in-law gave her a hard challenging stare. Then, turning away, she said: 'I have no time for people who lie to my face.'

A long uncomfortable silence followed. Then, as she was about to leave the room, the Countess stopped and spoke over her shoulder. 'I don't know what game you two are playing. But one thing I do know: my lascivious, perverted brother with his repulsive cravings would never share a woman's bed!'

Having delivered her harsh uncompromising broadside, the older woman swept out through the doorway, leaving Cecilie dismayed, furious and at a loss for words.

'You mustn't be sad, Cecilie,' murmured Alexander soothingly. 'She knows nothing of the deep friendship we share.'

The sound of Alexander's gentle voice close beside her instantly lifted Cecilie's spirits and lightened her mood. She drew a deep breath, allowing the anger and resentment in her to subside.

'You are kind, Alexander,' she said at last, forcing a smile. 'But I had wanted so much to be accepted by your family.'

'You will be, Cecilie, I promise you. I am so fond of you and so happy that you are here. And my admiration for you grows with each day that passes. I could never have wished for a better companion.'

'My tone was somewhat raw and vulgar, just then,' she reflected. 'You must excuse me.'

'She deserved it,' he smiled. 'Besides, I enjoy watching your wild, feline temper. I cannot understand where it comes from – it is not like the person I know at all.'

Cecilie, vaguely aware that intermittently she carried the spirit and courage of Sol inside her, smiled warmly and secretively to herself – but to Alexander and the world at large she said nothing at all.

* * * *

As the days passed, Cecilie wanted passionately to take Alexander home to Norway to introduce him to her family. But because the war situation was still tense and uncertain and his marching orders might come any day, Alexander could not obtain permission to leave his district. So they passed their days in a kind of limbo of uncertainty and waiting.

It was the carnival season and, to take his mind off the looming threat of war, the King had decided to enjoy himself come what may, and arranged some entertainment for the Court. Cecilie and Alexander were obliged to attend a number of functions, grand balls, soirées and receptions and on one occasion, Cecilie found herself swamped by a group of complete strangers. But she felt somehow that Alexander was watching out for her and so she did not allow herself to become too overwhelmed.

Looking around, she at last saw him smiling at her from the farthest end of the hall. Despite being engaged in conversation with a number of other men, he immediately hurried across to rescue her. He did not do this out of a sense of duty but – as he now frequently told her – simply because he enjoyed her company and wanted to be with her more than anyone else. This incident touched Cecilie deeply and she felt very glad that the closeness between them was continuing to grow significantly.

Then while they were attending another crowded ball, they suddenly heard a surprised and excited voice call his name from across the room. Cecilie could not immediately see who had called out and was puzzled at her husband's extreme reaction. The colour had risen suddenly in his face and she also noticed that his hands were gripping the back of a chair so hard that the knuckles had turned white. Then she saw that a young couple were making their way over to them – and the good-looking man who had called Alexander's name was beaming with joy.

'Alexander! How marvellous to see you! I haven't seen you in so many years! And is this your wife? May I present mine? Truly, we know how to choose the most beautiful, do we not?'

For once Alexander was speechless. He stood transfixed for some moments; then with an effort managed to gather his thoughts.

'Cecilie, may I present Germund, best friend of my youth,' he said haltingly. 'You will remember I have often spoken of him – and Germund, may I present Cecilie, my wife, as you correctly assumed.'

Germund bowed his head and took her hand formally. 'And this is my wife, Thyra. Mistress Cecilie, you will not believe how much I have missed Alexander! We were truly two of a kind. But then he just disappeared – transferred to another regiment. I was very hurt, Alexander. I missed you terribly!'

Alexander smiled, but Cecilie saw that the expression was strained. 'I soon regretted my decision, Germund. But by then it was too late.'

They all sat down in a quiet corner and chatted together animatedly for a long time. Germund, Cecilie realised, was a very compassionate man, but although his wife, Thyra, was pleasant enough she was just too conventional for anyone who had inherited the Ice People's temperament. Germund was short, slight of stature and sharp-witted. He had a lively and happy disposition and, while not particularly attractive, was extraordinarily charming. The reunion seemed to enliven Alexander and the awful tension Cecilie had noticed when he first met his old friend soon disappeared.

After that evening, however, something continued to bother him. He became edgy and distracted and his conversations with Cecilie became more and more abrupt and irritable. Eventually after several days, when she could tolerate it no longer, she took her courage in both hands.

'What is wrong, Alexander?' she asked as they sat eating supper. 'Are you still thinking of what happened at that last ball?'

He closed his eyes and it seemed from his pained expression that he wanted to tell her to be quiet and mind her own affairs. But in the end he simply said in a stifled voice: 'Yes, perhaps I am.'

'It was meeting *him*, wasn't it?'

'Yes,' he mumbled.

'Do you want to see him again?'

'I have told you before, Cecilie, that I don't *need* to be with someone just because I desire them! But meeting him opened up old wounds. You saw how happily married he is now, and he has never had the least suspicion of my predilections.'

'Can't we invite them here?'

'Why? I cannot go through all that pain again. Not to mention the indignity it would be to you – I could not put you through that.'

'He was your only *real* love? Is that not true?'

'I sometimes wish you were not so astute,' he said shortly. 'But you are right.'

'So do you still have a … weakness for him?'

Alexander drew a long breath, considering his answer carefully. Then he twisted his mouth wryly into a characteristic grimace that she knew well.

'Cecilie, I have no idea. That is precisely why I want to avoid his company. I do not want to discover that I still want … to be near him. The distress I felt at that time is not something I want to relive.'

'Then you had no such feelings when you met him this time?'

'No, only heartache over what had once been.'

'Yet you are so ill at ease these days.'

'Is that so strange, when I am so afraid? In fact I am frightened senseless!'

Cecilie could say no more. She did not know how to resolve the situation and she went to her bed that night with an unfathomable aching in her heart. For a long time she just lay on her back, looking blankly up at the ceiling, unable to gather her thoughts. Sometimes, she reflected wryly, she wished her husband were a less complicated man.

* * * *

Despite her open hostility, Alexander's sister Ursula stayed on at Gabrielshus and in effect kept a close eye on both of them. She knew of course that they had separate bedchambers, but Alexander habitually left some of his own personal belongings in Cecilie's room. In her turn, she slept deliberately on both sides of the bed each night to give the impression that he had been there at her side. Furthermore, their conversations had never before been so genuinely affectionate as they were now and as the days passed Ursula could find nothing whatever to criticise.

Most of the royal children had been moved back to Dalum Abbey to be with their grandmother, Ellen Marsvin. Only little Elisabeth Augusta remained behind at Frederiksborg because she was unwell and, as she lived close by, Cecilie's duties were to educate and care for the girl.

One morning at the end of March, Ursula came down to breakfast and found Cecilie sitting at the table, pale and out of sorts, unable to face any food.

'Were you not supposed to be at Frederiksborg some time ago?'

'I have sent word that I am unable to attend today.'

'Are you feeling unwell?' asked Ursula, who at last had begun treat her sister-in-law less formally.

Cecilie had always been adept at telling the occasional white lie whenever she thought it expedient. This was clearly yet another of her natural skills that had Sol engraved all over it, and she consequently employed it with the same relish.

'Alexander believes I may be with child,' she said, speaking very quietly. ' I can only hope it might be so.'

Ursula was horrified. 'Nonsense!' she roared. 'You *cannot* be with child!'

Cecilie was too weak to answer. Her head ached and she felt listless and sick.

'If that really *is* the case then who has fathered this child?' Ursula's words flew through the air like daggers. 'Tell me that – now this instant!'

Cecilie got slowly to her feet. Her mind was muddled, but her voice had the clarity of crystal. This would be her *great lie* and she could be good at those too, when they were called for.

'That Ursula, was an unbelievably insulting thing to say – first and foremost about Alexander!'

Countess Horn realised that she had gone too far. She could not withstand the righteous rage that burned in Cecilie's eyes and she eventually lowered her gaze to the floor. Then without another word she left the room. But her ramrod-straight back and self-assured step made it very clear to Cecilie that this matter was far from over.

* * * *

Alexander's orders to march came in April. The great host of mercenaries and the small Danish regular army were to assemble *en masse* in Holstein and then deploy from there. In the event Alexander barely had time to say farewell to Cecilie, who was truly sad to see him leave. Outside, his escort waited impatiently while he rushed hither and thither, hastily putting together everything he would need. Finally, he mounted his horse and as she stood silently at his stirrup, Cecilie felt a lump come into her throat. Without looking up, she quickly brushed away tears that threatened to betray her feelings.

'It's for the best this way, Cecilie,' he said softly, looking down at her.

'No, Alexander, no!' she cried. 'It's not. Please don't say that!'

'I'll write as soon as I am able.' He smiled sadly. 'And, Cecilie, make sure we have a fine little lad!'

Then in a moment he was gone. Cecilie stood and watched the troop ride away until they went out of sight. Inside herself, she was left with nothing but the dull ache of emptiness for company.

Chapter 5

Somewhere in the heart of the Holy Roman Empire, young Tarjei, son of Are and Meta and grandson of Silje Arngrimsdotter and Tengel the Good, was wandering distractedly through silent woodlands. He was hungry, worn out and completely lost. At one time he had been on his way to Tübingen to resume his studies, but that now seemed a distant memory.

He had managed to escape from the area where most of the fighting seemed to be taking place – but for all he knew it might just have been a local conflict that had flared up. Tarjei didn't know the facts or their background and there was nobody to tell him. Every door he had knocked at, to ask for information and seek a crust of bread, had been slammed shut in his face. He felt sure that this was because of his accent. He was clearly taken for one of the dreaded foreign mercenaries who laid waste, stole and raped without discrimination as they advanced.

Exhausted, he sank to the ground with his back against a tree in the tract of unknown forest. He had no idea where in Germany he might be; he had simply sought refuge deep among the trees, as any animal would do when death draws near. He was only eighteen years old, but young Tarjei was aware that he was one of the most promising talents in medicine of his generation. Now he feared that he would never use the skills he had learnt at the university in Tübingen and from his grandfather, Tengel.

In his small bundle he had a few of the rare herbal medicaments he had inherited from Tengel. He pulled them close to him, as if to protect them even in death. Everything else was still at Linden Allée, in a secret place that he and his grandfather had found together.

'What if I never return home again?' he wondered distractedly. 'And what if nobody ever finds that irreplaceable treasure?'

He was the one solely responsible for this unique and sacred treasure of the Ice People – all the ancient recipes and skills. Some of the recipes were bizarre, requiring lizard skins, dragon's blood, cats' heads and the skulls of newborn infants. Others were truly exceptional and based on lesser known herbs or special combinations of different remedies. The old witch, Hanna, had left her hoard of potions to Sol, while Tengel had his own inheritance. After Sol had died, her things, which were by far the more valuable, were left to Tengel. Now it all belonged to Tarjei. His grandfather had also made him swear that when the time came, he would find a worthy successor within their kin – so long as it was not the unfortunate Kolgrim.

The true successor had most probably not yet been born, he thought muzzily. Unless it was little Mattias – Kolgrim's angelic, mild and gentle-natured half-brother, born to Tarald and Yrja – whom Tarjei had helped bring into the world. But there would be more children born to the Meiden and the Ice People's families, wouldn't there? And what about his own children and grandchildren?

But no, this was just idle unrealistic speculation, he

reminded himself sombrely. He was obviously now close to death. Tarjei felt certain he could tell. He had no strength left, not even enough to search for something to eat here in the forest. There would be little to find anyway, this early in the year. He had not eaten for several days, and the last things he had consumed had been a few nuts from some hazels he happened to find.

He told himself for the hundredth time that he had to go on – that somewhere he would be certain to find help. But equally well he knew it was a fairly forlorn hope, for nobody dared speak to a stranger nowadays. The poor long-suffering population now had a deep hatred of all foreigners. Yet deep inside himself he knew that, for the sake of the sacred treasure of the Ice People, he must go on until he was no longer capable. But first he would sleep – just for a little while.

He was so tired – so very tired. The ground beneath him had not yet lost winter's raw chill and although Tarjei could feel the cold embracing him, he could do nothing about it. His body and his mind were both numb and without realising it, he slipped into unconsciousness before he slept.

And this is where the saga of the Ice People's secrets would have ended had something quite unexpected not happened. Through his haze of unconsciousness Tarjei gradually heard somebody shouting at him, as though from a great distance. But although he listened intently to the sound of the voice, he found he was absolutely unable to move. The unusual voice was young, insistent, impatient, demanding.

'Why are you lying here like this, you idiot?' the voice shouted in German. 'Answer me, you stupid man!'

Tarjei struggled again to claw his way back to a state of full consciousness in the world of the living – but without success.

'You must help *me*!' the voice squeaked, more impatient than before. 'You must!'

Somebody shook him roughly by the shoulder and Tarjei struggled again to climb to the surface of wakeful awareness. Finally he managed to open his eyes, or more precisely, forced his unwilling eyelids to part slightly. He didn't know how long he had been lying there, but his body was stiff with cold and he was so weak that he was unable even to lift a hand. But he could just make out the figure of a small person blocking out the frosty spring sunshine.

'Well, that's better! About time!' the angry voice rebuked him. 'I thought you were dead!'

'And so did I,' he mumbled almost unintelligibly in German. 'Who are you?'

'Do not address me as "you", stupid man!'

The shadow was gradually revealing itself to be a girl of about nine. As Tarjei's eyes began to focus, he could see that she was elegantly dressed, despite being dirty. She was also covered in pine needles and had dead leaves in her hair. He tried to speak again, but this time no words came out.

'Who might you be?' she was demanding again in a sulky tone. 'Tell me at once. Should you be one of those nasty mercenaries, then you shall not help me. I shan't even speak to you.'

'No, I am a Norwegian man of medicine,' muttered Tarjei after another struggle. 'I have nothing to do with this war.'

'You are a man of medicine? How splendid, because I have broken my leg!'

A broken leg was unlikely, thought Tarjei. You would not be standing there so at ease if it were. To his relief he was finding that the effort of focussing on a medical condition was helping to clear his mind.

'Why have you not yet properly introduced yourself, Norwegian man of medicine?' demanded the young voice imperiously. 'Come on, make an effort right now!'

'My name is … Tarjei Lind … of the Ice People,' he mumbled, then fell silent again. A new wave of tiredness engulfed him and his eyes closed involuntarily once more. 'Damn the girl!' he thought. How dare she demand an introduction from someone as they lay dying?

But Lind of the Ice People was indeed the name he had told her. This was the name the whole family had settled upon after long discussions. Lind came from Linden Allée, and they had decided to keep the clan name of Ice People, even though Grandfather Tengel had hated it so much. Many years had passed since the people of Tröndelag had hunted the Ice People to their death, and it had all happened a long way off. Nobody really remembered the terrible slaughter of witches and warlocks any longer.

'Lind of the Ice People? That sounds aristocratic,' the young lady chirped.

'Yes, you're right,' replied Tarjei, for the name did have an undeniably refined sound to it. 'And what is your name?'

'Do not address me as *you*!' she shouted and stamped her foot hard on the ground – the foot on the end of her 'broken' leg. 'I am *Mistress* Cornelia! My grandfather is Count Georg of Erbach am Breuberg. My Mama and Papa are both dead, so I reside at the home of my Aunt Juliana.'

'And now you want help with your foot?'

'You may not address me as *you*! Nobody may do so. It is forbidden.'

'I shall do as I please,' muttered Tarjei, still keeping his eyes closed.

'Then I shall leave!' she answered and turned on her heel.

'Yes, go. Then at least I can die in peace. You are of no help anyway. Nothing but a selfish, uninteresting little troll.'

Her young ladyship, the gracious Cornelia of Erbach am Breuberg contemplated the depth of this insult in silence, but did not move further off because her curiosity was getting the upper hand.

'Should I help *you*? What can you mean, you *commoner*?'

'Nothing. Now go away, you nasty little wench!'

She began moving off again then hesitated: 'Are you in pain?'

'No, I am not in pain, but I have eaten no food for seven days and I do not know where I am.'

'No food?' she echoed, taking a curious step closer again. 'Are you a beggar?'

'Would that I were! Then I should be alive now.'

'But you *are* alive!'

'Only just.'

The girl looked at him and said nothing for a few moments.

'If you put my broken leg back together again, then I shall permit you to come back home with me. You will be given food – at the scullery door.'

'Like a beggar?'

'No, perhaps not – you do have a title. Are you listed in the *Almanach de Gotha*?'

'What is that?'

'It is the register of the Royal Sovereign Princely and Ducal Houses of Europe. It lists all the imperial nobles of the Holy Roman Empire.'

'Then you can be sure that I am not listed in it.'

'A lower order of nobility, then?'

'No, I don't think so.'

'Well, in that case I'm not sure …'

'Oh, why don't you go and lose yourself in the woods!'

'It is *you* who are lost in the woods, silly man,' she retorted. 'Are you going to help me or not?'

'Hmm, show me the leg, then.'

Very cautiously she lifted the hem of her skirts just a little.

Tarjei stared in disbelief. While she did not have a broken leg, she did have a horrible gaping wound below her knee.

'How did you do *that*?' he exclaimed.

Seeing that he was suitably impressed with her injury, she played the role of heroine to its full.

'I tripped and fell over a tree root,' she told him, gesticulating to add to the drama. 'And it was a stupid branch that hurt me.'

'How long ago did it happen?'

'Just before I found you.'

'Did you cry from the pain?'

'I *never* cry, man of medicine!'

'No, of course not – but we must be quick. Come here!'

He found some dressing and a healing salve in his bundle. His hands were trembling and he had broken out in a cold sweat. Nausea washed over him in waves, like the sea breaking on the sand. Little Cornelia watched wide-eyed. Suddenly he groaned; his eyes wouldn't focus and he slumped forward.

'You've gone all white,' she said disdainfully. 'Wake up, man! You must help me!'

'Let me ... just … rest …'

'No! Get *up*!'

'I … must … eat …'

'I have told you – you will get food at my home at the scullery door!'

'You damned arrogant … conceited … little … troll,' muttered Tarjei, sheer anger driving him on. 'Now let's see if you cry or not, young lady! That wound needs to be sewn up – at once.'

'*Sewn up*!'

'Yes. Sit down and squeeze the edges of the cut together – unless you want to have a terribly ugly scar on your leg for the rest of your life.'

Little Cornelia sat down and did as she was told, deciding that pain was preferable to disfigurement, especially as Tarjei had pointed out that any blemish would make her less attractive to future suitors. Screwing up her face with distaste, she gritted her teeth as she watched Tarjei thread a needle fashioned from a fishbone.

'Ouch!' she yelled loudly, as he began work. 'That's hurting.' His making her cry in pain had affronted her tender dignity and she rewarded him with a slap. 'You stuck that *in* me!'

'Well, of course I stuck it in you. Do you want this sewn up or not, girl who never cries?'

'You carry on sewing, silly man! Don't concern yourself about me.'

His arms and hands were shaking badly, but he paused several times for a minute or two and eventually managed to sew up the wound. The girl flinched each time he pushed the needle into her delicate skin – three stitches were required in all – and although she was pressing her lips tightly together, she could not stifle an occasional desperate whimper. Tarjei dared not look up at her face; reluctantly he had to admire her fortitude and courage.

When he had finished, he rubbed an aromatic herbal unction onto the gash and finally wrapped a poultice around her thin leg. Having completed the task to his satisfaction, he closed his eyes and slumped back against the tree once more, allowing her the time to dry any shaming tears unobserved. She gradually brought her ragged breathing under control as the fierce pain of the stitching receded and Tarjei sensed she was slowly regaining her composure.

'You're almost handsome, you know,' she announced suddenly, without any warning. 'But in a quite unpleasant way.'

'Thank you!' he replied with an acid tongue.

'And what about me, then? I am beautiful, don't you agree?'

He opened his eyes again and strained to focus properly on her. She was a princess from a children's fairy tale, although a slightly chubby one, with dark hair in ringlets, now knotted and untidy, falling halfway down her back. Her well-defined mouth was small and pursed. There were dirty streaks running sideways from her large brown eyes to her ears where she had angrily wiped away some tears. Well, thought Tarjei, she could cry after all – he would have been amazed if she hadn't.

'You'll do!' he told her. 'Like a cake straight from the oven.'

'You are stupid!'

'Not as stupid as you.'

'I shall tell my Aunt Juliana's husband. He is Commander of the garrison at Erfurt, and he will have you flogged.'

'So that is how he treats people who have helped you, is it? Now let me just tighten that dressing and you can go – and let me say, you have been quite brave.'

His admiration obviously made her much happier and her face came close to relaxing in a smile.

'Come on, then,' she said, stretching out her hand to help him to his feet. 'Huh! You cannot even stand properly! I shall carry your bag.'

'No, thank you! I'll carry it myself,' he told her as he steadied himself against the tree, knowing very well that he did not have the strength to go on much further. 'Is it far?'

'No, no, no! Just beyond that little hill over there.'

The walk was gruelling for both of them and at first they limped along together, struggling with similar difficulty over the uneven ground. After a while, however, the youngster was supporting Tarjei's every step and she obviously enjoyed playing the role of the Good Samaritan, perhaps, he thought, because it was a novel experience for such a spoilt self-absorbed child.

Was it unkind of him to judge her so harshly? She was evidently a child of her time, defined by her rank and her status. The gap between the aristocracy and the common man was immeasurable. The Meidens were the only family he knew with a relaxed attitude to class differences. So, it was perfectly natural for little Cornelia to think of the masses as being there simply for her benefit and also to be shocked by Tarjei's lack of deference. She was begrudgingly impressed by him – or rather, she wanted him to be impressed by her and realised that being boastful and arrogant was not working.

'Let me tell you, Cornelia,' he said, breathlessly but in a more conciliatory tone, 'there are few grown men that could have withstood the sting of pain as well you did.'

She tried hard to look indifferent, but pride welled up inside her. His reward for this boost to her self-esteem was her immediate, if not wholly desirable, devotion. As they hobbled to the top of the hill, Tarjei was taken aback by what he saw. Below them lay a small hamlet and, on the hillside closer to them, stood the castle that it served. It was a tall, almost new and very beautiful building. In the distance, down the valley a larger town could be seen and he asked her its name.

'Do you know nothing at all? That is Erfurt, of course!'

Tarjei knew this was another university city and at least he had now discovered his whereabouts in Germany. He was in Saxony and this must be part of the border area being fought over by the Protestant and Catholic hordes. Now he fully understood why he had seen so much unrest and fighting.

'Are you Protestant or Catholic?' he asked her.

'Do you think I am a Catholic?' she demanded indignantly. 'They are Papists!'

'Thank heavens for that!' he thought, for although Tarjei was not deeply religious himself, he did regard himself as Protestant. It would not have augured well for him to have entered a hotbed of Catholicism, but at least no fighting seemed to have taken place here yet. If only he had known how close he was to an inhabited unspoilt valley, lying only a short distance from where he had sat in the forest!

After what seemed an age, they finally approached the great gate in the castle wall. He leant heavily against it, while he rested to catch his breath.

'Come on!' said the girl unsympathetically. 'We're not there yet. We still have further to go.'

They carried on, with Tarjei leaning more than ever on her narrow but strong shoulders. They continued in the shadow of the high castle walls for a time, until they spotted a crowd of people who had obviously emerged from the castle to meet them.

'Cornelia, my dear child, where have you been?' called one of the ladies among the crowd.

'I went out looking for spring flowers, Aunt Juliana,' the girl replied in her 'Good Samaritan' voice that sounded concerned, but more than a little smug. 'I broke my leg when I tripped and fell and this poor man made it better. He sewed in my skin! Then *I* saved *him*! He is a nobleman and a man of medicine who has not eaten for many weeks. He is not a mercenary – just a little stupid!'

The crowd had almost surrounded the pair, all talking at once, and then somebody lifted the girl up, leaving Tarjei to rest his back against one of the ornamental trees. He slid slowly to the ground, with the sound of Cornelia's high-pitched voice ringing in his ears as she tried to drown every other voice with the story of her bravery. That was the last thing Tarjei remembered, until he woke to find himself in one of the rooms in the castle. He was lying on a couch, and at a table heavily laden with food, sat Cornelia, waiting impatiently.

'Well! At last! It was horrible to see you sleep so long! They had to carry you in here, and you looked really silly with your head hanging over the manservant's shoulder! Now you must eat!'

Tarjei could see that her hair was brushed and tidy, and she was generally well groomed. Now that she was in her own familiar surroundings, there was no doubt that she was a very pretty and resolute young lady. Rising unsteadily from the couch, Tarjei carefully ate a little of the food and drank some wine. He was just finishing, when a young couple entered the room and introduced themselves as Cornelia's aunt and uncle, the Count and Countess of Löwenstein and Scharffeneck. Tarjei in his turn thanked them warmly and politely for their hospitality.

'It is we who should thank you,' replied Count Georg Ludwig Eberhardsson of Löwenstein and Scharffeneck, Colonel in the service of Sweden and Venice and commander of the garrison at Erfurt. 'Little Cornelia is a very adventurous and an independent young lady. Many's the time she has gone off on her own. Now you must tell us everything. Your treatment of her ugly wound implies a highly unusual knowledge of medicine. Who are you? She tells us you are a nobleman. And your dialect is unknown to us.'

'I am from Norway. My name is Tarjei Lind of the Ice People. My first name in full is Torgeir and any aristocratic connection has been exaggerated, I fear. I said only that it *sounded* like a noble name; I did not claim it to be one. My cousins however are nobility; they are born Meiden, a Danish baronial family. Nevertheless, I believe Lind of the Ice People is a name to be proud of.'

Count Löwenstein nodded. 'We know that the noble houses of Norway have been devastated. But continue!'

'Yes, I practice medicine. My grandfather was Norway's, and possibly Denmark's, foremost healer. I have studied under him and at the university in Tübingen. I was on my way there when the fighting stopped me – and nobody would offer any help because of my foreign dialect.'

'I can well understand. Wallenstein's mercenary knights have been plundering mercilessly. You will not be able to reach Tübingen now. Will you give us the pleasure of being our guest until you are fully recovered from your ordeal?'

'I cannot possibly burden you in that way,' replied Tarjei. 'At least allow me to show my gratitude by trying to treat the pains and sickness I might find among the folk here.'

The Count smiled. 'With pleasure, Master Tarjei! I wager you will find enough to last your lifetime! But wait – I have had a thought. A Protestant army is mustering, most likely under the command of the Danish King Christian. A field surgeon would be a heaven-sent gift. I will be pleased to recommend you, should you wish.'

The suggestion immediately appealed to Tarjei. 'I should be most grateful if you would. Thank you for your kindness.'

The Commander of the Erfurt garrison waved his hand dismissively. Then he said, 'First of all, I wonder if you might look at our newborn daughter, Marca Christiana. We are most concerned because it seems to us that her health might be failing.'

'I shall be pleased to do that at once,' said Tarjei. He tried to get to his feet a little too quickly and he swayed where he stood, feeling light-headed. 'I'm a great deal stronger already,' he said, as much for his own reassurance as for anybody else's. Then he stopped and bowed low to little Mistress Cornelia. 'A thousand thanks young lady for the help you have given me.

You fulfilled your promise in every way. Without you I would surely now be dead.'

She nodded gracefully, but now a happy smile was beaming back at him. She was flushed with a sense of knowing that she had been helpful and deserving of praise. It was indeed an unusual feeling for her.

'Uncle Georg, we must pretend not to notice his lack of manners when he addresses me as *you*,' she said still beaming. 'The poor fellow knows no better!'

Count Löwenstein's amusement showed in his smile as he looked at Tarjei, over Cornelia's head and motioned for the young medic to follow him from the room. The Countess joined them in their infant's bedroom and after Tarjei had examined the newborn Marca Christiana, he explained that she needed to be fed breast milk.

'Her stomach cannot tolerate other forms of nourishment,' he said quietly.

'But we have not been able to find a wet nurse,' the Countess told him anxiously. 'And the nursemaid weans her so well. With the best bread dipped in goat's milk.'

'That is no good,' said Tarjei thoughtfully. 'Not for her – she is too sensitive, it seems. Look at that rash – it is from the food. Can you not feed her yourself, Countess?'

'Me!' exclaimed the Countess in dismay. 'That would really not be appropriate!'

'It is the only thing to do, if you wish to save the infant's life. But perhaps Your Ladyship no longer has milk to give?'

Mistress Juliana was speechless. To have to discuss this sort of thing at all was so improper – and with someone so young!

'Well, my dear, do you understand the gravity of what our friend here is saying?' asked Count Löwenstein.

'Yes of course I do – but …'

'It is the only way,' Tarjei assured her.

91

'Juliana my dear, think of the baby,' pleaded the Count.

'But what if it becomes known! There would be such a scandal. I would be a laughing stock. And won't it ruin my figure?'

The irritation on Tarjei's face was plain to see. 'I do not believe so. But if you wish the infant to remain frail, become deformed or even die, then the choice is yours.'

'Oh, how embarrassing!' The cheeks of the Countess reddened even more. 'But I suppose if no one sees me – then ...'

Her husband smiled. 'Do it regardless, Juliana! And should anyone find out, well – it would not kill you. I think you will be very pretty. A Madonna with her child.'

The Countess, who had looked very downhearted, was slightly encouraged by what he had said and, despite remaining less than cheerful, she agreed.

By the following week Marca Christiana was much better and in that time almost everyone in the castle, nobility and servants alike, had come to Tarjei for help. Some of the pains were imagined, some downright fanciful, but everyone wanted to be treated by the sympathetic young healer with the fascinating features.

Little Cornelia sat with him all the time whenever he treated the sick. He was *her* discovery, a fact that she never failed to remind people. Sometimes she tried to dominate him, but soon discovered that it was like pouring water on a duck's back. Each time she failed, she resigned herself afresh to the fact that he *must* be stupid, as though it were the only explanation for his behaviour.

'Should you not be outside at play?' he asked her one day. She had by now graciously permitted him to address her informally.

'No, because I like to see how warm your eyes are whenever you feel sad for somebody. Why do you never feel sad for me?'

'For the simple reason that you have everything you could

wish for. But my eyes can still be warm for you, little friend, because I am very fond of you.'

Cornelia's sweet little face reddened with joy; in fact she was ecstatic. 'You are my true friend,' she said, with a catch in her voice. 'I have never had a friend like you before.'

He realised how alone she must have been as she grew up, orphaned, with her kind but strict relatives. She evidently had no one to play with and no one to whom she could chat.

'And you are my friend,' Tarjei told her solemnly. 'My best friend.'

She nodded, her eyes shining with childish devotion, and for a long time she could not take her eyes off him.

'Friendship is a fine and wonderful thing, Cornelia. The finest thing there is. It is the strongest, but also the most fragile thing in the world. Promise me you will never forget that.'

'Yes, you are right,' she sighed, gravely, despite not really understanding what he had said.

* * * *

A short time later, word arrived that the great Protestant army had begun to march south from Holstein. Tarjei was preparing to leave by then and Cornelia had gradually become inconsolable. As he made to depart, he crouched down beside his waiting horse and took the girl in his arms. Her heartrending sobs were muffled on his shoulder and her tears soaked his hair and his cheek.

'I am *crying*, Tarjei! I'm *really* crying. It's because I am so sad. You cannot leave me when I am so sad.'

He held her tighter, but said nothing, gently touching his lips to her hair.

'We are friends, Tarjei,' she tried again. 'You must not go!'

'I have to, my dearest child.'

'Then I shall go with you!'

'You know full well that you cannot. Besides, you have a runny nose.'

She drew her hand across her face and left a slimy trail all over her cheek.

'Oh, Cornelia! Where is your handkerchief?'

She gave him a delicate square of fabric and, very tenderly, he wiped her nose and dried away her tears. She made him promise that he would come back when 'this silly war' was over. Then she ran alongside him as he rode off and continued running all the way to the castle gate.

Before going out of sight, Tarjei turned in his saddle and waved sadly to the tearful little figure. Farewell, Cornelia, he thought. We shall never see each other again; you know that, as well as I do.

Colonel Georg Ludwig of Löwenstein and Scharffeneck had taken it upon himself to escort young Tarjei all the way through Saxony to meet the oncoming armies. So they rode steadily side by side throughout the day and when they finally met the advancing massed ranks of horses and foot soldiers, the colonel presented Tarjei to the Danish High Command. As expected, King Christian's troops were delighted to have the services of such a remarkable young field surgeon. He was quickly supplied with a complete field hospital and when it came to equipment, his every wish was granted. And Tarjei Lind of the Ice People had always known exactly what he wanted and how best to use it.

Chapter 6

The mighty Protestant hordes had disgorged themselves from Steinburg in Holstein and quickly overrun Northern Germany, like a torrent of migrating lemmings. Their Commander-in-Chief was King Christian IV of Denmark, although his appointment to this rank had not been unopposed. England, the Low Countries, Brandenburg, Lower Saxony and all the free cities of Northern Germany all belonged to the Protestant Union and none of them could quite comprehend what Denmark's interest in the war might be. They had refused to regard the war as a religious conflict, seeing it instead as a secular settlement of old scores. Sweden and France had decided to remain neutral for the time being, but were carefully watching events.

The final choice of King Christian as Commander was partly the result of family ties and influence. Not only was he ruler of two states, King of Denmark and Prince of Saxony, he also benefited from having his son, Ulrik, as Bishop of Schwerin and from other well-placed relatives in Bremen, Verden and Pfalz. The two men closest to him, as his armies advanced, were Duke Johann Ernst of Sachsen-Weimar, commanding the mounted troops, and General Johann Filip

Fuchs, who was commander of the infantry. While they marched, the 20,000 men or more who had set out from Steinburg found their numbers swelled by many knights from Lower Saxony and they were also joined by unexpectedly large numbers of Danish soldiers.

Alexander Paladin, with the rank of colonel, commanded a large cavalry regiment consisting mainly of mercenaries cobbled together from every part of northern Europe. Far behind him and his troops, among the infantry, marched the small contingent of men from Norway. What Alexander could not know was that there were among them three young men from the parish of Gråstensholm – the two brothers Trond and Brand of the Ice People and Jesper, the kind and considerate son of Klaus the stable hand. Nor would any of them have known who had arrived late one dark evening, far to the rear of the baggage train and begun to set up a field hospital. This was a welcome sight for soldiers and camp followers alike, who had already seen the first outbreaks of disease.

Trond, Brand and Jesper had all been issued with splendid uniforms – bright red tunics and yellow trews, which made them perfect targets for an enemy. They carried muskets and side arms, but as they had been given almost no training, they had not yet mastered their use. Of the three, only Trond regarded it as an adventure. The other two grumbled incessantly, saying that all they really wanted to do was return home.

'I should have been given a horse,' Trond declared one day at the height of summer. They had reached the town of Hamlin and had not yet seen or heard anything of the enemy. 'Then I could have been given command of a small company!'

'Why don't you go and ask for one, then!' barked Brand, who had grown tired of listening to his brother's never-ending ideas.

'Yes, I shall do so,' Trond retorted. 'First thing tomorrow, that's what I'll do!'

Brand and Jesper remained sitting on a hillside watching him storm off with brisk angry strides, evidently hurt by their lack of understanding. Brand was the youngest, heaviest and most relaxed of Are's three sons. He was a good-hearted soul, but was inclined occasionally to grumpiness and could then become very stubborn. He was the only one of Tengel's grandchildren who would brood over things, and when the mood took him, he would say nothing for days. Long after everyone else had forgotten what had upset him, Brand was still fretting over it. More than that, he expected everybody to understand just *why* he felt so aggrieved – something, alas, that is common to all who wallow in past slights.

Brand was stocky and well built, just like his father, Are, and had broad cheeks and deep-set eyes, of which nobody could clearly distinguish the colour. Only sixteen, he was too young to have discovered the pleasures and purpose of womankind. Equally, he was also much too young to have been taken off to war.

Klaus's son, Jesper, had a lot in common with Brand and they enjoyed each other's company. His flaxen hair was cut the same length all round – thanks to his mother's habit of putting the milk basin over his head and slicing off anything that showed below the rim. He was the same age as Brand's eldest brother, Tarjei, but they had no shared interests, although each had a friendly admiration for the other.

Jesper in fact was known for the simple directness of his thoughts and his friends often jokingly quoted his favourite example of reliable homespun wisdom: 'If all the haystacks in the world were one great stack, and all the farmhands in the world were one great farmhand, and all the pitchforks in the world were really one great pitchfork – damnation! What an awful lot of dust there'd be!'

There was not an ounce of malice in Jesper. All the evil he

saw in the world around him was beyond his grasp. Of the three, however, he was the one who spent most time watching women and girls. He looked at them whenever he got the chance and very often as he lay awake at night, surrounded by snoring soldiers reeking of sweat, he yearned for female company. Not that he would ever dare talk to any of them in the way the mercenaries did. The very thought made him blush and cast his eyes bashfully at the ground. Nevertheless, he grinned shyly at the thought that he might one day catch the eye of a young lass somewhere along the way.

Trond, always impatient and quick-tempered, was a totally different character from the other two. He was astute and quick-witted but, unlike Tarjei, he lacked the ability to put his ideas into practice. In addition, he was often ill at ease – a restless person, who always found it difficult to finish what he had started. He knew very well that he would be the one to inherit Linden Allée in due course because, despite being the eldest son, Tarjei had no desire to be a farmer. He also knew that the one most suited to the work was his little brother, Brand.

In short, Trond was seventeen and yearned to be a professional soldier – an officer – because he felt sure that was his destiny. The shadow of Tarjei had always loomed over him and he had never been able to match his elder brother, no matter how much he may have tried. Nor did he like the feeling that he was standing in the way of his younger brother. Was that why he wanted to be in command – to assert his authority? But Trond never wondered about such intangibles. To look at, he resembled Tarjei more than Brand, but both his build and his face were smaller. His grey eyes were quick, always darting to and fro, searching for new things to try.

That evening, their greatcoats wrapped around them, the brothers lay awake, talking softly while Jesper slept soundly between them.

'Why do we never meet our enemies?' whispered Trond. 'I want to fight – show what I'm good for!'

'I don't,' said Brand. 'I have no wish to die.'

'Who's talking about dying?' replied Trond, lifting himself up on one elbow. 'Obviously it's the enemy who dies.'

'There is nothing "obvious" about that subject at all,' said Brand shortly.

'Are we not kin of the Ice People?' asked Trond. 'We are almost immortal, you know that!'

'That's laying it on a bit thick. A few of our family have been special, that's true. But we are mostly just normal.'

Trond lay back down again. 'Do you know what I think?' he asked, musingly.

'No, what?'

'Well, you know how the Ice People had a treasure trove of magical herbs and such – even *mandrake*, they say. Now *that* is something worth having! And I think that if you had it all together, everything, then you could magic yourself to be really strong and immortal – maybe even invisible!'

'Humph!' Brand was sceptical. 'I don't think so. But a mandrake root? Just think!'

'Yes, but it doesn't really matter – the treasure is lost forever.'

Brand lay silent for a long time. Then he said in a ponderous voice: 'No, it isn't lost. I think I know who has it.'

'What do you mean?' Trond sat upright suddenly in his bed. 'You think someone was given it? By Grandpapa?'

'Yes, I think he told us all once – but we were so young then that it meant nothing.'

'Who was given it?' demanded Trond.

'Tarjei.'

'Tarjei? What could he do with it? He's got enough brains not to need it.'

Brand simply shrugged his shoulders. 'Did Grandpapa not say that Tarjei was the only one who could take charge of it?'

Trond had not listened to his grandfather, so he found it difficult to remember any of this. 'But Tarjei is in Tübingen in the south of Germany,' he said quickly. 'He cannot have carried everything with him down there! He must have hidden the things at home – and hidden them well, for I have never caught sight of them.'

'Yes,' said Brand thoughtfully, 'he probably has hidden them – so that little madman, Kolgrim, doesn't get his hands on them.'

Trond turned to look questioningly at his brother's shadowy outline in the darkness. 'Sometimes, little brother, you can be quite clever! Of course that's what he did. Because Grandpapa was determined always to stay on the side of good, wasn't he? But I think he was wrong. It's those who are cursed that should inherit the means to do witchcraft – like Kolgrim!'

'Yes,' agreed Brand. 'I think they were very unfair to him.'

'So do I.'

Brand chuckled. 'It would have been fun to be invisible – and own a mandrake root! It's said they have fantastic magical power. But to be invisible would be the best of all. Imagine what havoc one man could wreak in the enemy camp!'

'Untold mayhem!' laughed Trond.

They continued discussing their wild ideas about what they would do if they were invisible and other unlikely happenings. They became quite excited by their conjectures and long after all the other soldiers had fallen asleep, one of the two Ice People brothers remained wide awake. His mind was still racing, contemplating among other things the unfairness of the rightful successor, Kolgrim, not being given the treasure. But other more outlandish thoughts and fantasies began to play around in his excited mind too and he found that he could not sleep at all.

Eventually he sat up and stared out at the flames of the campfire that were dancing and flickering against the night sky. His imaginings began to lead him in strange directions, to places he had never known or visited before. The fantasies quickly grew more terrifying, but at the same time more wonderful, more alluring. They found their way down into a place of spinning blackness deep within himself that he would never have believed existed before that night. There he heard echoing words and saw vivid images to match them: 'Mandrake root! Become invisible! Find the secret store of potions!'

Jesper turned in his sleep, gasping for breath, his arms and legs entangled in his greatcoat. Eventually he opened his eyes sleepily, still panting for breath.

'What is it, Jesper?'

'Be careful!' Jesper hissed at him. 'I saw a big cat! A very big lynx! Right where you are now.'

'That's rubbish.'

'I did! I swear!'

'Did you truly see a cat – here?'

'No, not really a whole cat – but a pair of glowing eyes shining in the firelight. Really, like cats' eyes do. And they were there, really, just where your eyes are. It must have been standing behind you!'

'Variety with words has never been your strong point, Jesper,' said the other, changing the subject slightly. 'You have just used the word "really" three times in as many seconds.'

'Oh! Don't you understand it's *dangerous*! A great big animal!'

They got up and walked around quietly together, taking care not to wake the other sleeping soldiers. But they could find nothing. Jesper was still worried when he lay back down and pulled his coat around him.

'It must have been a nightmare, then,' he said in a mystified voice. 'But I thought it was really …' he stopped himself, remembering he had used that word too many times before.

The other young man spread out his coat on the ground and lay down. A slight smile played across his lips. 'I knew it! I knew that I was one of the chosen ones of the Ice People,' he murmured to himself. 'And Grandpapa knew it too! He looked so strangely at me that day. I am like them! After all this time it is wonderful to be able to acknowledge it. But this shall be my secret. Nobody is to know!'

* * * *

The very next evening and much to his comrades' surprise, young Trond went to see the commanding officer of his regiment, Lieutenant Colonel Kruse, and made the request of which he had spoken the previous day.

'What?' the high-ranking officer exclaimed with a mocking laugh, 'are you really serious?' He was in good spirits, having just finished an excellent supper in the company of his fellow officers and brothers-in-arms. 'Who does this cheeky Norwegian peasant think he is? So he wants to be an officer, does he? Ha! What practice have you had, young man?'

'Not much experience, sir,' admitted Trond. 'But I know that I have the qualities required for leadership.'

Good humour and wine were flowing freely and the officers and gentlemen all laughed heartily on hearing Trond's calm words. They exchanged mocking remarks and laughed some more before Colonel Kruse at last held up one hand to quieten the hilarity.

'You shall be given an assignment, soldier,' declared the

amused colonel. 'If you carry it out successfully, we shall consider your request. No, let's say we will make it two assignments! Do you accept?'

'Yes, Colonel,' said Trond, thrilled, 'I accept.'

'Excellent! We have a small band of foreign mercenaries that nobody can keep under control. To tame these wild animals is your first assignment. You will lead them to reconnoitre the small village south of Hamlin where scouts from the Catholic armies are said to be hiding. Obtain all the information you can, soldier, *without* giving away your position to the enemy – and without letting the mercenaries rampage through the village. Do all this and an officer's rank will be yours!'

Trond was beaming with delight as he saluted and returned to his quarters, but Kruse's comrades were observing him thoughtfully.

'Was that not a risky move?' one asked as soon as Trond was out of earshot. 'That young stripling might cause a disaster, you know.'

'Not at all!' boomed Kruse. 'First off, he'll never master those unruly troops – they'll *flatten* him! Second off, there *are* no Catholic scouts within many miles of us! Tilly cannot get his orders to march.'

The enemy of King Christian's force was the Catholic League, supported by the Holy Roman Emperor. Their Commander-in-Chief was Prince Elector Maximilian of Bavaria and their most successful military leader was the austere and fanatical Catholic general, Johann Tserclaes, Count of Tilly. By 1622, Tilly had conquered the whole of the Pfalz region and brought it under Catholic control. In 1623 he had defeated the Duke of Brunswick-Wolfenbüttel and in 1624 he had marched into Hesse. At this point the Protestants in the north were becoming alarmed.

Tilly boasted of three things: he had never tasted wine, never enjoyed the favours of women and never been defeated on the field of battle. He was now being held back, awaiting developments, while he watched the Protestants' progress and planned his strategy.

The other great Catholic general was von Wallenstein, Duke of Friedland. He was the opposite of Tilly in every way. It had been Wallenstein's militias, made up of mercenaries from at least ten countries, which had brutally ravaged the German states – with their leader's blessing. Wallenstein enjoyed luxury and savagery. To satisfy his marauding hordes, he allowed them to sack and plunder everything that lay in their path – which also enabled him to live in extravagant opulence. The mercenaries adored him. Many of them, his commanders included, were Protestants, but that was of no consequence to him or them. Their overriding interest was profit – and the opportunity to pillage the civil population.

Wallenstein was a swarthy, gloomy man with a piercing gaze and a mercurial temper that terrified many. Catholicism meant nothing to him; it was just a word. He put his trust in the stars and in astrology, not in God. He had no religious beliefs at all. But Wallenstein and his hordes were still too far away to pose any threat to King Christian's Protestants. There was also a third, younger Catholic general, named von Pappenheim – but it would be several years before his name was widely known.

The mercenaries in King Christian's service were hardly better than Wallenstein's militias and among the worst were the riff-raff that young Trond had been sent to bring to heel. They completely lacked any sense of battlefield ethics, were accompanied by a large band of camp followers, including many women and children, and only obeyed orders when it suited them. That evening, when Trond entered their encampment, he was confronted by a few quiet jeers and insolent grins from a group of ten or twelve men.

He had prepared himself well for the task before him. Suspecting that these men would not take kindly to a young outsider, he had designed a number of emblems and badges of distinction that he had sewn onto his colourful uniform. They meant absolutely nothing, but they did look very impressive. However, nothing had prepared him for the panic that welled up inside him when he saw what he had taken on.

To make matters worse they spoke several different languages. Because these men were mostly Germans and Italians, Trond had brought with him a Danish-speaking interpreter, who immediately introduced Trond as His Majesty's Emissary. None of them thought to ask why an emissary was dressed in such a colourful uniform. It was usual then for armies to go to war proudly dressed in bright, almost gaudy colours; camouflage was an unknown concept at the time, and besides, it would have been thought of as unprincipled.

Trond was convinced that he was a born leader but, as yet, only he was of that opinion. Somehow he managed to adopt a convincing air of authority and, without a second's hesitation, he pointed at a stocky brute of a man who was sitting, intimately fondling the girl perched on his lap.

'You!' Trond said coldly. 'You will speak on behalf of everyone!'

Intuitively he had made the correct choice. Although he wore no badge of rank, this man was their leader. He pushed the girl to one side and scowled at Trond.

'You're a cocky young thing, aren't ye?' he said offensively, but a slight note of uncertainty was detectable in his voice and he did not make any further comment.

This was a good sign, thought Trond. This indicated that

he might be able to manipulate this man and, through his interpreter, he explained to the group what they had been ordered to do. As the need for a go-between would take the edge off his authority, Trond kept looking directly at the mercenary as he spoke; he dared not even blink. But before long he was proved right – he was a born leader – maybe only in war as a soldier, because that was the life he had longed for. Those things we are really interested in are always likely to be the things we are best at. Conversely, back home in Linden Allée Trond lacked all authority, because he found farm work deadly dull and boring.

So in spite of their natural reluctance, the mercenaries listened to him – partly because he had the attention of their leader and partly because his voice had the quiet ring of authority. In addition they could also see there was a look of ruthlessness in his expression.

'There will be no plundering,' he warned them. 'We will do no more than ask careful questions of the local citizens, and to do that we must have their trust. You will not win their trust by preying upon them.'

'No, but y' will win trust when y' put a knife to their throat!' called one of them with a smirk.

Trond turned at once and fixed him with a glare. 'What value is there in that? Frightened people will say anything to save themselves. I want men who can ask clever questions and who have the courage to go unarmed where their enemies may be lurking.'

These mercenary vandals, who normally would not have listened to someone so young, found themselves reluctantly nodding in agreement. They had no idea who he was, but he wore the uniform of the 'Red Regiment', which was almost wholly made up of Danes. His officer's insignia was one they did not know; he had been referred to as 'Emissary' and that sounded like a title to be respected – although they remained puzzled that he looked so young. But no matter, they concluded, as they listened, he spoke of something that stirred the blood: a chance for action instead of marching, marching – all the time, marching. *That* was really dull and mind-numbing.

Trond quickly dismissed a couple of the men, who looked as though they were hangers on, there only because they were impressed by the raw strength of their comrades. This did him no harm; the remaining mercenaries looked at him with renewed respect.

'And I want to see no women or children in this camp,' he declared. 'We are an army on the march, not a bunch of wives on a Sunday stroll! And no other civilians either. They can all go and join Wallenstein's disorderly, good-for-nothing militia if they wish! Get them gone!'

There were murmurings of protest and dissatisfaction from all sides and the soldiers, as well as the women, immediately began to grumble audibly.

'Are you here to fight – or are you going to turn flabby and weak in the arms of women?' he demanded. 'We have no use for such men! I shall find others.'

He turned smartly about as he finished speaking, as if making ready to leave.

'Now, just hold hard there a minute, my eager young fellow,' called their leader, speaking his words slowly and with menace. 'Hold hard!'

Trond stopped dead, turned and said: 'Good! I'm glad you have understood and agree.' He looked even harder at the man who had spoken. 'You will ensure personally that all your men are ready tomorrow morning as soon as they have broken fast. If I see any civilians here then, I shall report the matter to His Majesty personally.'

The moment he left, the grumbling turned to uproar, but as he returned to his regiment Trond felt jubilant.

'I have done it,' he thought. 'And they had no idea who I was. If they had but known I am nothing but a young farm lad from Gråstensholm, they would have torn me to shreds!'

* * * *

At the agreed time next day, Trond presented himself and his ten men to Colonel Kruse. The officer looked a little taken aback on seeing them, but did not say anything immediately.

'Lieutenant-Colonel, Sir! His Majesty's Emissary reporting for duty with his chosen men. I am also pleased to inform the Colonel that the encampment has been cleared of civilians. We are ready to march. Are there any further orders, Sir?'

Behind his carefully controlled exterior Colonel Kruse was almost choking with surprise. But he managed to keep a straight face as he cautioned them to be careful then dismissed them.

'Well, I'll be damned,' said one of Colonel Kruse's aides. 'That lad's got some nerve – I'll say that for him. Did you see those insignia?'

Kruse laughed out loud. 'The boy's got guts. A pity on this occasion – because those men will ride roughshod all over him. And they'll eat him alive when they realise the whole thing is just a diversion.'

'But if his bluff works then I reckon he deserves some credit.'

'What was it I promised him?'

'The rank of lieutenant,' teased his companion, aware that Kruse had been enjoying a glass or two too many that evening.

The Colonel shuddered. 'Heaven help me! What will His Majesty say? Did I really say that?'

'No,' the other officer chuckled, 'but it was not very far from it!'

'Oh! Thank God for that,' sighed Kruse. 'Still, it's of little consequence. The boy will never bring it off.'

His fellow officers smiled and laughed as they nodded their agreement, but there was no sign of their smiles or their laughter at the same hour next morning when the same small band of soldiers stood before their commanding officer listening to Trond delivering his report.

'Yes, yes, yes! I know Tilly is encamped at Paderborn,' Kruse interrupted impatiently. 'He has been there for a long time.'

'Correct, Sir!' exclaimed Trond. 'But two of my men heard that he has been sent orders to march.'

'What! By Elector Maximilian?'

'Probably. It seems Tilly intends to advance towards the River Weser and cross it at Höxter, Sir.'

Their commander's face gave nothing away; his expression might have been chiselled in stone.

'And Wallenstein?'

'Nothing about Wallenstein, Colonel.'

'And has Tilly begun his advance?'

Trond turned questioningly to one of the mercenaries, who said: 'Nobody told nothing about that for definite, Colonel. The rumours wasn't that strong.'

'Thank you! Good work all of you! I shall convey this information to His Majesty at once.'

Having spoken, Kruse turned and walked quickly away, giving Trond no opportunity to remind him of what he had been promised, should he succeed. But for the moment Trond was not worried about his reward. Overjoyed by the success of his mission, he rejoined his two close comrades-in-arms and the three of them linked hands in a victory dance, swinging each other around wildly and cheering.

Colonel Kruse's fellow officers were no less astonished than Brand and Jesper when they had heard of Trond's successful exploits. Alexander Paladin was among those officers, and he too had previously allowed himself a chuckle at the expense of this delightful young fool – not knowing how closely related the two of them were.

But it soon turned out that the information Trond had obtained was true: Tilly had certainly decamped and was ready to march. At long last he was ready to strike down the Protestant horde. Tilly was a profoundly religious man and, as always, he went to pray to his Madonna. Unsurprisingly, he begged her to ask God to grant him victory over the ungodly. At the same time, King Christian and his closest followers were also deep in prayer, asking God to stand with them in battle against the blasphemous Papists. At that moment it seems quite likely that Our Lord was feeling more than a little confused.

* * * *

The Catholic army, led by Count Tilly, crossed the Weser on 18 July 1625 and continued its irresistible advance north along the river. King Christian IV, however, could do nothing because, on 20 July, he fell from his horse and suffered a severe concussion. He watched as his armies withdrew, without a shot being fired, to the fortress at Nienburg where Tilly caught up with them. The Protestants took refuge behind the ramparts where, in reasonable safety, they could await the King's return to health.

Just how poorly trained the regular Danish troops were had become apparent during their long retreat without a commander-in-chief, and there was a total lack of discipline among the mercenaries and irregulars. For these reasons alone, the well-needed respite provided by the fortifications was a godsend.

Trond of the Ice People was given the rank of corporal – to be promoted to lieutenant so quickly was obviously asking too much – and he was given the one thing he had longed for most: a horse. This meant that he was now parted from his brother Brand, and from his friend Jesper, although he was never far away from them.

His happiness, however, showed in his eyes: the in-between child, as he had often thought of himself, who had always been stuck in the middle, was making something of his life at last. He had found his calling. All he had to do now was prove himself worthy of the trust placed upon him – and that was something Trond intended to do, come hell or high water.

Chapter 7

Back in Denmark, a very resolute Cecilie was at loggerheads with the housekeeper of Frederiksborg Castle. Relations between the two of them were always distant and formal at best and acrimony was never far from the tone of their exchanges. But what the housekeeper had expected would be a routine discussion of Cecilie's immediate duties with the royal children had suddenly become something much more divisive, because Cecilie had decided it was time to make her condition public knowledge at the Court.

'No, I shall not be able to travel to Dalum Abbey on this occasion,' she said firmly when the housekeeper haughtily outlined preparations to take the children on a journey they had often made before.

'And why not, may I enquire?' asked the housekeeper in an incensed voice.

'Because I am myself with child,' replied Cecilie coolly. 'Therefore the journey will be far too arduous. What's more I shall no longer be able to care for the young royals as they have a right to expect. Apart from anything else, in my condition I shall no longer be able to lift or carry them.'

The housekeeper was furious. 'If that is the case, Countess, then you are dismissed immediately! Weaklings have no place here! Now go – right away! You will have to make your own way back to Gabrielshus.'

'No matter, I was intending to resign my position today anyway,' replied Cecilie evenly. 'My carriage, however, will not be here until evening.'

'That is no concern of mine! Borrow a horse from the stables if you must.'

'But she cannot ride in her condition!' exclaimed one of the ladies-in-waiting.

'What nonsense!' replied the housekeeper who, when it came to dealing with staff, considered herself Countess Paladin's superior without question. Furthermore, she knew that both Kirsten Munk and Ellen Marsvin would stand behind her, and they were a pair of terrifyingly powerful women.

'I rode every day when I was in my hallowed condition,' the housekeeper continued. 'What is more, I understand the Countess to be an accomplished horsewoman. She may take Florestan.'

'But that horse is the match for two strong men!' said the lady-in-waiting.

'Are you a good horsewoman or not?' the housekeeper demanded of Cecilie in a caustic voice. 'There is no other horse. Take it or walk!'

'Walk all that way? May I not be permitted to stay here, just until the carriage arrives?' asked Cecilie.

'You have just refused to obey an order! Refused to accompany the children of His Majesty the King to Dalum Abbey. That is unpardonable behaviour. Now go!'

At last the head housekeeper had found the perfect opportunity to exact her long-desired revenge on this impudent Norwegian girl, who was otherwise so well thought of by everyone at Court. Above all else she had dared to marry up and assume a distinguished title far above her station – this plain Norwegian hussy from 'peasant' nobility who had become a Paladin overnight. It had all been quite insufferable.

Cecilie took a deep breath, but said nothing more. Yes, she could ride competently; there was no doubting that. But whether she could handle the fiery-tempered horse Florestan was decidedly another question. Yet if she was to return home, then she was left with no choice. Feeling anxious, she gathered together her few belongings and bade farewell to the young housemaids with whom she had worked, all of whom had become her friends.

The King was far away in Germany, and to everybody's astonishment, Kirsten Munk had joined him. In her absence, the housekeeper was now the unopposed head of staff. As a result of her insistence that she be allowed to share the hardships of war with her husband, there was now plenty of gossip at Court suggesting that marital relations between Christian IV and Mistress Kirsten had begun to blossom anew. If true, this would have been heartily welcomed by the King, because he cared a great deal about his family circle.

People had often held Kirsten Munk in low esteem, and referred to her disparagingly as a simple-minded housemaid, but they were wrong. She had been born into a very distinguished family – her father was the powerful Ludvig Munk of Nörlund, one time Governor General of Norway, who had amassed a vast fortune in that country before he was removed from his post by a very young King Christian.

Her mother was Ellen Marsvin of Lundegård and Ellensborg, one of Denmark's wealthiest and most influential women – and also one of its most cunning. Mother and daughter were both arch-schemers, avaricious and hungry for riches. Unlike her mother, however, Mistress Kirsten was both foolish and shallow. Her sudden desire to leave for Germany with the King was seen by most, not as a token of love, but more likely a taste for adventure. Whatever it was, nobody at Frederiksborg missed her, particularly the ill-tempered housekeeper, who relished the greater freedom this allowed her to rule the domestic fiefdom in the castle in her own dictatorial way.

As Cecilie left, the housekeeper was watching from a discreet position beside one of the castle's upper windows and she smirked with satisfaction at seeing the Norwegian governess carrying her belongings a little disconsolately towards the stables. The stable boy who greeted her showed he was very concerned when Cecilie asked him to saddle up Florestan.

'Make sure you keep him on a tight rein, Countess! But not *too* tight, mark you. He's not that easy to handle.'

'Is there no other horse I can take?'

'Everyone's out hunting, Your Ladyship.'

'You'd better wish me luck, then!' said Cecilie and climbed into the saddle. 'Will somebody fetch him back later?'

'I'll see they do. Good luck, My Lady!'

She would certainly need all the luck available, she thought as she set off homewards, because Florestan began immediately to prance and skitter in an alarming way. But she succeeded in getting him under some sort of control and settled as best she could into a very bumpy and nerve-wracking ride. Countless times she wrestled with the strong-willed beast to keep him on the right path, and everything went reasonably well until she entered the courtyard at Gabrielshus. There she and the horse were promptly greeted by a number of barking dogs, at which point the horse reared up wildly.

Cecilie had no chance of holding him and to her dismay she was unseated and fell heavily to the ground. Luckily she avoided the horse's flailing hooves as it turned and made off through the archway of the courtyard, heading back towards Frederiksborg. Cecilie found she could not move and the dogs clustered round and started licking her face. Shocked and exhausted from the ride, she cried out for help in a voice that was weak and tremulous.

Alexander's manservant Wilhelmsen hurried outside, followed closely by several housemaids and servants.

'Help me,' whispered Cecilie. 'I fell from the horse.'

'We saw it all,' said the manservant in an agitated voice. 'That was such a difficult mount you were riding!'

'I was given no choice,' she gasped. 'I was made to ride him, because I did not want to go to Dalum. I didn't have to go, did I, Wilhelmsen?'

'Certainly not, Your Ladyship. Come, take my hand.'

Cecilie screamed with pain as she tried to rise, 'Aah! The baby! Please help me!'

Many willing arms lifted her bodily from the ground and carried her anxiously inside. With great care the servants settled her gently on her large bed.

'Send for the midwife – I forget her name!' shouted the manservant. 'But do it quickly!'

Cecilie felt waves of pain rising and falling through her whole body. She suspected she had banged her head badly as she fell and now everything around her became hazy as she drifted into troubled unconsciousness. When she awoke, she was still in great pain and her head ached, but her sister-in-law Ursula was sitting by her bedside.

'The baby,' she whispered, her eyes wide with fear. 'Alexander's baby – will I lose it?'

'There, there,' Ursula said soothingly. 'Just lie still! The physician will be here soon. All will be well.'

'No!' Cecilie told her in an agonised voice, 'all is not well. I can feel it.' She began weeping and the wrenching bout of tears sent daggers of pain through every part of her body.

'Try not worry,' said Ursula soothingly. 'Lie quietly if you can.'

'I want so badly to give Alexander a child,' she groaned. 'He seemed so happy that … the family name … would not die out. Now everything is going to be … ruined.'

In her eyes Cecilie had not wantonly misled Ursula. In every practical sense she thought of her baby as Alexander's and now considered the part that had been played in the matter by Pastor Martinius as totally irrelevant. After all, she often told herself, it was Alexander she had really been thinking of that day in the churchyard tool shed.

This thought triggered a new flurry of tears and as she observed Cecilie's anguish, Ursula was herself overcome with emotion. Reaching out, she embraced her and held her close. 'My dearest sister-in-law,' she murmured, choking back her own tears. 'My dearest Cecilie!'

Cecilie held on to Ursula tightly as pain seared through her once again. 'I so wanted to make him happy,' she sobbed. 'He has been …' She struggled vainly to finish her thought, but her voice tailed off and she found that she no longer had the strength to talk.

'Oh, what a beast I have been,' said Ursula as tears ran down her cheeks. 'Can you ever forgive me, Cecilie? And Alexander? I hated him for dragging our family name down – and all the time it was nothing other than slanderous lies!'

'Oh, Ursula!' whispered Cecilie. 'Ursula!'

The next moment she let out a terrified shriek. It seemed as though her whole body was being torn apart from within and she felt a sticky warm wetness in the bed.

'Alexander!' she screamed and his name echoed again and again through the corridors and passageways of the house. 'Alexander! Alexander!'

Ursula held her more tightly. 'To think I doubted you both,' she said in an agonised tone. 'To think I doubted your love for each other.'

Cecilie did not have the strength to get out of bed for several days. The injury to her head made her feel dizzy if she sat up, so she lay on her back most of the time. She could do little but stare out through the window into the gardens, lost in her thoughts, and consequently her mind wandered, and jumbled impressions came and went without making any real sense.

One evening after her supper had been cleared away, Ursula came and sat with her. She took Cecilie's hand, smiling at her as she did so.

'And how are you feeling?' she asked with friendly concern.

'I don't know,' replied Cecilie with a little shake of her head. 'I truly do not. I seem incapable of feeling anything.'

Ursula squeezed her hand sympathetically and smiled again. 'I feel I have judged you both so unfairly – Alexander most of all.'

Slowly Cecilie turned her head and looked straight at her. 'No,' she said kindly, 'you were not completely wrong. Alexander has had some difficulties.' Her sister-in-law stiffened visibly. 'Try to look upon him with more compassion, Ursula. Alexander has been a very, very unhappy person.'

'Is he – restored to health, now?'

'He is trying to be. And we are very happy together, as you must have noticed.'

'Yes, yes – that is true. But …'

Cecilie interrupted her. 'Ursula, will you do something for me? Will you tell me all about Alexander when he was a child and how he grew up? He remembers so little, you see.'

'Why do you want to know that?' the other woman asked, uncertainly.

'Because it would mean so much to me. That part of his life may hold the key to what happened to him later on.'

'His … weakness for the wrong type of person. Is that what you mean? Oh – the whole thing is so sordid! It's repulsive!'

'But you cannot believe he wished it to be so, Ursula? He was just as shocked as you and I.'

'Was he?' asked Ursula in a cynical tone. 'I doubt that. I think Alexander has probably always been the way he is. For example, I can recall …' She stopped talking abruptly, her sudden distress plain to see.

'Ursula, *please* go on. I have a right to know.'

'But it is not something I can bring myself to talk about.'

'Do try! Snuff out some of the candles, if darkness will help to make it easier to confide in me. Alexander remembers nothing at all.'

'He *must*! How can he not? What happened was so awful!'

'Perhaps that is exactly *why* he doesn't remember,' murmured Cecilie. 'It might all have been so vile that he buried it away deep inside himself.'

'I shouldn't be surprised,' said Ursula quietly.

There was a long silence.

'Well?' prompted Cecilie.

'No, I really cannot do this.'

But Cecilie, encouraged by the fact that her sister-in-law did not get up and leave, decided to persist.

'Ursula! Alexander and I have talked through everything – or everything he can remember. It wasn't easy for either of us. I was also disgusted by it all at first and couldn't understand how anyone could be like him. But you see, he couldn't help himself. It was almost like a sickness – although I don't believe he would think of it in that way. And he is such a wonderful man.'

Alexander's sister nodded. Her red-painted lips were grim

and unsmiling. 'I suppose I can try – but not without misgivings.'

And so she began her story: she told first how the plague had robbed them of all their siblings, and about their miserable mother, who doted on Alexander. She spoke too of their father, who had not been a warm family man and had in fact been self-indulgent and given to extremes of debauchery.

'What about the pictures?' asked Cecilie, 'Alexander spoke of some pictures in a room that he did not like.'

'Ugh! That! That was our father's room – the pictures were truly repugnant. They were mainly obscene depictions of alluring women – often with strangely bloated bodies. It wasn't art; it was more ... uh ... what should I call it? Fulfilment of men's filthy imaginings. Mother hated that room, and when father died she burned every one of the pictures.'

'Do you think that might have had some effect on the way Alexander is now?'

Ursula thought for a minute or more. 'That I cannot say. I hardly think so. But he did get an awful lot of beatings because of those pictures.'

'What do you mean?'

'Well, he managed to sneak into the room on his own quite a few times. It was otherwise forbidden for us to enter, you understand. Father ordered his valet to give him ten lashes with a birch after he had been in the room once too often.'

'So are you saying Alexander *liked* to go into the room and look at those wretched pictures?'

'I don't know. Besides I think that episode is irrelevant.'

'No,' thought Cecilie, 'I don't think it is.'

'You said before that Alexander had always had unnatural affections?'

'Yes, there's no doubt about it,' replied Ursula. 'He was not more than twelve years old when he was discovered in some very suspicious circumstances.'

'With a man?'

'Yes, with father's old valet who had been kept on after father died. He was dismissed at once, of course. Despite pleading his innocence, the old man's punishment was harsh.'

'And then nothing more after that?'

'Not until these unpleasant rumours started.'

Cecilie stared up at the ceiling. 'That was when he was twelve years old, you say? And when was he given that beating for sneaking into the locked room?'

'It must have been … oh … I think it was during the last year of our father's life.'

'Then Alexander would have been about six or seven years old,' said Cecilie reflectively. 'Did you *see* him being beaten?'

'I cannot remember that now. It was so long ago. But no, I do not think so.'

'Yet until then, you had noticed nothing strange about Alexander?'

'No.'

'Just *why* was the valet kept on after your father died?'

'Because he begged and pleaded with mother to be allowed to stay on.'

'Aha,' said Cecilie sombrely. 'Could that be because he had discovered a young boy that he could mistreat after promising him, on that first occasion, that he would not be beaten?'

Ursula stared back at Cecilie, but said nothing.

'If that *was* the case, then perhaps the valet was later able to threaten him with the birch if he told tales or refused to do as the valet asked. Here was a little boy whom you have said was naturally curious about looking at naked women, as I imagine most growing boys are. But then he might have been forced to do things that were not normal to him. Could that not have been so?'

Ursula stared at Cecilie wide-eyed, perhaps without really seeing her. Her expression suggested she might be silently considering the whole of her brother's childhood properly for the first time.

'You are making me think, Cecilie,' she said very quietly.

'You said just now that you were sure that Alexander could *never* have forgotten one awful situation … Was that the time he was found with the valet, when he was twelve?'

'Of course – it was the most terrible day. Mama had always worshipped Alexander and she burst into a terrible rage after he was seemingly found with the valet. She hit him over and over, howling and screaming the most horrible words at him. Alexander did not speak for many weeks afterwards.'

Ursula fell silent for a while, staring straight ahead. Cecilie thought she was unable to say more, but eventually she straightened on her chair and looked again at Cecilie.

'After that he behaved very strangely for a long time. Perhaps he was so shaken and distressed that he forgot his earlier childhood.' She paused again and shook her head in a little gesture of distress and bewilderment. 'Imagine poor little Alexander, first being discovered in shame, then beaten red-raw by his beloved Mama. Yes, and I even hit him as well …'

Ursula's voice died away and this time her expression showed clearly that she could no longer hide her shame. Cecilie swallowed, but said nothing. After another long interval Ursula turned to her sister-in-law again.

'Do you truly believe, Cecilie, that he was seduced and then mistreated by our servant?'

'Perhaps we will never be certain of that. It was only a presumption on my part.'

'Can you not ask my brother?'

'Of course I shall. When he returns home – or should we say *if* he returns home!'

Without saying anything further, Ursula rose and walked very quietly out of the room, obviously deep in thought. Cecilie returned to her own inner musings, but her mind now seemed to have become much clearer.

By evening she found herself in a more optimistic mood. She decided she believed what Tarjei had told her, namely that only a person *born* with unnatural tendencies was 'incurable'. Now she could see a tiny possibility that Alexander had started life as any normal person – and if that was true, then perhaps he could be so again. Her spirits rose on reaching these conclusions – yet at the same time, she felt she heard a very small voice deep within her saying quite contrarily: 'Ha! Foolish heart! Your ability to hope knows no bounds!'

* * * *

As that warm summer of 1625 reached its height, two personal letters began their journeys by courier along contrasting routes travelling to and from different parts of Scandinavia and Germany. They carried confidences, confessions, reactions and revelations important in differing ways to their senders and recipients, and each on arrival would bring comfort and have other important bearings on the lives of those concerned.

The first, sent from the country estate of Gråstensholm in Norway, made the long journey to Copenhagen. It was from Liv to her daughter Cecilie and it read:

'My Dearest Little Girl, How awful it was to learn that you had lost your unborn child. Your dear husband will be heartbroken when the news reaches him. What can I say? What can I do? If only I could make the journey to see you and be with you for a while. But we may not travel to

Denmark because she is at war. It is, however, a comfort to know that your sister-in-law is with you. I would judge her to be strict but sincere. The letter she wrote to us telling of your sad condition was both friendly and compassionate. You must convey our greetings and our thanks to her.

'Try now to look to the future, my dear Cecilie. Your Alexander, whom I am so longing to meet for the first time, will soon be home again. All wars must end eventually, even though this one has already lasted seven years. We cannot come to terms with why Denmark had to poke her nose into it at all.

'Here at Gråstensholm and Linden Allée life goes on peacefully. We are thrilled to see that your little protégé Kolgrim is becoming so clever. It is hard to believe how kind and considerate he is. He behaves like an angel towards his little brother, Mattias, and all the women at Gråstensholm adore him. I cannot describe how much he has changed. My dear Cecilie, all the misgivings we felt at his birth have proved unfounded and all is well with Kolgrim now …'

That might be what you think, Cecilie reflected cynically, as she paused in her reading of the letter. Who knows what you are up to now, my satanic little fox? Have you discovered that there is more to gain by showing a friendly face to the world? Or is there some other explanation for your strange change in behaviour? Unable to decide one way or another, Cecilie returned eagerly to the rest of the letter.

'All is well with Tarald and Yrja,' Liv had written. 'Yrja scratched her hand badly on a rosebush when she was picking wild strawberries, but it has healed now. One of the maids cut her hand with a kitchen knife and the barber treated it with a poultice of something called "Devil's Dung", which is perhaps better known as Giant Fennel. This is something neither father nor Tarjei would ever have done – but despite that, the girl is better.

'Poor Meta was devastated when both her youngest lads were taken off to war. Are has become sombre and introverted in the absence of Brand and Trond, although he was never one to show his feelings very much. But far worse, we have heard not a word from Tarjei! They wrote a letter to the university in Tübingen, but it was sent back with a message that Tarjei had never arrived there! We are all terribly worried. Have you heard anything?

'And pity poor Klaus, who stands each day down by the road, hoping to see the wagon that drove away with his son, Jesper, bring him back once more. It is so tragic, and it pains me so to see that poor man in such distress.

'Father is well, but I do not like to see him working so hard. He works more and more at home, sitting up in bed late at night ruminating over difficult cases he has dealt with. But everybody says he is an excellent notary. Perhaps that is because he takes his duties so seriously.

'You met our dear priest, the young Pastor Martinius, I think? Unfortunately he has left us. You remember that all was not well between him and his wife? It seems that their relationship had improved of late and he was offered a deanery or bishopric, I forget which, in Tönsberg, I think it was. I am not sure. In any event, the wife became much more accommodating before they left, a colossal change which was nice for his sake, because he is such a fine person who really merits the love of a good woman. We all miss him so much.

'That is all I have to write at this time. The flowers you planted in the border are all in bloom at the moment, except for one that didn't take. I have put something else in its place, but I have no idea what it is. No matter, it is mauve in colour and looks well.

'Try not to dwell on what has happened, little Cecilie. You know that so often we women must see our infants die. I knew someone once in Oslo who lost nine infants; one after the other, and not one reached their first year. You have all your life before you, and the children of the Ice People have always been hardy.

'Father wishes you well. Our thoughts are always with you. And do not forget to place a sprig of lavender in your linen cupboard. It gives a lovely scent to everything and keeps the moths away. Sent as always with my heartfelt good wishes,

Your loving Mother.'

* * * *

The second letter took longer to reach its destination. It had been sent to Alexander Paladin by a courier taking messages from the Copenhagen Court to His Majesty King Christian IV at the battlefront. Ursula had just managed to catch the courier before he left and he had promised to deliver the letter in person to her brother.

When it arrived, Alexander was sitting in a private house in Nienburg that had been requisitioned for officers. Looking at the letter, he could not help but feel surprise at seeing Ursula's handwriting. It had been many years since she had written to him and a feeling close to panic gripped him as he opened the seal.

The letter said: 'My Dear Brother, You will without doubt be surprised to receive a letter from me, as we have not enjoyed cordial relations for a long time. However, the time has come to put this right.'

'Get to the point!' thought Alexander, feeling worried and impatient. He ached with a sense of foreboding and for a moment he looked away from the letter, fearing to discover what it might contain. Then, plucking up his courage, he resumed his reading.

'I don't know how best to reveal this to you my dear Alexander,' the letter continued, 'but I have to tell you that Cecilie has recently suffered an unfortunate accident. And of course it grieves me greatly to say that she lost your child as a result of falling from her horse. I have not dared tell Cecilie this detail, but had it lived, Alexander, the infant would have been a boy who would have passed on the name of Paladin.

'All blame lies with Kirsten Munk's head housekeeper for forcing Cecilie to ride home when she declined to undertake the journey to Dalum Abbey because of her condition. Cecilie was immediately dismissed and given the most unmanageable mount. I have naturally made a complaint about this matter involving the death of your heir, but of course His Majesty is not in residence. Nevertheless, I pray the housekeeper is severely disciplined. But who is there left here to chastise her?

'Cecilie has become very quiet now. She says very little and spends most of her time in bed staring out of the window, although she did get up for a short time today. I cannot tell what she thinks or is feeling. But since she lost the child we have grown close. She is a fine girl, Alexander, and it gladdens me that you chose her. I try as much as I can to comfort her and help her, but what can anyone say in a situation such as this? One feels so desperately helpless.

'Furthermore, your wife has taught me to understand your difficulties. For my part I told her about that horrible valet who treated you so badly for so many years, and of the number of beatings you received, most of all for entering Father's room where he kept those ghastly paintings of women. I also spoke to her about the appalling episode with the valet, when mother became panic-stricken. I realise now that you should never have been blamed for what took place. Can you please forgive me, Alexander?'

He stopped reading, shaking his head distractedly and

found that he had partially crumpled the letter in his hands without meaning to. After smoothing out the creased pages again, he resumed his reading.

'Your beloved wife is very dear to every one of us here at Gabrielshus,' Ursula had said. 'We all share her grief and do what we can to spare her further upset. And you must not distress yourself over the lost child! You can still have many more. Never forget, please, that our thoughts are with you every day and both Cecilie and I are anxious for your safe return. Please take the greatest care of yourself and do not put yourself in harm's way without good cause. You already know how much we need you. I remain, Your affectionate sister, Ursula.'

Alexander held the letter loosely between his fingers and looked up, gazing out absently into the distance over Nienburg. Half a dozen words from the letter were ringing and reverberating over and over again in his mind.

'You can still have many more … You can still have many more …'

At that moment, his orderly knocked sharply on his door and entered the room. Without saluting or observing any other subtle points of military etiquette, he handed Alexander a formal written order.

'His Majesty has called an immediate Council of War, Colonel,' said the orderly. 'The whole army is to make ready for battle at once.'

Chapter 8

The convenor of the War Council, King Christian himself, had not been having a very enjoyable campaign up to that point. Feeble and ineffectual due to his indifferent health and the after-effects of the head injury suffered in the fall from his horse, he was lying in his magnificent camp bed – complete with velvet curtains and other finery – looking laughably out of place in the bleak surroundings of an army at war.

'We shall get up!' he announced impatiently, 'and cut Tilly down to size. When we have finished with him he will be no taller that the boots he stands in!'

'One more week of rest, I beg you, Your Majesty,' his physician replied anxiously. 'Your Majesty's strength has not fully returned.'

'It is only you who tell us this. You are nothing but a witless broody hen! We shall get up!'

The Court Physician was offended. 'I will send for the field surgeon, should Your Majesty wish to confer with him also.'

'Field surgeon? May we be spared the attentions of those butchers.'

'They have an exceedingly talented surgeon now. He is a young Norwegian boy – and he is educated to boot! I have spoken to him myself and found his knowledge to be exceptional.'

'Norwegian … hmm?' mumbled King Christian. He had always had a soft spot for his second country. 'Our foremost healer came from there, but sadly he is now dead. Tengel was his name.'

'This man is his grandson, Majesty.'

The King sat up at once. 'Aah! Oh, no!' he gasped. It felt as though someone was stabbing daggers into his head and he fell back against his cushions. 'Then fetch him! At once! We wish to meet this boy.' His Majesty gave a satisfied grunt. 'Herr Tengel's grandson – admirable!'

It took some time to bring Tarjei from the field hospital to the King's private quarters in Nienburg, but the moment he arrived, the Court Physician presented the young man to King Christian.

'Tarjei Lind of the Ice People, eh?' said the King. 'We never had the pleasure of meeting your grandfather, or perhaps it should be said that we were lucky enough to enjoy such good health that he never had to be sent for. By coincidence, we recently made the acquaintance of another of his grandchildren – our dear wife's lady-in-waiting.'

'Of course, Cecilie,' said Tarjei smiling. 'My cousin – she has always spoken most warmly of Your Majesty.' They both understood the words left unspoken: 'but not most warmly of Kirsten Munk'.

The pleasantries over, Tarjei was given free rein to practice his medical skills. His Majesty could not have imagined what he was about to undergo, but not one inch of the royal personage escaped Tarjei's scrutiny.

'The liver is not at its best,' said Tarjei.

'Really?' replied the King. 'Is it serious?'

'Not yet, but it is a little enlarged.'

'What can be done about that?'

'The problem is caused by strong drink, Majesty,' answered Tarjei, tactfully.

'Humph!' grunted Christian. 'Then we shall suffer a poor liver.'

The young Norwegian investigated further and soon discovered one or two more minor ailments. Then when his diagnosis was completed, he turned frowning slightly to the King.

'In general I will say that Your Majesty is in remarkably good health considering his age and the great amount of work required of him. It is pleasing that Your Majesty enjoys such a robust constitution ...'

The nearly fifty-year-old monarch was delighted by this and opened his mouth to make some light-hearted remark. But Tarjei, quite deliberately, cut in ahead of him.

'However, Your Majesty's chief physician is correct,' he continued in a sombre tone, 'and Your Majesty ought to continue to rest for at least one more week.'

'But Tilly will be regrouping – and Wallenstein's army remains a threat. God knows where he is lurking now.'

'That cannot be helped. Your Majesty's health goes before all other considerations. A head injury can have consequences for life – especially if it is not cared for properly and early.'

On hearing this, His Majesty agreed reluctantly and with no little ill grace to continue resting. By the middle of August however, he was fully recovered and, with his usual vigour and foolhardiness, he immediately summoned his advisers to another Council of War and, not long after that, the real fighting began.

* * * *

The battle for Nienburg was never destined to go down in the annals of history as a great confrontation. It was vague and imprecise, too unpredictable – and last but not least, fairly unimportant. The conflict lasted one month, during which there were no major encounters, only occasional small skirmishes here and there. Eventually it was Tilly who gave way and the elated King Christian, dizzy with victory, recklessly pursued the retreating Catholic forces.

But the battle for Nienburg was notable for one thing; it was where, on a hillside outside the town, the accursed descendant of the Ice People killed his first human being. He stood with the corpse of his victim, a mercenary knight, at his feet and gazed in reverence at the bloody sword in his hand. The blood in particular fascinated him. Looking at it, his eyes began to glow and sparkle and he chuckled softly to himself.

'I am immortal, invincible!' he whispered. 'Truly, I am one of them!'

Thrilled and aroused, he crept back into the undergrowth in search of more Catholics and before evening he had slain a further five men, most of them ambushed from behind. With each successive death, the fiery amber colour glowing in his eyes grew deeper. He had nothing but contempt for the musket; he preferred to kill using cold steel and was deeply enthralled by the blood that spattered his blade. Thus, finally the evil spirit of the Ice People had taken control of the chosen one among Tengel's grandchildren.

* * * *

That evening Jesper, son of Klaus from Gråstensholm, accompanied a bugle boy with an injured hand down to the large unsightly tent that was the field hospital. The boy, on his first campaign, was very nervous and Jesper had to push him ahead of himself into the tent. As soon as Jesper himself stepped inside, he stopped dead in his tracks.

'What in Jesus' name have we here?' he exclaimed 'It's Tarjei, isn't it? Yes, indeed it is. What in hell are *you* doing here?'

Tarjei stared, surprised in his turn. 'Well, if it isn't the stable lad's foul-mouthed son! What in the world brings you here?'

Each was delighted to see the other and their greetings were warm and heartfelt. Then Jesper ran as fast as he could to fetch Tarjei's two brothers, who were thrilled beyond measure to be reunited with him. For a long time, after Tarjei had treated the bugle boy's hand, they all sat talking, sharing news and wishing they were back home. Then a large new batch of wounded men was brought into the field hospital, and Tarjei was forced to return to his work. As they went their separate ways, three of the companions felt deeply relieved that they were all together once more. The fourth, however, felt a much greater sense of elation – an aching, eager, vaulting sense of the highest exhilaration.

* * * *

Following the defeat of Tilly's troops at Nienburg, a new battle ensued not many miles south of the town itself. It began without warning in the dead of night, so unexpectedly that King Christian's armies were roused from their sleep by wild discordant trumpet calls.

Tarjei had already been working in his field hospital for twelve hours and was about to make his way to bed. He put the thought from his mind and ordered his assistants to be prepared for the worst. Not far away, as Trond swung himself into his saddle, he barked some orders to his section. Riding away, he knew exactly what he planned to do.

Rising blearily from his sleeping place, Jesper rushed to and fro looking for his leggings, until Brand brought him to a halt and handed him the clothes that had lain in front of his nose all the time. Brand's heart was racing, as together he and Jesper hurried to join their company.

Alexander Paladin wasted no time looking for his helmet or breastplate. Astride his charger, black hair flowing behind him and cloak billowing in the wind, he galloped ahead of his squadron. Alexander was an excellent and respected leader who inspired all under him and his cavalrymen followed him wherever he led them without question.

There had been several fateful nights in the history of the Ice People since that night long ago when newly orphaned young Silje found Dag and Sol within minutes of each other at Trondheim in the midst of the deadly plague. Then within the next hour she had encountered, in quick succession, Tengel the Good and Heming the Bailiff-killer. Not long afterwards, they had survived the dreadful events of the night when their homes in the Valley of the Ice People were razed to the ground, and almost everyone else living there had been brutally murdered. More recently there had been the landmark night that saw the birth of the dreadful Kolgrim and the simultaneous death of his poor mother Sunniva. This then, although none of those concerned was aware of it, was to be another night like those that had gone before when the fates of many of the surviving Ice People would be decided.

Once it had begun, the battle raged throughout the dark hours. Early on, Alexander Paladin paid the price for not wearing his breastplate, when he and a small number of his soldiers were engaged in close combat with Catholic mercenaries. It looked as though Alexander's men would emerge victorious, when suddenly a musket shot rang out and he felt a searing pain in his back. Two of his men caught him in their arms before he could fall to the ground.

The fierce fighting continued without let-up and much ground was quickly won and lost again by both sides. The dull heavy thud of cannon from all quarters underscored the sound of musket and pistol fire and the screams of men; repeated infantry charges were ordered and positions were frequently overrun and then sometimes speedily recaptured. The pace of the fighting was relentless – but throughout the strife Alexander Paladin remained oblivious to all of this.

When he did regain consciousness, he saw flames all around him. I must be dead, he thought, and they are holding my wake. Slowly, before closing his eyes again, he realised he must be in the field hospital. He felt so tired, so unbearably exhausted.

He could hear a gentle voice talking to him, saying something about a musket ball near his spine. It's Cecilie, he told himself illogically, despite the fact that it was a man's voice. He could feel no pain and he was not afraid, because the deep voice was so comforting and calm. It's Cecilie, he thought once more, before losing consciousness completely.

* * * *

Brand and Jesper were both still fighting the enemy, but somehow they had become separated and Jesper was distraught. He knew nothing of combat and had no desire to kill anyone, so when nobody was watching and he felt himself unobserved, he moved stealthily away to a wooded mound.

At least he thought he had not been seen. There was a strange luminosity in the night sky, a dim shadowy grey half-darkness and it was that curious half-light when the eyes play tricks on a man: something that is there one moment is gone the next.

Further down the line, Trond had gone on the offensive with his troops. He gave his men sensible orders that, now that they had learned to trust his warrior skills, they carried out at once. Separated somehow from his unit, Brand fought on single-handedly, wielding his sword in isolation yet always undeterred.

In the field-hospital tent, Tarjei was tired beyond exhaustion. His last operation on a back injury had been complicated. The faint light of dawn, a pale strip of grey just edging along the horizon, greeted him as he wandered out of the great tent and over to a nearby wooded knoll, where he could be on his own for a moment. Despite being unsure of his bearings, he crept upwards until he chanced upon a large boulder that offered some shelter. There he stretched out and fell asleep, forgetting completely for the moment all the bothersome assistants and suffering patients he had left behind him.

He had not chosen the boulder as a hiding-place, but simply as somewhere to rest from his toil, and was therefore unaware just how clearly he could be seen from the trees on the other side of the mound. He had hardly fallen asleep, before his sixth sense jerked him awake again with a strong sense of threat. Someone, or more precisely some *thing*, was coming up the slope. At first he was confused, then terrified, as he stared at the ghastliness which seemed to be moving closer and closer with a rolling wraith-like gait.

Tarjei thought it must be a monster from the underworld, or possibly that most feared spectre of battlefield superstition, the 'Devourer of Corpses'. With sluggish heaving steps and slowly swinging arms, the giant dark figure approached. It moved ponderously, as though it was straining to free its feet from an oozing, cloying mud. Although he stared hard, Tarjei could not see its face, which was shadowed by a pair of enormous hunched shoulders.

Tarjei soon found he was frozen to the spot. He wanted to yell, 'I am no corpse. Stay away!' but the words would not come. Then he thought: No, I'm dreaming. This is nothing but a nightmare and I'm sure to waken soon.

As it came closer, he began to imagine what the face of this horror would look like. Men spoke of it in fearful terms; the long, pointed, jagged-edged teeth; the slavering mouth; half the skull shining through the shredded flesh on its face. No, he told himself fiercely, stop this nonsense! These are vile thoughts. Wake up, Tarjei! Wake up from this nightmare!

But now the monster had reached him. It stood poised above him, leaning forwards, powerful and overwhelming, and Tarjei found himself staring straight into a pair of glowing catlike eyes that peered out at him balefully from the dark silhouette.

'No!' he yelled, terrified. 'No! Have you gone mad? I am Tarjei, your brother! What is wrong with you? What have you done?'

'Yes, you are indeed my brother,' hissed the hateful figure, throwing off the large black ornamental caparison he had snatched from the haunches of a fallen warhorse and wrapped around himself to alter his appearance. Tarjei could now clearly see, not the sickening face of the Devourer of Corpses, but that of a very familiar human being – and yet to him this sight was far more distressing and much more horrifying than anything else could have been.

'Yes,' hissed the voice again. 'Yes, you are my brother Tarjei and you were given everything that is rightfully mine!

Why did Tengel not see that it was I who should have it all! He knew, I am sure of it.'

'In the name of God, is this a hoax?' yelled Tarjei – but in the depths of his being he knew that it wasn't. Those eyes could only belong to one of the Ice People's tainted creatures and at this realisation, Tarjei's heart filled with grief and fear.

'Where are they, Tarjei?' shrieked the demented-looking figure before him. 'Tell me now! Where have you hidden all the potions? Are they here? In the tent?'

'I will never tell you; you know that. You cannot have them. Grandfather …'

The eyes burned yellow. 'Tell me now! You will tell me!'

Brutally a pair of hands gripped his throat and Tarjei summoned all his strength to fight back. Maybe because there was some remnant of the respect his younger brother had always had for him, Tarjei managed to break free and throw himself to one side. He fell and tumbled headlong down the bank, but the terrifying creature that had once been his own brother followed swiftly and was upon him before he could get up again.

'Where are they?' The voice was now low and threatening. 'The mandrake! Give it to me! And the other potions – give me everything! I want everything – they are mine, mine!'

At that same second the thunderous sound of a musket rang out close by, almost deafening Tarjei, and the monster jerked upwards with a wild scream before falling forward heavily across his chest. Trembling, Tarjei struggled free and got to his feet, although his legs felt shaky and barely able to hold him.

'I fired the shot,' said Jesper, his frightened childlike eyes staring from beneath his fringe of barley-coloured hair. 'I fired the shot with the musket!'

'Thank you,' was all Tarjei managed to utter before sinking to his knees, weeping beside the body of his dead brother.

'I fired the shot,' repeated Jesper, still with a shocked expression on his face. 'I thought it was a Catholic wanting to kill Tarjei and so I shot him – I killed my friend!' Then he too broke down in tears.

Tarjei pulled himself together. 'What you did was right, Jesper. Think no more of it! You saved my life and you saved him too. He would have lived a terrible existence as an outlaw, cast out, despised and filled with wickedness.'

Jesper cried mournfully, 'He has got such scary eyes, Tarjei. I want to go home!'

They heard footsteps running toward them and both knew that neither of them had any strength left to defend themselves. It was not an enemy, however, but Tarjei's other brother.

'What's happened?' he asked. 'I heard … ' He looked down in dismay at the dead figure. 'Dear God, it's Trond!'

They all stared down at the dead figure in a dreadful silence.

'But why does he look like that?' gasped Brand. 'What has happened to him?'

The sightless eyes, their amber glow now dulled, were staring glassily up at the dawn sky. A strange howling grimace had distorted the features and the outstretched hands and fingers were clenched like a clawing eagle's talons.

'He was the one who was cursed, Brand,' said Tarjei in a strangled voice. 'Grandfather knew that there would be one among us – Cecilie once told me so. She had also heard Grandmama talking to herself about it years ago.'

Without thinking, Brand said aloud: 'Yes, because there ought to be one in our generation as well …'

'It has always been so among our kin, that the accursed one, the evil one, was the inheritor of the spells and medicaments. But Grandfather changed all that because he wanted them to be used in the service of good. That is why he forbade me from sharing anything with Kolgrim. And that's why I refused to say anything about them to our poor tainted brother.' He sniffed, but he could not stop the tears, as they started to stream down his cheeks again.

'He attacked Tarjei,' stammered Jesper, still choked by what he had done. 'It was like he had gone mad!'

In despair, Brand shouted: 'But how could it be? What made him so?'

'The war? The killing? The blood? Any or all of these things,' replied Tarjei, in a grieving tone. 'All those things must have released his evil powers – and don't forget that Trond always wanted to go to war. There must have been something stirring inside him already, long ago.'

He walked over to where his brother lay. To his surprise the dead man's previously agonised expression had relaxed and become serene. His hands too had relaxed their clawing talon-like grasp on the air and fallen to rest at his sides. When Tarjei knelt reverently and closed his brother's eyes, they bore no trace of evil.

At that moment a couple of officers spotted the group and marched quickly up the mound.

'What is going on here?' they demanded. 'What's happened? Why is our bravest warrior lying dead? You should have seen him only two hours since! He showed such outstanding bravery that Lieutenant Colonel Kruse had decided he should be promoted. With my own eyes I watched him dispatch at least six Catholic devils. Aah! Such a pity!'

'He shall be buried with full honours,' said the second officer. 'As one of Nienburg's heroes!'

At first the three Norwegians stood in silence saying nothing. Then Tarjei spoke up quietly, 'He was our brother.'

The officers expressed their sympathy formally before one of then turned quizzically to Jesper. 'Isn't this the young pup who brought disgrace to our ranks? He was seen to desert a short while ago, if I am not mistaken.'

'No, Captain,' Brand said quickly. 'This was his first time in combat and it took him badly. He had to run to the bushes, because he was in dire need to relieve his bowels.'

The officers both gave a wry grin and Jesper smiled uncertainly, grateful to have been saved from an awkward situation.

* * * *

Trond's body was treated with great reverence as it was carried away. As Tarjei walked back to the dark and ugly hospital tent with its sagging canvas, he reflected on the fact that the more lives a man takes, the greater the honour he receives, while the man who wishes to harm no one is despised and snubbed.

Similarly dispirited, Brand and Jesper walked in silence back towards their company's lines. They were both so shaken by the unfathomable events they had witnessed that they did not notice where they were going. Suddenly they found themselves close to the fighting once more and a musket ball ricocheted, hitting Jesper in the foot.

'I'm dying,' he screamed as he writhed in pain on the ground. 'I'm going to die! Mama! Mama! Take me home!'

'Hush! Hold on to me and keep your mouth shut!' ordered Brand in a harsh whisper. 'We have to get away from here – back to the tent, and Tarjei.'

'Mama! Papa! Dear kind Papa,' snivelled Jesper as they hobbled away. 'I don't want to be here any more. It's all so horrible. I don't want people to be angry with each other and fight to the death.'

The naïve words of the rough peasant boy poured out of him in a rush, expressing in the very best and simplest of terms that which portentous statesmen struggle to convey in their more complex speeches and rhetorical flourishes.

* * * *

A day or two later, at the field hospital, Alexander Paladin swam hazily back to a state of consciousness, although he was not fully aware of everything that was happening around him. Most things remained a blur, but still he felt no pain. He could see daylight coming from outside and from the sounds and moaning close around him, he realised he was still in the hospital tent. He wondered how long he had been lying there – it seemed like an age.

He recognised the foul smells of warfare, the stench of old blood, for he had been in tents like this before. But this one looked to be unusually clean, at least the little he could see of it. There were no piles of amputated limbs, which in other hospital tents were simply thrown and left to rot. There was the smell of smoke, probably from a fire close by, where such tragic, unpleasant objects were disposed of.

His eyelids felt heavy and his arms lay weakly at his side. He could not feel his legs at all. Alexander had a vague memory of a face appearing over him from time to time. It was a friendly face, with features that he had seen somewhere before; or to be more exact, features that reminded him of somebody.

He was almost certain that a gentle voice had spoken to him, but he had never been able to answer. Now he heard that voice again, but it was somewhere else in the tent, a long way off, and he could not distinguish the words. Above all else, Alexander felt sluggish and sleepy and he thought he was about to lose consciousness once more. Then someone shouted out loudly nearby.

'Tarjei!' yelled the voice. 'Tarjei, come over here! I'm dying, I'm sure of it!'

The next moment, the gentle cultivated voice replied again from somewhere close at hand, speaking in a language he only partly understood.

'Easy, Jesper. You're fine. Don't worry. All will be well with you.'

'Thank you, Tarjei,' said a younger simpler voice. 'I'm glad you're here.'

Tarjei? On hearing the name again, Alexander was at once wide awake.

Tarjei was such an unusual name. Could it possibly be Cecilie's cousin, the young physician? But of course! It had been the lilt similar to Cecilie's Norwegian dialect that he had heard earlier while they were working on him. And perhaps it had been the traces of her family's features and eyes that he had imagined in the young doctor's face. As realisation dawned, he too called out feebly and Tarjei came over to him straightaway.

'Ah! So you are awake now, Colonel. That is good.'

Alexander took an immediate liking to this young man. He had never known such sympathy in a person's expression. His eyes were warm and sympathetic and his mouth was set in a friendly pleasing smile.

'You must be Cecilie's cousin Tarjei, aren't you?' enquired Alexander in a hoarse voice.

The young field surgeon's eyes widened in surprise. 'Yes, I am. Do you know her?'

'She is my wife,' said Alexander, smiling.

'Is Cecilie married? I did not know. We met last Yuletide and then …'

'We were wed in February. My name is Alexander Paladin.'

'But …' Tarjei broke off before he betrayed his thoughts, but he could not hide his dismay.

Alexander smiled bitterly. 'I know that she has told you about me. You were the one, I believe, who explained for her the background about my – let's say "peculiarity", shall we?'

The young field surgeon nodded uncertainly. 'Yes, but I do not quite understand.'

'It was a marriage of common sense. I was threatened with the gallows and she was with child. We saved each other.'

'Cecilie was with child? How?'

'Yes, but please, you must not tell a soul that it was not mine! Neither Cecilie nor I want people to know.'

'No, of course not.' Tarjei pondered for a moment, then said, 'Aha!'

'What is it?'

'Nothing, just that I was wondering … We had a friend who was completely enthralled by Cecilie all the time she was there over Yuletide and before. He was very much like you. And she was deeply upset because of what I had told her – about you.'

'This friend, he was a priest?'

Tarjei nodded.

'Unfortunately, it happened,' Alexander continued, 'that Cecilie lost the child not long ago. I received the news by letter.'

'Poor Cecilie,' Tarjei murmured, mostly to himself.

'Indeed, and it pained me as well. For her sake, of course, but also for my own. I had been prepared to take the child as mine.'

Tarjei did not say anything, yet it was clear he was mulling over what he had just heard.

Alexander was surprised by how quickly a bond seemed to have formed between them and he wondered if it might have been because Tarjei was Cecilie's cousin. Or was there another reason? Putting such thoughts aside he looked up at Tarjei.

'Well?' he smiled hesitantly. 'Will I recover?'

'I have just been asking myself that same question, and …'

He was interrupted in what he intended to say by the arrival of Brand, who had come to see Jesper. The peasant boy was lying not far from Alexander, but Tarjei waved Brand over.

'Come and meet Cecilie's husband,' he called. Turning back to Alexander he said: 'This is my little brother Brand. We were three brothers, but Trond the third one, sadly fell a few days ago quite near here. And that straw-haired youngster lying there is Jesper, the son of our neighbours back home.'

'Are you badly wounded, Colonel?' asked Brand, noting the insignia of rank on the folded cloak lying beside the simple bunk.

'Please call me Alexander! Am I not part of your family now?'

Brand smiled slowly. 'Of course you are, and you are most welcome!'

'Thank you. And I was just asking your brother what was wrong with me.'

At once Tarjei's businesslike manner returned. 'You are able to speak and move your head, eyes and arms. I can see all this, and it is good. Do you feel any pain?'

'No, none at all.'

That was what I feared, thought Tarjei, but he did not give voice to the reflection. Looking down speculatively at Alexander, he asked: 'Can you move your feet at all?'

Alexander laughed. 'Move them? I cannot even feel them!'

Deeply concerned by this, Tarjei went to the end of the bunk and prodded Alexander's toes with the point of a knife. But there was no reaction.

Tarjei sighed. 'You have a musket ball in your back, Alexander. I attempted to remove it but it is lodged in a difficult place.'

As the seriousness of the situation began to dawn fully on him, Alexander asked in a hushed voice: 'Do you mean to say that I am paralysed?'

'Yes, for the time being. From the small of your back to your feet. However these things can right themselves. We must wait a few days and see what happens.'

Nobody spoke, but it was evident that they were all dejected by this news. There was silence around the bunk for a time before Alexander finally perked up.

'And what ails our straw-headed comrade over there?'

Brand grinned and answered for Jesper. 'He has suffered just a few broken bones in his foot, and never before or since in the history of warfare has a man been more terribly wounded than he! But Tarjei is so bold as to believe that the wounds will heal themselves, if only he is allowed to rest. Though it has to be said that Jesper's greatest ailment is homesickness.'

'Yes, it is pointless that Norwegians should fight in this war,' said Alexander ruefully. 'Did you volunteer?'

'No, we were press-ganged.'

'You both seem so young. I shall speak to someone very soon and see that you are sent back with the unit taking the wounded.'

On hearing this from his nearby bunk, Jesper's face lit up and Brand too looked relieved.

'That would be very welcome,' said Brand. 'Thank you.'

'And when you reach Denmark you must stay at my house, with Cecilie,' Alexander continued. 'She will be very pleased, I know. But you, my young man,' he added, pointing at Tarjei, 'I fear we cannot do without you.'

* * * *

That night Alexander Paladin lay awake reflecting on his life – what had already been and what might be. It looked fairly bleak on both fronts, he thought. The only high points were his profession – in which, until now, he had been a success – the fact that he had been born with reasonable wealth, and his meeting with Cecilie. But what would she say now, if his condition did not improve and he remained paralysed? Would she quite simply be relieved? No, he could not believe that of Cecilie. There was one thing, however, to which he gave no thought at all: his own sense of honour. But then it would never have crossed his mind to do so.

As the evening drew to a close, he watched Tarjei, lamp in hand, walking among the wounded one last time before retiring to his bed. There was something very admirable about him and his obvious gift for treating the sick and wounded. As he watched him going from bed to bed, Alexander found himself thinking: 'This is a man I must not become too friendly with, because he is far too much like Cecilie.'

He felt a little twinge of apprehension as this phrase slipped naturally into existence in his mind. Far too much like Cecilie? Why had he expressed the thought like that and what exactly had he meant by it? Was it something to do with this hazy state of mind brought on by the severe wound? He did not know and in the end felt too weary to consider it further. Before long he fell into another exhausted sleep, wondering vaguely if he should have paid more heed to his curious choice of words.

Chapter 9

It was October before the great transport column of sick and wounded finally set off for Denmark. Among those travelling with it were Brand of the Ice People and his friend Jesper. Alexander Paladin however had remained at the camp, because Tarjei dared not move him. The young surgeon had tried several times to retrieve the musket ball from his newfound relative's back, but on each occasion he had been forced to give up. Now he had promised Alexander that he could return home on the next transport, because it was impossible to say how the fortunes of war might turn out.

For the time being there was stalemate. King Christian's forces had not succeeded in driving Tilly from Lower Saxony, but a new threat was also looming over the horizon. Wallenstein, with his army of 20,000 mercenaries, had already taken Magdeburg and Halberstadt and was advancing swiftly towards them.

To compound the problem, the allied Protestant princes were unable to agree on anything. The union was coming apart at the seams; promises of soldiers, weaponry and money were being broken and Christian was apparently isolated. Despite this, he remained in good heart and was determined to be victorious. He hoped to win a great deal of personal honour and acclaim as well, although this was something he did not want widely known.

Among the sick and wounded, Jesper was one of the most anxious to get back home to his beautiful safe farmstead and his mother and father. He would gladly have hopped all the way on one leg, if that had been quicker. He thought the column moved at a snail's pace. Brand, however, was not quite so eager; the burden of the news he must share with his parents lay heavily upon him. He and Tarjei had agreed to let Trond remain the fallen hero that the army had made him, but they feared that Jesper might possibly be the problem. Could he succeed in staying silent about the macabre events he had witnessed? Of course, the flaxen-haired lad had promised not to breathe a word to anyone, but Brand was not certain that this kind simple soul would be able to cope if he found himself in an awkward situation. Perhaps an innocent throwaway comment from him might arouse their parents' suspicions.

The column of wounded men had reached the halfway stage on their journey to Denmark when dysentery broke out, worsening the already dire conditions of the hapless and battle-weary men. This time there was no Tarjei to assist them and Brand, who was not himself wounded, helped as best he could to keep the stretchers and palliasses clean. Jesper was fortunate in that, with the aid of a crutch, he was able to take care of himself. One of the unfortunate consequences of Brand helping the other men was that he himself also contracted the sickness.

Sadly they were forced to leave many behind along the way, resting finally in hastily dug graves at the roadside. One after the other, the unfortunate men fell into a slumber from which they never awoke and eventually there were so few left that they could not be considered a military unit any more. In the end, scarcely twenty survivors were struggling to help each other to keep going.

Brand's condition was so dire that he was thought unlikely to survive and a reluctant decision was taken to leave him behind. Jesper remained loyally beside him and together they watched the small contingent of stragglers disappear into the distance, across the heath lands of Holstein.

'According to all the rules of heroism, I probably ought to tell you to go on home and not think about me,' Brand told Jesper with a weak smile. 'Papa Klaus and Mama Rosa are both eagerly waiting for you. But I want so much to get home too, you understand. I want to see our beloved Linden Allée once more. Otherwise there will be nobody to take over the farm.'

'I will not go without you,' said Jesper, resolutely.

'Thank you, old friend, from the bottom of my heart,' said Brand warmly. 'But how are we to travel now? You with your foot and me with a tortured belly that has a will of its own.'

Jesper had only suffered a mild case of 'the flux', as it was called. It would have taken a lot more to get the better of such a tough farm boy who had been accustomed to every sort of bacillus and bug in Mama Rosa's little cottage. Had it not been for his foot, he would almost certainly have been considered fit and well again.

'So! Let us try our best!' said Brand vehemently, although he was completely exhausted. 'There is something that might help us which I learned from brother Tarjei. I remember when he and grandfather Tengel helped during the plague at home many years ago, all they spoke about was boiling and boiling everything.'

'Why?' asked Jesper, looking puzzled.

'I'm not sure, but perhaps it's because you destroy things when you boil them? Anyway let's be foolish enough to do what they said. We certainly won't survive as we are. I can't move from here myself, so can you start a fire and find something to boil our clothes in?'

So much talking had taken most of Brand's remaining strength. His heart was pounding like a smithy's hammer and there was a ringing sound in his ears. Jesper could see that he would have to act alone and he looked around wildly. Boil their clothes? Nobody eats clothes! And what should he use to boil them in?

'You must try to imagine,' Brand whispered, 'that after we've done it, we shall have got rid of all the evil that is upon us. Tarjei told me that. You must also wash yourself and me in the boiling water. And I must have boiled water to drink. Clean water, not the water you boil the clothes in. Nothing else, do you understand?'

'Not really,' replied Jesper, unable to grasp fully how all this was to be done. 'I'm confused.'

Jesper's alarm and confusion grew more acute a few minutes later when Brand lost consciousness. As night closed in he was beginning to feel lonely and isolated on the exposed heath and he tried desperately to shake his friend back to life. But Brand did not stir and Jesper eventually gave up. With a sob of despair, he sat down and began cudgelling his brain on how he might help them survive. What exactly had Brand told him to do? He was not given to praying, but inside his mind he asked silently for help in this desperate predicament.

* * * *

The night was well advanced before Brand regained consciousness – and then he remained aware of his surroundings for only a short time. However, the sight that greeted his eyes, when he opened them, was astounding. A grotesque figure, naked as the day he was born, with a grimy crutch under one arm, was dancing around a large fire which burned close to him. Brand was glad to feel the warm glow of the fire on his body, for he was also naked and chilled to the bone. He saw their glamorous but worn out uniforms flapping among the trees and bushes where they had been hung out to dry, and all the garments looked suspiciously reduced in size.

'Brand, I'm so glad you're awake again!' said Jesper fervently. 'I thought you were dead. But look! I've done everything just like you said I should.'

'How have … you managed it?' Brand tried to speak, but his lips were parched and his throat was dry.

'Here, drink this. And I've washed you all over too!'

Jesper produced his water jar and held it to his comrade's lips. The water was far too hot, but Brand drank it anyway, knowing his body desperately needed the fluid. Jesper, anxious for approval, started to recount all that he had done in a fast gabble in case Brand lost consciousness again.

'I walked back along the way because I remembered passing a few farm cottages. I found a nice girl there who helped me.' His eyes were shining as he told his story and if anything, his words poured out of him faster than ever. 'She was so kind and gave me all that I asked of her. I promised I would return later with the pot and the fire irons. You don't mind if I go back again, do you?'

'No, Jesper, of course not. You must take them back and thank her properly for helping us.'

'Well, she said something about being paid, but "not with money". What do you think she meant? What have I to offer in payment?'

But Brand was no longer listening; he had fallen into a torpor and Jesper was left in a quandary again, sitting beside his friend. However, when he returned to the farm the following day, he quickly learned how he was expected to show his gratitude to the farm girl. Afterwards it was a very jovial, beaming and liberated Jesper who returned, hobbling and somehow swaggering at the same time, to where Brand lay. His shrunken uniform jacket was askew and there were handfuls of hay stuck in his hair, but he gloried in the knowledge that he was now a man.

No prouder cockerel was ever seen, thought Brand as he watched the confident, colourful and slightly comical figure limping towards him, leaning more lightly now on his crutch. His jacket was stretched tightly across his chest and its arms finished well above the wrists; his leggings were also impossibly short, but there was a telltale and unprecedented brightness in those mild eyes. Brand patiently listened to the whole story – several times over and in every minute detail. Broad concepts and paraphrases were not things his friend had ever grappled with and his narrative was earthy and direct.

'Ah, Brand! It was so wonderful, so marvellous!' Jesper told him with a look of ecstasy. 'You have to try it sometime! It's just like … like … I don't know…' He searched for something to compare with, the best thing he knew. 'Like eating rye porridge with cream!'

Brand felt his stomach heave. He had no wish to try to eat anything at that moment, when his stomach was making him feel so terrible that he would gladly have embraced death. With an effort he thanked and praised Jesper generously for all his outstanding achievements, then closed his eyes gratefully again to rest.

They remained on the heath for a second night and Brand gradually regained his strength. At dusk Jesper sneaked cautiously back to the farm again while Brand was sleeping – but his heroics of the previous day were not to be repeated, because an old crone came out and chased him away with much screeching and waving of her skinny arms. The following day they both knew they would have to move on – and as it turned out, luck was with them. A farm cart came rattling down the road and the farmer took pity on them. Brand was careful to say nothing about the flux, and in the eyes of the farmer they remained simple soldiers, wounded heroes from the war.

From then on, day after day they journeyed north. Their progress was erratic and depended entirely on whether or not they were able to find transport. In the first few days Jesper had to take care of everything, which he did admirably but in his own way, having learned that young maidens were more than happy to give a strapping fair-haired lad a morsel of food or a night's shelter in a barn – in return for half an hour in his strong brawny arms, hidden away in some secret corner of the farmyard.

Brand's condition improved slowly and he was soon able to take over the decision-making once more. This pleased Jesper, as leadership was not his strong suit. His gratitude was tinged with regret, however, since he had so recently discovered his powers of persuasion with young ladies and to his intense disappointment, Brand flatly refused to contemplate the further use of such 'questionable' methods.

On the long journey, the two young men continued to suffer periods of great hardship. They froze, were drenched by rain and often went without food for several days. But at no time did either of them ever feel they wanted to give up. When they reached the coast, they had no money to pay for the sea passage over the Lilla Bält and Stora Bält, which in turn separated Jutland from the large island of Funen and the more distant Zealand. But once again their ragged uniforms proved helpful.

People regarded the two weary, battle-scarred young men with admiration and respect and, after only a few days of waiting, a kind-hearted wealthy nobleman paid for their passage. They were lucky enough to board a boat that was sailing directly from Jutland to Zealand without putting in at Funen. Finally, after they had asked directions at least a hundred times, they reached Gabrielshus in late November.

Cecilie was overjoyed to see them both. She had already known that they were on their way, because she had received letters both from Alexander and Tarjei. She had been fretting during the past weeks, having heard that the remnants of the wounded column had arrived and that they had not been with them.

Tarjei had written a warm letter, in which he had also discussed Alexander's paralysis in considerable detail. He had urged her to be positive about the condition, but also warned that she should not automatically expect any early improvement. She felt encouraged by what he had written, but in contrast, Alexander's letter had left her deeply upset and troubled. She could be free now, he had said, because he had no right to cling to her when the two reasons why they had married no longer existed. She had lost the child and could therefore marry again, while he would never again be able to engage in any foolish attachments that might endanger his reputation. It had been impossible for her to answer his letter, because she could not know how long Alexander would remain in the temporary camp. She could only wait, feeling distraught and impatient, saddened by what fate had decreed for him.

Brand and Jesper stayed at Gabrielshus for a few weeks until they had recovered sufficiently to make the long sea voyage home. Because Cecilie had known longer than anyone else that one of her cousins had inherited the curse, Brand told her the whole tragic story of what happened to Trond. She had, of course, already known from Tarjei's letter that Trond was dead, and Alexander had written to tell of his determined bravery when facing brutal mercenaries and how he had been buried as a hero.

Brand also told her of the warm relationship that had developed between Tarjei and Alexander, a piece of news that had caused her to lose a night's sleep. Her imagination proved a burden to her and she stayed up late, restlessly pacing the corridors, nervously going from one room to the next all through the large house. Eventually she decided to do what Alexander had always done before going to bed, fastening the shutters on every window and closing every door, snuffing every light as she went, before finally closing the door to her bedchamber. Hearing him perform this routine had always made her feel safe.

She would be on her own now, she decided. Nobody could say if he would be coming home again. And what if he did return? Would he be condemned to a highly restricted life, lying in his bed? She could accept that, she thought, but not if he had strong feelings for another person who was close to her – her own cousin.

'Oh, Alexander! You were born to suffer,' she whispered hopelessly to herself over and over again as she tossed and turned through the night in her lonely bed.

* * * *

The autumn and early winter saw little change in the progress of the war. But back home at Linden Allée and Gråstensholm and in Klaus's small cottage there was jubilation at the return of the two young men. Are and Meta had already received the news of Trond's death, so their initial sense of grief had abated, making it easier for them to welcome the return of their youngest son.

They were also very happy to know that Tarjei was alive and well. Both his parents were immensely proud of him. But of course Meta went off and wept in silence at not seeing both her 'little ones' – Brand and Trond – return. To her, Tarjei had somehow never been 'little'.

However, the greatest excitement and happiness erupted in the small cottage when Jesper made his entrance. Klaus wiped away his tears of joy, fetched his keg of finest homemade *brännvin* and got himself heartily drunk. This time, an understanding Rosa forgave him; she was absolutely beside herself with joy and could hardly believe her Jesper had grown so tall, handsome and self-confident. He had seemingly become such a man of the world. But look at the state of his hair, she thought nevertheless and was about to go and get the sheep shears, when both father and son laughingly objected.

This was a moment for celebrating and storytelling, they insisted, and Jesper duly obliged and told them of all his adventures. Every anecdote quickly became a tale of valiant daring exploits, so that in the end everyone in the cottage was convinced that without Jesper, the Danish armies would have been lost. All through this, his little sister sat affectionately beside him, inspecting his fine, somewhat shrunken, uniform in every detail, listening wide-eyed to descriptions of places she had never imagined and lands and towns that were so far away, they couldn't possibly exist!

Her big brother was coming out with the strangest place names, ones that the folk living in German towns would have had trouble recognising! His interpretation of Brunswick became Brunnsviken, followed by Stenborgen, Hammern and Paddybom for Steinburg, Hamelin and Paderborn.

Over and over Klaus begged him: 'Tell us again how you saved King Christian from that terrible enemy fiend with a single musket ball!' This had come about because Jesper had not been able to keep completely quiet about the shot that had killed Trond; he had simply decided to dress up the story and change the names a little bit to protect the truth.

* * * *

As the first snow began to fall over Zealand, Alexander Paladin arrived home at Gabrielshus. Cecilie was waiting outside in the courtyard to meet the stretcher-bearers. She squeezed her husband's hand, gently brushing away the snowflakes from his face, and wished him welcome home in a voice so overcome with emotion that only he could hear her. But her face held a bright and cheerful expression at seeing him again, while his melancholy eyes held only a single question: 'So you have not left me?' When he said, 'Thank you' to Cecilie, it was meant for both things.

He was extremely tired after his journey and was immediately put to bed. He slept very soundly through the night, never once stirring or waking. He did not dream, but inside his mind the words 'Home at last ... home at last!' repeated themselves over and over and their very sound was the best sleeping draught he could wish for.

When they were first told that Alexander was coming home, Cecilie and his manservant Wilhelmsen had discussed the situation in great detail. They were aware that his condition would have a very considerable impact on the way life at Gabrielshus proceeded. Many things, they realised, would have to change immediately.

'How are we to deal with this?' Cecilie had asked the manservant. 'Do we need to find someone to nurse him independently or will we be able to manage by ourselves, you and I?'

'I believe His Lordship would set great store by our managing it ourselves,' Wilhelmsen replied. 'I am sure it would mean a very great deal to him.'

Perhaps, thought Cecilie, perhaps not. She was personally determined to care for Alexander herself, but she had a suspicion, a fear even, that he would object most strongly to the idea.

'Yes, I definitely believe we should not involve his sister,' she added hastily.

'Indeed not!' the manservant answered. 'I am sure His Lordship would never consent to such a thing.'

Ursula had in fact moved back to her own mansion on Jutland, which had been owned by her deceased husband. She had said she planned to spend the winter there and Cecilie was really quite relieved at this, because she wanted to be alone with Alexander on his return.

'It seems from Tarjei's letter that my husband will be housebound and bed-bound, does it not?' Cecilie asked Wilhelmsen.

'Yes, My Lady,' replied the servant.

'But will that really be necessary?' she asked. 'It will be an incredibly passive existence for a man like Alexander – and humiliating as well.'

'But he is paralysed from the waist down, My Lady,' he reminded her.

'Yes, but his arms will not be paralysed! I have been thinking over and over again … What if he could sit in a chair!'

'His Lordship is a powerfully built man. I do not think we would be able to lift him between us.'

'No,' she smiled absentmindedly, casting a glance at the diminutive servant. 'And in any event a chair would be of little use unless …'

'Unless what, My Lady?'

She remained lost in thought for a time then looked excitedly at Wilhelmsen again.

'I have been lying awake at night wondering how we can make life easier for my husband. And I have come up with some far-fetched ideas. But first, tell me do we have a small handcart or …?'

The servant looked horrified and was lost for words.

'No, I do not mean that we should pull him after us in it!' she explained hastily. 'But the wheels, Wilhelmsen! If we had four wheels and fitted them to some kind of a stool – no, that doesn't sound right, does it?'

The manservant smiled, having been following her thoughts. 'I can always speak to the blacksmith, Your Ladyship. He has a practical turn of mind.'

'I shall come with you,' said Cecilie without any hesitation. 'As I said, I have several ideas.'

In no time at all the whole estate had heard that the blacksmith was building a strange contraption for His Lordship. His large favourite armchair had been carried down to the smithy and the blacksmith had been rooting around in the coach houses, closely examining every wheel he found. Eventually he selected and removed the wheels from one of the family's finest miniature carriages, formerly used for transporting children, and attached them to the solidly built chassis he had made.

Everybody was interested in what was going on, offering advice and suggesting improvements, until at last the 'wagon' stood finished. To look at, it was clumsy and bizarre – but it worked!

And now the master had come home and there was great excitement among all the staff about how he might adapt to these new challenges. On his first full evening, Cecilie went in to see Alexander while he was eating supper in his bed and explained that she and Wilhelmsen had agreed that they would manage to care for him between them.

'No, out of the question,' he said decisively. 'We will get another man in.'

'But *I* want to help you,' she insisted.

'Why?' he asked suspiciously.

'I believe it is obvious. I am your wife, and despite our relationship being somewhat unconventional, our friendship is surely strong enough to carry this burden? What is more, it would look peculiar if I were not permitted to help you.'

'But I have no wish to be tended to by a woman!'

Cecilie regarded him sternly. 'So you see me as a woman, then? Not as a friend?'

'I see you as both,' he answered with a fleeting, embarrassed grin. 'You are far too womanly for anyone to ignore that. But you do not know what tending to my needs will mean.'

'Oh, I can well imagine what is needed. And I can also understand how you will feel humiliated, because you have always been a proud man.' She got up to leave. 'Naturally I shall not force myself upon you. If you are so absolutely mortified by the idea I shall …'

'Cecilie!' He grabbed hold of her arm. 'You must not think like that! Do you truly mean that you can understand how I feel?'

'Yes, Alexander,' she said softly, 'I do.'

She sat down on the edge of his bed and after a brief moment's hesitation she bent forward until her cheek lay against his. Alexander in his turn wrapped his arms around her and they lay quiet and unmoving together for a long time – he making his silent, impotent pleas for understanding and comfort, and she anxiously and wordlessly providing the answers he needed.

'If you believe in your heart – that you are able to …
manage this,' he said haltingly, 'then perhaps …'

'I do not think there is anything I want more than to care for
you,' she broke in quickly. 'It is my heart's desire.'

'Then it is decided.'

'Thank you, Alexander.'

He laughed out loud suddenly: 'But you know, I shall be
terrified the first time you tend to my needs!'

'I too,' she admitted with a self-conscious smile. 'So
everything will be well.'

She released him and sat up again, patting her hair back
into place. She looked at him for a moment with a fond
expression in her eyes. Then she stood up.

'By the way,' she announced suddenly. 'We have a surprise
for you.'

'Who are "we"?'

'Wilhelmsen and I. Now wait!'

'I can do nothing else,' he muttered with a trace of
bitterness.

When she had called for Wilhelmsen and told him to bring
the surprise, she returned to the bedside.

'Where is Tarjei now?'

Alexander's expression showed no inkling of that which
she had feared most.

'He stayed behind. He is a remarkably clever lad – and so
like you!'

'Is he? I have never given it any thought.'

'Very much. That is why I felt so warmly towards him.'

'Thank you.' She smiled, not knowing quite how she
should interpret his words.

The servant coughed discreetly and Alexander turned his
head to look at him. Then he stared in amazement at his new
'carriage'.

'What in all the world?'

'A gift for you, Alexander,' announced Cecilie, grinning with pride, 'from me and Wilhelmsen and the blacksmith and … everyone. Because we are all so fond of you and want to make life as easy for you as we can.'

Alexander had raised himself up on his elbows. 'It's my old chair – with wheels!' He burst out laughing. 'What a monstrosity!'

Cecilie's smile waned. 'Will you not try it?'

'And how do you expect me to get into it?'

'If Your Lordship will allow,' said Wilhelmsen, pushing the chair closer, 'we have placed a strong handle here so Your Lordship is able to lift himself across using his arms. Then, with a little help from us with your legs, you will be sitting in the chair, My Lord.'

Alexander said nothing; he was weighing up the possibilities for and against.

'You can sit up, can't you?' Cecilie chipped in anxiously.

He nodded. 'With support, yes. But without it, I really do not know.'

'And you have always had strong arms, haven't you?'

'Of course.'

Wilhelmsen stepped forward, lowering his head respectfully. 'We have also made a similar arrangement in … ahem … your small private chamber over here.' He pointed discreetly to the door of a little cubicle in the corner of the bedchamber.

'So you mean that I can be wheeled everywhere? With somebody pushing behind me or …?'

'That will certainly be quicker. But we had thought that this way Your Lordship would be able to manage virtually everything on your own, except for getting into bed. That will not be possible.'

Alexander lay very quiet and still for a long time. He seemed deeply moved.

'Thank you,' he said at last. 'You have solved a proud man's greatest challenge.'

'Not proud – noble,' Cecilie corrected him.

'Noble men are not bothered by such worldly considerations.'

'Noble folk are also human, and that is something we often forget.'

'You have an answer for everything,' muttered Alexander, amused. 'Now it remains to be seen if my arms have the strength you attribute to them.'

'If they don't now, they soon will have,' she assured him. 'Almost every person on the farm and the estates has helped with the chair and all the other things, Alexander. They all wish to see you live your life as fully as possible.'

'You must thank all of them,' he said, overcome with emotion. 'Give every one of them my sincerest thanks. It is wonderful to come home to such kindness and thoughtfulness.'

That first day Wilhelmsen looked after Alexander, but after that it was Cecilie's turn. It turned out that her first task was to settle him for the night.

'Tell me what you want me to do,' she prompted him nervously.

He was feeling just as awkward as she was. 'Cecilie, are we really going to do this?'

'There is a first time for everything. Then it always becomes easier.'

Alexander swallowed. 'Tarjei says that my whole body must be washed every evening. I sweat a little and that can cause bedsores. But we can ignore that when it is your turn.'

'Such foolishness!' Cecilie replied with more courage than she felt. 'Have you been … to the closet?'

'I can manage that by myself,' he answered tersely.

Cecilie knew he had been practising all day to get in and out of the chair unaided. It must have strained his arm muscles, yet several times he had told her how pleased he was with what he called his 'chair-cart'. Most encouraging of all, was the fact that he had taken an interest in something. He had absorbed himself in the practical details of his chair and made some changes of his own, including obtaining some small brake blocks that he was able to put in place by himself. Although he was adapting to his surroundings, occasionally his frustration showed. At those times Cecilie and Wilhelmsen exchanged knowing smiles – above all else he was recovering, and that meant more than anything to both of them.

Cecilie had earlier prepared a bowl of water ready to wash him. When he was ready, she carefully drew up his nightshirt and he helped her to pull it over his head and shoulders. If I hesitate now I shall be lost she thought, closing her eyes briefly before she folded back the bedclothes to the foot of the bed.

She noticed immediately how evident it was unclothed that he had an absolutely magnificent body. There had been a moment when she had wished that he had not been so attractive, and then perhaps things would have been easier. His skin was tanned and Cecilie imagined this was a family characteristic, because Ursula was also dark-skinned. A thin line of black hair ran down his chest and his whole body was still well muscled, although his legs appeared thinner than they ought to be. Soon they will waste away, she thought, if we don't do something to prevent it. Oh, Alexander! My dear, dear Alexander!

She tried not to stare at his body while she washed him with a small cloth. As she did this, he turned his face away, not wanting to meet her gaze. But this is my husband, she was thinking. I have known him more than five years and we have been wed for one year, yet still we are shy in front of each other. Why should this be? What sort of marriage was this?

That was indeed a question to ponder and she was glad that nobody else was privy to it.

'There, that part's done,' Cecilie told him cheerfully. 'Now turn over!'

With his help she managed to roll him over onto his stomach and taking care not to spill water onto the bed, she gently washed his back.

'The scar is not very pretty,' she told him.

'No, you're right. Tarjei opened the wound twice to try and remove the ball. He was unable to reach it.'

'Is it lodged deeply?'

'I don't believe so. Tarjei says it is just behind my spine.'

'And does it hurt at all?'

'Not in the slightest.'

She turned him onto his back and helped him put on his nightshirt again and pulled up the bedcovers.

'There! That went very well,' she said, but her smile took a little effort. 'Is there anything more you want?'

'No, everything is fine now. Thank you. And Cecilie, you have very gentle hands.'

'Is it good to be back home?'

'It's heaven! I feel in truly safe hands with you and Wilhelmsen.'

'It gladdens me to hear it. Goodnight, Alexander. Gabrielshus has waited too long for your return.'

'Thank you! Sleep well, my friend.'

She snuffed out the candles and walked out carrying the bowl of water.

'Dear God,' she whispered leaning against the closed door. 'Dear Lord, help me to be strong! Not just in caring for him, for that I do very gladly do. But also help me be strong in – other things too – I am sure You above all others, dear Lord, know exactly what I mean!'

Chapter 10

On the fourth night after his arrival home, Cecilie saw a line of light shining from under the door of Alexander's adjoining room. She lay in her own bed for some time staring at the beckoning glow; then making a sudden decision, she got up and knocked on the door.

'Come.' His deep voice was gruff, not very inviting.

She crept in and closed the rarely used door behind her. She found him lying on his back as usual, but with his arms covering his head, hiding his face. A candle burned beside his bed.

'Are you finding it hard to sleep?' She spoke softly, despite there being no one who could overhear them here in his bedchamber.

'Yes. I did not mean to wake you.'

She curled up in an armchair close to the bed. 'I was not sleeping either.'

Grudgingly he took his hands away from his face. In the weak flickering light from the candle he looked very tired and drawn.

'It's been bitterly cold – a real winter's day. You must be freezing there.'

Cecilie took this to be an invitation. 'May I creep in beside you for a while?'

Alexander chuckled. 'I don't think that can do any harm!'

She wriggled her feet down against his. How limp and lifeless his legs feel, she thought, as she stretched out on her back beside him.

'Your bed is warm and cosy.'

'Is it?' He smiled at her. 'We have never lain together like this, you and I.'

'No,' she replied simply, but at the same time she was thinking that it was no fault of hers.

Alexander smiled again and took her hand in his. 'I am so sorry for your sake. Losing the child, I mean. Does it still grieve you?'

Cecilie held tightly to his hand, so that he could not take it away. 'Both yes and no. I had begun to feel for the little life within me, as a child, for its own sake. It was someone who needed me to care for it. And, if it had been a boy, I would have given you an heir to the family name – I had completely forgotten the real father, who I had never had feelings for, except as a friend. And yet … I don't know, Alexander, perhaps the fact that the child was not truly yours might have caused problems.'

'How do you mean?'

'I mean for me. I cannot help wondering whether I might have been afraid that you would have seen the child as a cuckoo in the nest, or something like that.'

'I don't think I would have.'

'No, but that fear would always have been with me.'

'Are you saying that what happened was for the best?'

'Of course not. What happened was a tragedy for me. But perhaps it was a way I found of comforting myself. Or …'

'Don't stop. What were you thinking?'

'You remember what I told you about the witch, Sol? She

had a daughter, Sunniva. But she was never able to love the child. She felt fondness for her, but never love – all because she hated the child's father.'

'But you do not hate the priest?'

'No, I feel pity and shame – which is almost as bad.'

They lay together in complete silence for a long time, still holding each other's hands. Inside and outside the house, the winter's night was hushed and still. No sound broke the timeless quiet.

'Why could you not sleep?' she asked at last.

'Oh, that's easy to understand, surely.'

'Yes, it was a foolish question. Alexander, your sister told me much about your childhood.'

Abruptly he turned his head away. 'Why did she have to bring all that up again?'

'So you do remember it all?'

'Yes, I remember.'

Cecilie was hurt. 'But you told me you didn't …'

'Dear Cecilie, I did not lie to you. Not really. You believe I have hidden those memories deep within me so I can no longer be troubled by them, is that not so?'

'Yes, that is what I thought.'

'Well, that is not how it is. I remember it all – horribly clearly, but can't you see, those events *must* be forgotten? I have sworn to myself that I shall never speak of them. They have never taken place. Can you understand that?'

'Yes, but that was not a very practical …'

He interrupted her sharply. 'But that is why I said I did not remember.'

Cecilie waited a moment or two then said: 'But now that I have heard it all …'

Again he interrupted her brusquely. 'You have heard Ursula's account – not mine!'

Again, Cecilie waited quietly for some moments before she asked: 'Do you not think I have the right to hear your account as well?'

'Oh, what purpose will that serve?'

'Understanding.'

'Cecilie, you cling on to some sort of idea that I can change myself. You must forget such imaginings – it will never happen. And what does it matter now, anyway?'

'I know it is easy for me to say this, Alexander, but please don't sound so bitter! I want you to tell me what happened only because your life interests me. You, as a person, interest me. There are so many puzzling gaps in your life.'

'So let me remain a little mysterious,' he countered.

'A *little* mysterious? Alexander, when you were small, you were normal about the relations between boys and girls. That was why you often sneaked in to your father's chamber of sin. With a young boy's natural curiosity, you probably enjoyed very much looking at all those naked women. So you were … '

'No, no,' he said, stopping her. 'You are quite wrong. I did not like them at all.'

'Then why did you go to look at them?'

'Because my mother forced me to! To horrify me, and deter me from liking other women! "Look at those vile creatures," she would say to me. "Stay away from all women, Alexander darling! Stay with your Mama, always, always. Never leave your Mama, Alexander!" Those are the sorts of things she would say.'

'So it was your mother who forced you into an unnatural way of love?'

'No, Cecilie, it was much more complicated than that. You must not try and make this into some sort of emotional inquisition.'

'But you admit that you were not born so?'

'How was I to know what a man should feel about love when I was only six years old? At that age it is of no importance.'

'Yes, that's true. So what did happen? Where did things go wrong?'

'Did things have to go wrong somewhere, Cecilie? Can't you simply accept that I am who I am?'

'I want to know what happened!'

'Oh, it was all so complicated and I cannot recall everything. Only bits, here and there.'

'So let me hear them!'

'You are the most insistent person I have ever met!'

Cecilie waited for him to continue. She felt sure he would, because now he was holding on firmly to her hand. And eventually he began speaking again in a very quiet voice.

'I remember my mother's fear of being abandoned, and in some way I can sympathise with her. She had lost so many of her children, and father cared nothing at all for her.'

'Not at all?'

'No. You see, on one occasion when mother sent me to the portrait room to learn to despise everything about women, well ... my father was there, naked – and disporting himself with two naked women besides. It was then that he decreed that I should be beaten for intruding upon his privacy.'

'Your mother knew nothing of these women?'

'I don't know. It might be that she sent me in there knowingly; or perhaps she was completely unaware. But that had no bearing on what befell me.'

'Of course not. But did you get ten lashes with the birch?'

'No.'

'So I was right? About the servant who was ordered to beat you?'

'I don't know what theory you have, but he promised me that he would not beat me if I ... did certain things ...'

Cecilie nodded. 'That is as I thought! So it began then?'

'Yes. Six years of purgatory, Cecilie. I should have taken the birch, but I was a child, and a coward. I did what he wanted me to. At first it disgusted me so much that I felt sick, but I became accustomed to it. He threatened me with the most terrible punishment if I told anyone. But equally he rewarded me well if I did as he asked. The punishments he threatened were really ridiculous. But I was young and foolish, so I believed him.'

'And then you were found out?'

He stiffened instantly at the bluntness of her question. 'Yes. There was a terrible scene. I shall never forget it, however much I try. My mother's unbalanced mind left her that day, Cecilie. She went mad. And in fact she never recovered and died the following year. I felt that I had caused her death.'

'And the manservant?'

'Hanged!'

'Oh, Alexander, what torment you have suffered!'

His silence told her he agreed with her and he gripped her hand more tightly. Feeling suddenly impatient, she turned towards him.

'Now I am able to understand better the despair you must have known on discovering that you had no passion for girls – but felt passionately for boys instead.'

'Yes, the servant's abuse of me as a child had made its mark. Or perhaps it was my disgust at seeing those paintings. It may even have been my father's episodes with other women – or my mother's love that clung to me like a leech.'

'Perhaps it was all those things.'

'Most probably. But do not forget my natural tendency. We have not considered this in any way, Cecilie … '

She interrupted him. 'I don't believe that at all!'

He turned towards her as far as he could and grasped her hair tightly as a sign of warning.

'Cecilie, you have been trying to fathom out the reason for my attitude to women. Maybe you will, maybe you won't. But you have no reason to look down on those who are born with a different view of love! You, who are strong and compassionate, cannot condemn them! Not you of all people! It is enough that we must suffer the condemnation, the hatred, the contempt and the persecution of so many "normal" people. Do you understand?'

She nodded; there was a lump in her throat. 'Trust me, I shall never judge anyone,' she assured him.

'There are good and bad people amongst us "outcasts", just as there are amongst you "normal" people. Our tendencies do not provide us with an excuse to do evil things. Most of us are normal pleasant human beings. You should understand by now that I will never be different – nor do I wish to be. People want to *save* us from our misery, but none of us is miserable! We have no desire to be like everyone else. Once we have accepted our situation, Cecilie, we are happy. If only we could be left alone! It is all of you who are our greatest problem. The ruthless invariably hunt to seek us out – to seek out *everyone* who is different. But it is no longer of any consequence to me now. My future … '

He fell silent suddenly without reason or warning. Cecilie said nothing, but she hoped he would be aware of the sympathy she felt, as she lay close beside him. When it became clear he had no intention of resuming, she sat up in the bed and looked down at him.

'When you were away at the war, you were among many men. Did you feel any attraction to anyone there?'

'No,' he laughed, 'the only person I grew to like at all was your dear cousin Tarjei – and I think that was that was simply because he is like you in so many ways.'

'Does that mean you like me?' she whispered.

He squeezed her hand. 'You know I do. As my dearest friend. Just as you like me.'

'Yes,' she said feebly, 'just as I like you.'

She ought to have left him then to sleep and returned to her bedchamber, but she did not want the wonderful harmony they had found at that moment, to end.

'Is there no feeling in your legs?'

'None at all.'

'Not even the slightest?'

'No, from the waist down I am a cripple. The only thing I have felt is a very slight tingling in my right leg once or twice.'

Cecilie lifted herself up on one elbow. 'So you have felt *something*?'

'My little Cecilie, it was so very unimportant. I told Tarjei about this some time ago and he called it a "phantom pain". Perhaps you have heard of such a thing? It happens to soldiers and others who have lost an arm or a leg. Suddenly they will sense pain in fingers or toes that are no longer there. It is a strange phenomenon, but not uncommon. I did not feel pain, however, merely a tiny twitch or tingling, no more than an ant crawling on my leg.'

'But it was *inside* your leg that you felt it?'

'Oh, dear God, Cecilie! Please don't start trying to transform me all over again! Sometimes you can be very wearisome.'

But Cecilie had already jumped out of bed and, ignoring the cold floor, she stood at the end of the bed, near his feet.

'The right one did you say?'

'Cecilie, please! You are only giving rise to hope where there is none.'

But she was not listening to him. 'May I borrow your slippers?' she asked briskly. 'Thank you! Oh, they are too big, but perfect for cold feet!'

She began to pinch the skin on his leg, little by little from his toes to his thigh, but he showed no reaction.

'I shall be black and blue,' he grumbled.

But Cecilie carried on, ignoring him.

'Bend your toes,' she ordered.

'Don't be foolish!'

'Bend your toes! Try! If you convince yourself that you can, then by your power of will, your toes will bend!'

He made no sound, but she knew by his expression that he was trying as hard as he could. But no, his toes did not move. Not the tiniest twitch or shiver could be felt.

'Cecilie,' he begged her, 'please stop torturing me!'

'Have you tried to do this before?'

'What for? Why? Tarjei stuck needles into every inch of me and I never felt them.'

'But did he ever ask you to use your power of will?'

'Of course not! What is dead is dead!'

'Then we shall try something else.'

She raised his knee and held his right foot with one hand, while her other hand supported his unresponsive leg.

'Push your foot against my hand,' she told him.

Alexander swore at her between clenched teeth, and she was thankful she hadn't heard *every* word.

'Try!' she said again. 'Harder! Concentrate every ounce of your will on this alone.'

'I am!'

'No you are not! You are angry with me, aren't you? Then use that fury, push with all that rage!'

'Have you understood nothing? I have no legs any more.'

'Yes, you have! They were long and beautiful and strong, but soon they will be pale and withered like flowers without the sun. You could once fence wonderfully, like a god and …'

'The gods do not fence.'

'Alexander, make the effort! At least for my sake! Whatever happens, you will not get better just lying here bemoaning your fate …'

'What interest is it of yours that I get better – only to find a new "friend" and cause you more humiliation? Would you not rather I remain as I am, crippled, helpless and in your power? At least then I will be faithful to you.'

She let go of his leg and it dropped back onto the bed. 'That was a horrible spiteful thing to say! Is it impossible for you to believe that I want only what is best for you? It hurts me to see you defeated and downhearted – is that so strange? Why must you make everything so complicated, you damned bull-headed fool!'

A broad smile spread across his face. 'That was magnificent, Cecilie! You looked like a dazzlingly beautiful witch – your eyes were on fire with rage and your hair was shining in the candlelight.'

She smiled back at him. 'I suppose I looked a lot like Sol. When I feel like that, I can swear like a trooper. Forgive me!'

'I am the one who should beg forgiveness,' he said soothingly. 'You were right to be angry. So, shall we try again?'

Cecilie raised his leg once more, thankful that he had at last decided to do his best. For a whole hour they continued to work together, but there was no sign of any change. By then they were both tired out by their efforts.

'At least one good thing has come from this,' Alexander said when Cecilie finally decided to give up. 'I am so tired now that I shall fall asleep at once.'

'I will, too. Goodnight, Alexander. Oh, here are your slippers, well warmed and downtrodden. We will try again tomorrow – and every day.'

'Slave driver,' he muttered, but he was no longer feeling so dismally pessimistic.

She resisted the urge to stroke his cheek as she left. She knew there were limits to their relationship.

* * * *

Over the succeeding days, Cecilie was as good as her word. She came to his room every morning before he was up and dressed. She pinched and prodded him, told him to move his feet and push against her hand. Although there was no difference from one day to the next, she refused to give up. Alexander, realising that he might just as well resign himself to this treatment, had stopped protesting, although in his quiet moments he did wonder how much longer she would persevere.

He was able to sit at the table for meals and this alone raised his spirits. Furthermore, as the strength in his arms increased, he was able to achieve much more than anyone had imagined. During the evenings they would play chess or some other board game and each day they took short walks around the estate with Cecilie either wheeling him along or walking beside him as Wilhelmsen pushed the chair.

Occasionally, by way of a change, she invited friends who lived in the area to call on them. Although these visits seemed to cheer him, after their guests had left, he was often low-spirited because most of their conversation reflected a world in which he was no longer involved.

Cecilie received constant approaches from Court inviting her to return and take up her position with the royal children again. They missed her calm, friendly but disciplined presence. She respectfully refused every request, however, saying her duty now was to be at Alexander's side.

Occasionally she did leave him on his own and went off on trips by herself. She told herself that she had her own life to live as well – and it did not hurt for him to miss her presence now and then.

And to her delight, it seemed that he did miss her. He always brightened up whenever she returned and had lots to tell her about the farm and estates, and things he had discovered. He never missed the daily walk, always happy to ride in his chair. Above all else, he still retained a realistic sense of his own worth and this Cecilie knew was a very good sign.

* * * *

In the late summer of 1626 they received family guests – Liv and Dag were finally able to realise their dream of travelling to Denmark to see their hapless daughter. It was natural for them to think of her as unlucky and unhappy – had she not first lost a child and then had her husband return home to her crippled by war? They could not see that Cecilie was happy in spite of these things. She was needed, wanted and sometimes she was conceited enough to believe that she was indispensable. Almost everyone wants to enjoy such feelings and Cecilie was no exception. But the long, silent, lonely nights were her greatest dilemma – and she could not see any way of ever resolving that tantalising situation.

Her thoughts on such matters, however became secondary during the visit of her parents, at which she was truly overjoyed. Its impact was heightened by the fact that they brought Kolgrim with them, who had been yearning to see her for years. She could not get over how wonderful it was to see them all once more. So she fussed and rushed around, to and fro, her head filled with all manner of things to do and tell, forgetting in her excitement what she had been meaning to do or say in the first place. From the comfort of his wheeled chair, wrought so skilfully by the farm's blacksmith, Alexander watched all her comings and goings with affectionate amusement.

Mama Liv had not changed in the least. Warm-hearted and as understanding as ever, she had kept her youthful looks longer than normal folk, perhaps as a consequence of being a kinswoman of the Ice People. Baron and Notary Dag Meiden however, had for his part aged considerably. His hair had thinned and turned grey and he had even lost some of the 'weight' of authority that Cecilie had teased him about when she had last been back home.

'Father is growing old,' she thought gloomily, 'and I don't want him to. Not my kind, dignified father who has always listened so absent-mindedly to all our small childish worries, before letting Mother decide.'

Forty-five years had passed since the young Silje had discovered her two foundling infants in the midst of a devastating plague – the two-year-old girl and the newborn babe she had respectively named Sol and Dag. That had been the same night when Tengel saved them all and Silje had rescued Heming the Bailiff-killer, the scourge of the Ice People, from the gallows. Yes, Heming … who had been Sol's downfall, Sunniva's father and was also Kolgrim's grandfather. They were all long dead now, all except Liv – who had been born out of the love between Tengel and Silje – Dag and Kolgrim. How rare that for once they were all together again, here at Gabrielshus with Cecilie.

She had always thought that Tengel and Silje's other child, Are, had to some extent stood apart from the family, despite becoming the chief clansman of the Ice People when Tengel died. She had never had much in common with his two younger sons, Trond and Brand, but she had always shared a close relationship with his eldest boy, Tarjei. And now Trond, afflicted by the curse of the Ice People, was gone too. But while she grieved with her parents over Trond's fate, had it not perhaps been for the best, quickly over and done with?

Tengel and Silje's home had been Linden Allée, where Are and his wife Meta now lived, but Gråstensholm had become more the focal point of the family after Dag had inherited the estate from his mother, Charlotte Meiden. However, only Cecilie believed this to be so, because she saw things from her own perspective. Tarjei, for example, still considered Linden Allée to be the centre of the world, because it was his home.

During the visit to Gabrielshus, Dag and Alexander got along famously and Cecilie thought how good it must be for her husband to be able to hold conversations with someone so experienced in national and local affairs and so widely read. For her part, Cecilie spent most of the time chatting about womanly things with her mother, having passed so much time of late in the company of men. Liv was surprised to find her daughter so happy and she found Alexander to be very amiable and was soon speaking very fondly of him – such a pity of course about his injury. Cecilie had obviously never said anything about his unusual tendencies – in that respect she was rigidly loyal to her husband.

From day to day during the visit, it was Kolgrim who commandeered most of her time. What Liv had written about him being as kind as God's little lamb – something about which Cecilie had the gravest doubts – seemed indeed to be true. In addition with his idiosyncratic looks, he was indeed a fascinating person. God help those girls who cross his path when he is older, she thought more than once. There was still something a little grotesque about him; his looks, which had put so much fear into everyone's heart when he was born, were still there but had softened a lot, giving him the kind of attractive, sensual aura that often appeals to people who are drawn to the exotic and the unusual.

His eyes were narrow, like the yellow slits in a nocturnal cat's face, and his teeth were slightly pointed. His face had a triangular shape with broad cheeks tapering towards a strong mouth and chin. Straggly black hair reached down to his shoulders and he moved with a fluid, sinuous gait that Cecilie found somehow devious and a little unsettling.

Kolgrim in his turn worshipped her and stayed at her side from morning till night. He never once spoke of the pair of them attending the 'Troll's Great Feast', which she had spoken of when last at home, possibly because he had come to understand that it was just a fairy tale. Nonetheless he would happily have sat listening to her imaginary stories for hours, had he been given the chance. The genuine empathy they had shared then, still remained and it was clear to Kolgrim that Cecilie was the only one in his family who was able to understand his way of thinking. Only she knew and fully understood his yearning for the shadows and the darkness of night, how much he longed to visit the land of shadows where strange spectres moved and evil was good – and good was for fools.

On one occasion she asked him very seriously and pointedly: 'What are you planning for your life now, Kolgrim?' But instead of replying, he had simply laughed uproariously and run away.

On another occasion she asked him: 'And how is your little brother?'

'All right,' was his rather indifferent reply.

'And are you fond of him?'

'Yes! Mattias is nice. Watch me swing in this tree!'

Cecilie stopped to admire his antics, but nothing more was said about little brother Mattias.

Towards the end of their stay, Kolgrim asked suddenly: 'Will you come home soon, Aunt Cecilie?'

'As soon as Uncle Alexander is well,' she replied.

But when will that be, she wondered to herself with a pang of despair. There was no end in sight and she ached for him to make some progress. She was as determined as ever to help him, but there were days when her optimism dipped in the face of the arduousness of the uphill struggle. Realising suddenly that she might be seeming pessimistic to the young boy, she smiled at him again.

'I have not been able visit you before this because Alexander has been so sick,' she explained quietly. 'But I am looking forward to being with you all again, Kolgrim.'

The boy was watching Alexander, sitting defenceless in his chair, holding a conversation with her parents. Something inexplicable in the boy's demeanour at that moment caused cold fear to run through Cecilie suddenly. But Kolgrim's eyes, when she looked at him again, held only a look of innocence and friendliness. In that moment she was shocked to find that she wished that her parents and the boy would leave at once.

Yet when that day actually came for them to depart, Cecilie found the prospect hard to bear. As the time for departure drew nearer, however, Alexander said something unexpected that lightened her mood.

'I know my dear Cecilie yearns to travel home to Norway,' he said to her parents. 'So rest assured we will arrange it before long.'

'But I want you to be with me,' she said. 'I want to show you all the places I knew as a child, I want to show you Norway, my country.'

Alexander smiled. 'And one day I will see it, I promise! But for the time being I have not quite got used to the many changes in my life.'

They all smiled, understanding too well what he meant and then they were on their way, her parents and the mysterious, charm-filled little troll, Kolgrim. As she and Alexander waved them goodbye, Cecilie was aware that she was the only one among them who felt anxious when she looked into Kolgrim's seemingly virtuous and honest eyes.

* * * *

As summer quickly turned to autumn, something unbelievable was about to occur at Gabrielshus. A year had passed since Alexander had been paralysed and in the world beyond its walls, many other things had been taking place. King Christian, ignoring the warnings of his officers, who beseeched him not to, had decided to take Silesia for the Protestant cause – and his own gain. Near the small village of Lutter am Barenberge, his army clashed with Tilly's hordes, supported by almost 5,000 of Wallenstein's men.

Unfortunately this became a crushing defeat for King Christian, and his troops were routed. Whole phalanxes of mounted men and infantry fled the battlefield *en masse*, with their officers saving themselves as best they could. The King stood his ground until the end, vainly trying to call his men back to the fight and openly lamenting the death of so many.

The King held General Fuchs to blame, and may well have had good cause to do so, but the general was unable to speak in his defence because he too, was killed. The same fate had befallen Lieutenant Colonel Kruse. On the other hand it must be said that it had been General Fuchs who had been most vocal in warning the King against going after Tilly at that time.

Christian IV himself was a very brave leader, but he tended

to rush headlong into conflict with very little idea of wider strategy. Lutter am Barenberge, however, marked the end of his participation in that great and seemingly unending war. From that moment on, Christian played only a minor, and an often less than honourable role in the historical events of that period.

The defeat promised to release Tarjei from his onerous duties as field surgeon, which he had continued to perform right up to the debacle at Lutter am Barenberge. As this possibility dawned on Tarjei, he realised that he was not very far from Erfurt and his mind went back to the events which had led him to join King Christian's forces. As a result he began to ponder whether he should perhaps consider visiting little Cornelia again?

But this plan would have to wait at least a little while; because King Christian's defeated soldiers needed him now more than ever. Granted most of them had fled north, back to Holstein, but many wounded were left behind on the battlefields where they had fought, deserted by their comrades, disabled and incapable of making their way home. Reluctantly he reminded himself that his first duty was to help them.

* * * *

Meanwhile, at Gabrielshus, Alexander had been brooding, silently, for some days.

Cecilie, always sympathetic and supportive, did her best to cheer and encourage him, but it began to appear that he was beyond consolation. Finally Cecilie was unable to endure his moodiness any longer and one night at the supper table she turned on him.

'For Heaven's sake, Alexander, what is it? Have you developed a fondness for Wilhelmsen, or what?'

'That was a particularly poor joke, Cecilie.'

'Yes, I know it was! But I had to get your attention somehow. Please tell me what is going on! You are driving me out of my wits with your faraway looks and bizarre answers. Yesterday I asked you what you wanted for your evening meal and you replied: "They are under the table."'

He smiled wanly at her. 'I did? Please forgive me!'

'Yes, I forgive you, but what is *wrong*?'

'If I was only sure, I would say straightaway. But it is so vague.'

Cecilie's heart began thumping against her chest. He sighed and reached out for his fork, but she grabbed his hand.

'Tell me, Alexander!'

'It's really nothing my dear friend.'

'Then tell me about *nothing*!'

'I know you. There is nobody more stubborn when they get something into their head.' He paused and grinned. 'I had not wanted to say anything for fear of giving you false hopes.'

'Oh, Alexander,' she gasped.

'No, Cecilie, no! It is nothing, I'm sure! Only that when we do the movement when you press against my foot ...'

'Yes?' it was almost a scream.

'Calm, please, I cannot *feel* anything – nothing at all. But I sense that I am more *aware* of it when I strive to push against your hand.'

She stared at him, open-mouthed.

'Close your mouth, Cecilie dear,' he admonished with a grin. 'It makes you look so unintelligent. Anyway it is only my imagination that is making me aware of this. You must see that? The result is the same as before – nothing.'

'Are both the same legs?' she demanded so quickly that the

words also tripped over each other. 'I mean do you sense the same thing in both legs?'

'Only the right leg.'

'Yes, but don't you see what that means? Had it been the same in both legs then it would have been your imagination playing tricks on us. But only one leg! That must mean something.'

'Yes,' he replied matter-of-factly, 'it means that we have concentrated too much on the right foot because that was where I felt the tingling.'

'And you have not felt that again?'

Alexander took a gulp of his wine. 'Yes!' he answered abruptly.

Cecilie drew a breath. 'And you never thought to say anything? When was that?'

'Once or twice, a couple of weeks ago – and last week.'

She forced herself to stay in her seat. 'Don't you understand?'

'Cecilie, please! Do not raise any hopes! We, neither of us, can bear to be disappointed.'

'We will see,' she said firmly. 'As soon as you have finished eating you are to return to bed at once and we will begin another session of treatment.'

But she could see no difference and in her eagerness and frustration she became heavy-handed. With too hard a grasp on his leg, she bent it back against his body. Alexander wheezed.

'Oh!' she said, frightened. 'What did I do? Where did it hurt?'

'All over my body, you fool!' he panted. 'Now leave me in peace!'

'Yes, I will. I'm sorry Alexander, I did not mean to cause you pain,' she said carefully arranging his legs in a more comfortable position. 'Is that better?'

He nodded, saying nothing, and after making sure his call bell and other items were within reach, she left him on his own.

But even as she prepared herself for bed in her own room, she could not subdue a sense of certainty that progress of some kind was at last being made. She slept fitfully as a result and sure enough on the very next day something truly wonderful did happen.

She eagerly began another treatment session in the morning, working with even greater caution and consideration and it was while she was manipulating Alexander's toes, in exactly the same way as she had done all year, that he let out a sudden tiny squeal of surprise.

'What was that?' she asked.

'I don't know. It was as if I felt something!'

'Where? Here?' She pressed her fingers all over his foot.

'No, there's nothing there.'

She was excited, but still felt mystified that she could not identify anything tangible. 'Try moving your toes again,' she said a little wearily. 'Just try please.'

Alexander did as he was asked for several minutes, but without success. 'Cecilie,' he panted at last, 'the will is there, stronger than ever! It is as though the leg is listening. Is it working?'

She stared hard at his feet. 'No,' she replied flatly.

'But I can *think* I can *feel* it, Cecilie!'

Once again she examined his feet. But once again nothing moved and Alexander sighed unhappily.

'No more today, my friend,' he said. 'Let us give it a rest.'

She drew the bedcovers carefully back over him and left the room, feeling more bemused than ever before. The rest of the day passed without event and that evening when she had settled him for the night, she lifted the corner of the covers at the end of the bed.

'Move your toes, Alexander,' she said, thinking how these seemed to have been the only words in her vocabulary for the past twelve months. 'Don't argue please. Just move your toes.'

'As you will,' he sighed.

Cecilie stared as he said this – and drew a long deep breath, a genuine sigh of wonder.

'Alexander!' she squealed.

'What is it?'

'You … mo … moved something!'

'What? Are you sure?'

'I cannot say what it was. It was just the sense of a tiny movement – like a leaf trembling on an aspen tree. It was so feeble that I cannot even say truly *where* it was.'

'Good God,' he prayed silently, closing his eyes. 'Dear God, please don't let her be mistaken this time!'

But when he opened his eyes again he saw that Cecilie was already out of the room.

'Wilhelmsen!' Her falsetto yell could be heard all through the house. 'Wilhelmsen! Wilhelmsen! Come quickly!'

Within fifteen minutes the news had spread all over the estate – and everybody was overjoyed. But in their hearts they all knew that the battle was not yet won. A slight movement in his right foot, so tiny that it might almost have been imagined, was all there was to celebrate so far. The retinue of staff and farm workers had all heard of Her Ladyship's strange notion that she could make His Lordship's lifeless legs work again – but most had shaken their heads in disbelief at such foolish ideas.

But now all doubts were being pushed aside. Soon the words on everybody's lips were: 'What did I tell you?'

Chapter 11

In the days that followed, Alexander's ability to feel and make any further movement showed only the faintest signs of improvement. Cecilie was joined by his manservant, Wilhelmsen, on several occasions and both agreed, as they worked diligently together, that they did see a slight quivering now and again. Although it required a lot of concentration and persistence, neither of them had any doubts.

They continued to apply themselves very diligently to the task, refusing to be discouraged by the slowness of his progress. They took it in turns to exercise his legs and give him massage and sometimes worked together on these and other tasks. As a result, the setback, when it came, was a big shock to them both.

It was Wilhelmsen who brought the first hint of it to Cecilie about ten days after Alexander's first breakthrough. She was resting in a drawing room after her earlier exertions, while Wilhelmsen worked alone with her husband after supper and she could immediately see the signs of alarm in the manservant's expression.

'I am not happy with the way the His Lordship's back looks this evening, My Lady,' he said in a tense voice. 'I think you should come and look.'

Cecilie rose from her chair at once and went with him to the bedchamber, where Alexander was lying on his stomach, with his head resting on his arms. A small red blotch was clearly visible in the small of his back and although he reassured them that it was not causing him any pain, Cecilie immediately began to share Wilhelmsen's anxiety.

'We must have exercised you too much,' she said in a worried tone. 'We will not do anything tomorrow. You can rest.'

'Must I?' he muttered into his entwined hands. 'Is that the wisest course?'

'Why? Are you starting to enjoy it at last?' asked Cecilie with surprise.

Before Alexander could reply Wilhelmsen said gravely: 'I believe it will be for the best, My Lord.'

'But what if we lose what has already been won?' Alexander wondered.

Cecilie said nothing. 'What exactly have we won?' she wondered dejectedly. 'Whatever it is, it does seem fleetingly small.'

The next day the red blotch was more noticeable and the day after that it had become swollen. Soon Alexander was complaining that it was becoming painful – he had an ache above his waist, he said, and the whole area was tender to the touch.

'Dear Lord,' thought Cecilie, 'what are we to do? Tarjei! If only Tarjei were here!'

Later that day she went to her rooms, shut the door behind her, and lay down on her bed. Was she not a kinswoman of the Ice People, she asked herself? Had she not inherited some of Sol's skills, just as Tarjei had been born with Tengel's gift for medicine and love of his fellow man? Tengel and Sol had both been chosen ones, so would it be unthinkable if she and Tarjei had been granted even just a small crumb of their talents? Especially now, when they were needed so badly. She did not really know what she could do to encourage any latent energies to surface in her, but come what may, it seemed foolish not to try. Keeping this in mind, she closed her eyes and emptied her head of all other thoughts.

Tarjei! Tarjei! Tarjei! She found her cousin's name was going round and round inside her head. The words seemed to be forming a spiral that went down, deeper and deeper inside her as if they were falling into a dark well. After a time her consciousness seemed to leave the world about her and reach unfathomable depths within her soul, where nothing existed but the desire for Tarjei to come to her. The intensity of her effort was so great that she could not stop herself drifting into a seemingly disillusioned slumber.

She began to dream, and in her dreams she saw a pair of gleaming wicked demonic eyes and a mouth, laughing silently at her. She was certain she knew that face. Yes, she had seen it somewhere before! Where had it been? Ah yes, it was all coming back to her now. It had been in the hallway at Linden Allée – it was Silje's portrait of Sol, the witch whose looks Cecilie shared. In her dream Cecilie gazed steadily into the compelling face and although she remained deeply asleep, a slow grateful smile spread slowly across her own features.

* * * *

In reality, Tarjei was not very far away. Having done all he could in the field hospital for the wounded of the battle of Lutter am Barenberge, he was completely exhausted and wanted nothing more than to go home again. It had been two years since he had set eyes on Linden Allée, and Tübingen, he decided, would have to wait.

191

He knew without any shadow of doubt that he did not have the willpower or energy to begin studying again immediately. Besides, he had gained so much practical experience in the field hospital that it had more than made up for the time he had missed sitting in university lecture halls.

Yet he had still found it hard to set off on his journey. First of all he needed to rest and, after some consideration, he began walking to the castle at Löwenstein. The temptation to recuperate in the company of friends, in luxury and abundance, proved overpowering.

In the event, it took him two days to reach the castle. On arrival, he beat his fist loudly against the enormous door and it was opened by a friendly watchman who recognised him at once, not least because Tarjei had removed the man's painful corn when last there. As soon as she saw him, Cornelia began squealing with delight. He went to great pains to tell her how weary he felt, but could not free himself from her joyfully unbreakable embrace. Finally her uncle and aunt took pity on him and hurried the girl away, so that he could lie down and rest. He barely had time to admire the lively and pretty little one-year-old Marca Christiana, before he was asleep. Later the following day he was awakened by somebody softly whispering his name, again and again.

'Tarjei! Tarjei! Are you sleeping, Tarjei?'

'Yes,' he mumbled.

'What a pity,' said Cornelia, giggling at her prank.

He opened his eyes. 'Good morning, my young friend!'

'Good morning?' she chirped. 'The sun is already setting!'

'What,' he exclaimed sitting up. 'Have I slept all through?'

'Yes. I was thinking of pouring water into your mouth, but I didn't! That was considerate of me, wasn't it?'

He laughed and ruffled her hair. 'My goodness, it's lovely to see you again, Cornelia! A real living little girl, instead of great brutes of men in a sea of blood and death. Dear Cornelia!'

'I have said my prayers for you every evening and begged that you would come back,' she said, taking the opportunity to give him a real hug.

'And there I was, so certain that we would never see each other again,' he muttered, his face crushed into her pleated dress.

'You are my best friend ever,' she declared emotionally.

He pulled himself free from the pleats and folds of her dress. 'You know I cannot stay for long.'

'But why not?' she protested. 'The war's over, isn't it?'

'For the time being perhaps – but my father and mother know nothing of where I am. They do not even know if I am alive or dead. I have not seen them in over two years.'

Cornelia tried hard to produce a few tears. 'I do not want you to go, but I feel sorry for your parents.'

'Well, that's some progress! Cornelia, born Countess of Erbach am Breuberg, is able to give thought to others!'

'Now you are being horrible,' she said, pouting.

'Dear Cornelia, we are both much older now. I am nineteen and you must be, let me see – how old are you?'

'Nearly eleven.'

'Exactly. And that is why we must be wiser. I have to leave; you know I must. Can you read and write yet?'

'Of course I can! Surely you do not think me uneducated like those peasants and servants in our village?'

'Listen to me, you conceited and arrogant little pup!' Tarjei warned, shaking her. 'Part of me belongs to those of whom you speak with such contempt. I will hear no more of that from you, or else our friendship will be at an end. Is that clear?'

This time she had no difficulty making tears run down her cheeks. 'Don't be angry with your Cornelia,' she sniffed. 'Not you, Tarjei. I'll be kind now, I promise.'

'Good. So you can write letters?'

'Yes,' she said, cheerful once more. 'Aunt Juliana has taught me.'

'Wonderful! Then as soon as I have somewhere to stay, I shall write to you, and then you can write back, can't you?'

'Oh, yes! Now I shall have a friend to *write* to! And you will have to leave soon so that you can write to me!'

'Ah, how we are betrayed by women,' he muttered half to himself in Norwegian. 'It was ever thus.'

When he was ready to leave, the Count presented him with a horse as a gift, in gratitude for all he had done for them, and most especially for saving the life of their treasured Marca Christiana. Once he got going, his journey was uneventful and much easier on horseback. Before long, he reached Denmark and found himself waiting in Copenhagen for a boat sailing to Norway.

The journey couldn't go quickly enough for Tarjei. He began to convince himself that all his family were at home, perhaps at death's door, waiting for their lost son and heir to return. Perhaps there were only hours to spare, perhaps all were anxiously watching the driveway leading up to the house for him to appear. Then he smiled at his own melodramatic self-centredness.

'Utter foolishness,' he said to himself and put the fanciful ideas out of his head. But no sooner had he done so than he was overcome by a sudden and much more powerful urge to visit his cousin, Cecilie. This, he knew, was no irrational idea that he had dreamed up in his vivid imagination. It was expressing itself as a relentless and heartfelt longing.

But where did she live? He had written letters to Gabrielshus, yes, but had no real idea where it was. A few judicious questions later, he had the information he needed about the home of the well-known Marquis Alexander Paladin, whom Cecilie had married – and it was not very far from Copenhagen. Would he have time, he wondered? What if he should miss a ship?

But despite these considerations, the urge to see Cecilie grew stronger. Then other more tangible reasons clarified themselves in his head. Of course he ought to visit his cousin, he thought, especially while he was so close. He had always enjoyed Cecilie's company, but more than that, what had become of Alexander Paladin? How was he? Was he still alive? Recovered a little perhaps? Or still crippled and miserable?

Tarjei had planned to spend the night at an inn near the harbour, but driven by a fast-growing sense of unease, he changed his mind and set off at once for Gabrielshus.

* * * *

At Gabrielshus Cecilie was sitting beside Alexander's bed, her hands clasped tightly in prayer. She had never been one to pester Our Lord for every little thing, but this time she felt she had good reason to ask him to look down with compassion and mercy on Gabrielshus and its master. Alexander was lying on his stomach to ease the pain in his back, and his face, bright with fever, was turned towards her. His eyes were closed and his breathing was rapid and painful.

'Cecilie,' he whispered.

'Yes, dearest.'

'It hurts to lie like this. Please turn me onto my back!'

'But …'

'I have cramps in my belly. For two days I have lain like this! Do as I ask!'

Reluctantly she obeyed him. When the swollen part of his

back touched the bed linen, his face twisted with a grimace of pain and he cried out softly. Then he fell silent and lay still.

'Cecilie,' he gasped a few minutes later. 'There was something I wanted to say.'

'I am here, my friend. Wilhelmsen went to fetch the healer. But they say that the healer himself is sick.'

'Cecilie, I forgot to give you the Paladin family heirlooms. The jewels – they are yours now. You should have had them long ago.'

'No, they are Ursula's, surely?'

Painfully he shook his head. 'She has her own. These are yours. Wilhelmsen will show you where they are kept.'

'Oh, Alexander, stop talking about such needless things! Is there anything I can do for you?'

'No, thank you, Cecilie. What happens will be for the best. Both for you and me.'

'Don't say that!' she implored him.

'It's true – my dearest … it's true.' The act of speaking was becoming harder for him and he was beginning to struggle to get his words out. 'My life – has been a misfortune from … beginning to end.'

'It has not!'

'Beloved Cecilie! My mother – only loved me because it served her purpose. It was for her own sake. My friend and comrade … young Germund – do you remember? He never guessed my affection for him. And Hans Barth – well! He only stayed as long as he profited from it.'

'Did you give him things?' she asked, shocked.

'Gifts of money; a loan sometimes. He was never without money. Yet when he found another, more generous man he left me. So – what is left?'

Cecilie laid her cheek on his chest. 'Oh, but you have been loved, Alexander! Loved, loved! Far more than I dare say.'

As he lay there he could feel the warmth of her tears soaking through his nightshirt.

'Cecilie?' he sighed, almost impossible to hear. 'Oh, you poor young girl!'

With that his arm fell limply back onto the bed. Cecilie stood up and saw his eyes were closed.

'Oh, God, be merciful,' she whispered in prayerful desperation. 'Please, dear God be merciful …'

She opened her eyes again, sensing a presence and found Wilhelmsen was standing in the doorway.

'My Lady, please pardon this intrusion,' he said, speaking in a hushed voice. 'But there is a young gentleman at the door asking to see you.'

'Oh, not now, Wilhelmsen,' she sniffed. 'Who is it?'

'I could not really understand his name. It sounded like "Tar-something of the Lind", I believe.'

'Tarjei!' gasped Cecilie in amazement. 'Thanks be to God! Thanks be to God!'

She hurried out to the front hall, never thinking that God may not have been the right authority to thank for the remarkable telepathic ability of the Ice People. After the briefest of greetings, she explained rapidly to Tarjei about the sudden deterioration in Alexander's condition and led him back to the bedchamber at a run. As soon as he saw Alexander, Tarjei told Wilhelmsen to light every candle he could find around his master's bed. Then he turned the Marquis onto his stomach.

'But what have you *done*, Cecilie,' he demanded, alarmed.

'I know it was my fault,' she sobbed unhappily. 'We were exercising his leg. You know, I told you about the wonderful thing that happened.'

'Yes, yes,' he replied impatiently. It was obvious that he gave little credence to these imaginary improvements.

'Then just a few days ago I became too impatient and bent his leg too much. Alexander screamed and said the pain went right through his body. After that, the changes came more easily – but they were very small. Almost invisible.'

'I can understand that!'

Cecilie's voice rattled on almost incoherently. 'And after a few days Wilhelmsen noticed a small red patch here – and then it got worse. So I tried to contact you – by supernatural means and …!'

'And you succeeded,' he said tersely.

While she had been pouring out her tale, he had been cautiously running his hands over Alexander's back. The problem seemed to be centred in the middle, low down.

'I believe …'

'What?'

Tarjei moved his hands to a new position, probing very gently with his fingers. 'I believe the musket ball might have moved!'

'Oh, no, Tarjei! Have I killed him?'

'You could have, perhaps. Now, Cecilie, we shall try and remove it.'

'Oh, will you, Tarjei, will you, please?'

'Me? You will definitely be helping! And you too, Wilhelmsen!'

'Of course, sir,' said the manservant, looking distinctly pale.

'But Tarjei, what if he dies?' wondered Cecilie.

'It is very likely that he will. But if we don't try, he most *certainly* will.'

* * * *

Because the patient was her beloved Alexander, Cecilie did not really want to take part in this operation. She didn't have the courage for it and, more than that, had not the slightest wish to see what her husband looked like when he had been cut open. But at the same time she was prepared to do anything at all that would help him stay alive. When all the basic preparations had been made, Tarjei gave his instructions.

'Wilhelmsen, you fetch a bottle of *brännvin*! Alexander is unconscious at the moment, which is good. But if he wakes, he must be made drunk to kill the pain. I have treated him before and he knows what to expect. But before you do anything else, you must both wash yourselves! Cecilie, take this powder; it is to stop the bleeding. Stir it into a bowl of warm water and have it ready at the bedside. My travelling clothes are quite dusty, Wilhelmsen. Please fetch me some cleaner ones!'

The servant stood wide-eyed and stared at Tarjei. What strange ideas were these? There could be no doubt that Tarjei was ahead of his time in the field of medicine, but he was far from perfect. He did not object, for example, to Cecilie helping him whilst wearing a dark dress with many layers of skirts and folds that could hold dirt and dust. Neither did he ask the servant to change his clothes. Nor did he order them to change the bed linen, which was sweaty and soiled, since Alexander had been bedridden for some days.

However, Tarjei did have his things well organised. His chest, which he had carried with him all over northern Europe, was soon open and everything was ready to begin the operation. When he brought out a very sharp knife and ran it back and forth over a candle, letting the sterilising flame play along its well-honed edge, Cecilie felt the blood drain from her cheeks. If only she could run away and hide, with her hands over her ears, and wait until Tarjei called her to say that it was all over and Alexander was well again. But that would be the act of a coward, and Silje's granddaughter ought not to be a coward. So she stood her ground, although her nervous swallow was loud enough for the others to hear.

'What shall I do?' she asked in a tentative voice.

Tarjei passed her an empty bowl and one of the white napkins she had found in the linen store.

'Use this to wipe up the blood! Wilhelmsen, you must see to Alexander. Hold him down if you must!'

The servant nodded obediently. The atmosphere in the sick man's room was bizarre. A large wardrobe that Alexander had ordered to be made in the new baroque style was in sharp contrast to the stricter lines of the other Renaissance furniture. The dark brown cupboard too, was extravagantly decorated with an orgy of creeping flowers and pompous cherubs blowing horns; the keyhole was conveniently hidden behind a swivelling flower. The bed, around which they were all standing, was crafted in the same wasteful baroque fashion, with turned bedposts and extravagant flowing decorations on the headboard and footboard.

I lay in that bed once, Cecilie thought absentmindedly. And now Alexander is lying there in this, his most fateful hour. She could see that the muscles in the upper part of his back had become well defined, an obvious sign that he had been using his arms a great deal. He was sweating slightly and his shoulders glistened in the light from the many candelabra. Just above his waist, she could see the vicious red swelling and Tarjei studied the injury for some time.

Then he moved decisively and sliced directly into the infected area. Cecilie closed her eyes tightly for a few seconds. Alexander did not move, as blood and pus began to pour from the incision. Cecilie focused on swabbing the wound clean and soon found she had no time to be afraid. Tarjei expertly applied the cauterizing solution to the edges of the cut flesh, but one napkin after the other had to be discarded before the bleeding stopped. Tarjei motioned to Cecilie to help Wilhelmsen keep Alexander perfectly still. Even the tiniest movement at this point could spell disaster. Very gingerly Tarjei eased the point of the knife into the open wound.

'It *has* moved,' he whispered. 'I can see it, beneath the muscle.'

'Can you remove it?'

'Not without endangering his life. He has been fortunate, for it might have moved to a less favourable position. Instead of which, it has come to the fore – almost.'

Cecilie found she had been clenching her teeth so hard that her jaw hurt.

'Try Tarjei. Please try!'

'I am about to.'

'Why is the swelling so great?'

'It's the musket ball. I believed that it might get drawn out when the pus began to flow, but it did not. The inflammation was in the flesh where the ball entered his body. Now stay quiet; let me see.'

The silence in the room grew heavy. The dark sheen of the furniture reflected the warm glow of the candlelight and looking at Tarjei, Wilhelmsen was terrified. He did not know this boy, had never heard of his grandfather, and had no idea what secrets lay behind the high wide forehead, which at that moment was wrinkled in thought. He was saying a silent prayer that the youth before him would not do anything intemperate or ill judged.

Little by little Tarjei's fingers probed deeper into Alexander's back. All his actions were wary and deft, and from time to time he was making new small careful cuts with the knife and asking for more napkins. Cecilie watched anxiously as the contents of the bowls gradually disappeared.

She could feel the sweat dripping from her brow, caused as much by her anxiety as by the heat from the candles.

Throughout the makeshift operation, Alexander had not moved at all. He was lying so still that Cecilie stretched out her hand and rested it lightly on his back to feel if he was still breathing. To her enormous relief, she found that he was.

Then Tarjei gritted his teeth and pushed his fingers downward with a sudden determined thrust. In response Alexander jerked violently on the bed for the first time and recoiled twice more in a fierce spasm.

'Hold him still!' hissed Tarjei. 'Both of you.'

As Tarjei spoke, Cecilie was sure she saw a grimace of satisfaction cross his face – and a sudden surge of hope coursed through her, because she thought she knew why. Alexander had reacted and felt pain where before he had been lifeless. Now she and Wilhelmsen were having to do their best to keep Alexander from moving by pressing down across his shoulders.

'I think I have it,' Tarjei told them with a little murmur of triumph. 'Just one minute longer!' His left hand riffled among his instruments and found a strange sort of knife with a very twisted blade. Seeing the questioning look on Cecilie's face, he said simply, 'I have done this before!'

Wilhelmsen and Cecilie were now restraining a patient who was regaining consciousness and she leaned closer to him to whisper in his ear.

'Tarjei has come, Alexander. He is operating and he has the musket ball. Try to lie very still!'

Alexander did his best, but she could feel his body tense and become rigid as he fought the pain. He began to sweat and became difficult to hold down.

'Relax,' said Tarjei, but it was easier said than done.

Wilhelmsen picked up the glass of *brännvin* he had poured earlier and assisted Alexander in taking a few deep gulps.

Tarjei waited while the spirit took effect, but his fingers kept a firm grip on the ball. Blood was flowing freely and Cecilie gently wiped away as much as she could. Then, as Tarjei had done earlier, she washed the wound with the cauterizing solution wherever her fingers could reach.

Tarjei had produced a new instrument, a thin pair of tongs, which he asked her to hold in readiness. She watched as he pushed the twisted knife carefully down and around the ball and took the tongs from her. Then, very quickly and decisively, he positioned them both to get a good firm grip on it. Alexander screamed very loudly, but suddenly it no longer mattered that he moved: Tarjei was holding the musket ball in his hand and there was a look of triumph on his face.

But this moment of triumph lasted for only an instant.

'Quickly, Cecilie, put your finger here! And the other hand here; we must stop the bleeding! Press as hard as you can!'

Alexander took no notice of what happed after that. He had fainted, as did Cecilie. The room began to spin dizzyingly and the last thing she felt was Wilhelmsen's strong grip on her arm. A little later she woke to find herself slumped in a chair in her own bedchamber – and decided at once that it would be best if she remained there.

* * * *

In the next room Alexander let out a yell. Tarjei's heavy-handed treatment had obviously brought him back to consciousness. He yelled again, less loudly the second time, but it was clear he was in some agony.

'That's enough,' said the young physician, harshly. 'I can tell you, Alexander, that last year I sewed several stitches in the delicate skin of a young girl who had not had a good draught of *brännvin* beforehand, as you have. She made not a sound! She was not more than nine or ten years!'

Alexander responded to this with a long heartfelt chant of foul abuse, but at least it put a stop to his screams. A few minutes later, Tarjei allowed Cecilie back in to see Alexander, explaining that he would have to remain on his stomach for the first few days. Because the danger was not altogether past, Tarjei promised to stay at Gabrielshus for one more week.

Once the others had left the room, Cecilie crouched down beside her husband's bed, determined to overcome the embarrassment of her ill-considered declaration of affection earlier that day.

'Hello,' she said softly.

'Hello to you!' he replied, still sweating with fever. 'You did very well!'

'And what would I not do for you?' she retorted. 'Now you must rest. One of us will stay close by.'

'Thank you.'

Because she had sat recovering in her room for some time, Cecilie watched over him first, while Tarjei rested on her bed in case he should be needed urgently.

There were only two candles burning by the bedside now and she could just make out the dark hair that formed curls in the nape of Alexander's neck.

'So now he knows,' she thought, feeling slightly pitiable. 'I have revealed my true feelings. But what else could I do? He was dying, and believed he had nobody in the world who cared for him. Of course it was foolish of me. It did not gladden him. It only made him feel uncomfortable – and feel pity for me. And yet I could not let it remain unsaid. The urge to tell him came from deep within me.

'But at least I know he was pleased that I stayed here with

him after I had lost the child and no longer needed his support,'
Cecilie told herself, drawing comfort from the memory. 'And
this was also despite the fact that he would never be able to
leave here and form dangerous relationships again. And he
told me once how happy it had made him. So he does care for
me – a little. As a friend.

'It is as well I did not tell him about the secret dreams I
have of him in the silent hours of the night,' she thought,
blushing inwardly. 'Those irresistible temptations, the
forbidden yearnings! Those are things for which he would
never have forgiven me.' She stopped her flow of thoughts,
considering painfully the biggest question of them all. 'Can
an intimate friendship such as ours really continue in this
fashion between a man and a woman? I do not believe it
can – not over time. Sooner or later one of them will want to
cross over the line between friendship and love. And perhaps
that is where friendship comes to an end. All that remains then
might be despair for the unhappy one – and icy coldness from
the other.'

* * * *

Alexander lay in a critical condition for several days, during
which time everybody at Gabrielshus was on tenterhooks.
Cecilie was probably the worst of all. But slowly, very slowly,
he started to recover. After ten days Tarjei told them that the
wound was healing well and that he was therefore going to
continue his journey home. On the day when he was preparing
to leave, Cecilie went to ask him something about Alexander
and found him composing a letter.

'To whom are you writing?' she inquired. 'Mama Meta?'

'No,' he replied smiling and putting his hand over the paper. 'I am writing to a young lady.'

'Well, Tarjei!' she exclaimed gleefully. 'How exciting! Who is she? What does she look like?'

He inclined his head thoughtfully to one side. 'Very pretty – long dark tresses, big beautiful eyes and sweetly shaped lips. Skin soft as a rose petal.'

'She sounds wonderful. Is she of good family?'

'Born a countess. She lives in a fine castle.'

'Goodness me! And how does she conduct herself? With confidence, would you say?'

'Oh, yes! I have to say that she does like to embrace a lot …'

'That is a little outrageous.'

'It is. And she is often snotty-nosed!'

'Tarjei! Please!'

'And she will soon be eleven years old!'

Cecilie stared at him and he gazed mischievously back at her. Then she burst into laughter.

'You scoundrel! You tricked me! And I was happy to believe that you had found a young lady at last!'

'At last? I am only nineteen.'

'You have always seemed older than your years, Tarjei,' she said seriously.

His smile waned suddenly. 'Yes, I suppose I have. I grew up quickly working with Grandfather all those years ago.'

'Yes, you inherited the treasures of the Ice People far too young. But he knew that he was soon to die.'

'That is so. And he taught me so many secret things that a child ought not to know. But what made me a man was when Sunniva died and Kolgrim was born. That was when my childhood also died, Cecilie.'

She nodded. 'I was not at home then, but I cannot think I could have endured such a terrible thing.'

206

'No. It was as though fear itself had burst upon a doomed world. That was how it felt to me. I was held by something horrifying – something that foretold of uncertainty. It was a feeling that I have never been able to explain. I was in fear of my life, Cecilie.' He paused significantly. 'Kolgrim has changed since then.'

'Has he?' she asked softly.

Tarjei looked at the floor. 'I have been away for so long. I have only heard how pleased everyone is over the change in him. Neither should we forget that he is but a little child, and thinks as a child. That being so, I believe the future bodes well for him. But now I want to return home as fast as I can. I shall see if I can involve him in good things – it will certainly be interesting to see him again. Oh, Cecilie, I shall be so happy to get home at last!'

She had been thinking of something else while he was speaking. Now, with a slight start, she said: 'Yes, I remember what I was about to ask you. What are we to do about the treatment I was giving Alexander?'

Tarjei sat and thought for a moment. 'It seems that inadvertently you might have done something good – and unusual. Perhaps with the musket ball gone, the worst is past. Allow the wound to heal in peace! When only a scar remains, try your treatment once more, but with great care. I cannot say yet how much injury the ball caused to the other organs.'

Cecilie nodded and her cousin turned to gaze thoughtfully out at the trees in the parkland outside. Their leaves were already betraying the yellow and orange hues of autumn and a light breeze was beginning to riffle through the branches, stirring the colours in a gentle magical dance.

'I do not know for certain, Cecilie,' said Tarjei in dreamy voice, 'but it may be that you have done something far-reaching.'

She blushed with surprise, and delight. 'How? What do you mean?'

'Well, the ball had obviously been a hindrance to something, although I cannot guess what – the blood perhaps. We know so little about the body, but blood is most important. It controls the limbs and the senses and contains the very essence of life. Yes, I think the ball stopped the blood from flowing and if nothing had been done his legs would probably have withered and died. I think your actions kept life in them and stopped that from happening.'

'You mean it kept the blood running?'

'In a way. A sort of channel.'

Tarjei was thinking correctly, but with one flaw. He had mistakenly focussed on the circulation of blood, without also considering the nervous system. But few, if any, physicians of the time had his insights and understanding and his theory was basically correct. Cecilie had indeed succeeded in keeping alive the delicate nerve fibres leading from the brain to the legs, which the musket ball had been pressing against.

Hearing such praise from Tarjei made her feel very proud. She had at last done something good for her beloved Alexander, the husband to whom she could only show affection by making life as comfortable as possible – and by being an understanding friend, always at hand when he needed her and always discreetly out of sight when he did not.

When the time came for them to say their farewells, Cecilie embraced her younger cousin with great tenderness and gratitude. For his part he returned her hug warmly and in equal measure as they exchanged fond smiles.

'Thank you again, Tarjei, for all you have done for Alexander,' said Cecilie cheerfully. 'And take our good wishes with you to all and sundry at Linden Allée and Gråstensholm. And tell them that Alexander and I shall see them there soon!'

Tarjei smiled a little more sadly. 'You are an incurable optimist, Cecilie. But of course I shall do as you ask.'

After Tarjei had gone, they left Alexander's wound alone, as he had instructed, so that it had time to heal. Neither Cecilie nor Wilhelmsen gave any more of her treatments and Alexander was incensed at the need to lie on his stomach day after day. He often railed impatiently when Cecilie, without help, changed the dressing on his wound. It was not until much later that she understood the reason for his tetchiness.

To begin with the wound looked very ugly. The edges were red and swollen and it suppurated continuously. Cecilie cleaned it every day and night as best she could, but was unable to ignore the profound sense of hopelessness that swept over her from time to time. It seemed to her that, despite what Tarjei had told her, the sore was never going to heal and on top of that, Alexander's irritability made her very unhappy. On many occasions after she had tended to him, she went outside and wept.

As time passed, however, she realised the wound was becoming slightly smaller and she was surprised that she had not really noticed that before. Alexander was overjoyed that he was, at last, able to lie on his back for short periods. On one particular day, about a month after the operation, he called to her. His voice sounded like a festival fanfare, or so it seemed to Cecilie, and she hurried to see him.

Alexander was lying in bed flat on his back under the covers, but his eyes were shining brightly.

'Cecilie, watch!' he said, with a note of joy in his voice. 'Watch!'

He pointed to the end of the bed. Following his finger, she looked and saw the thin bedcover move. She tore it away from his feet and as she did so, he wiggled all his toes on both feet in triumph.

'Alexander, oh Alexander!' she whispered. 'How wonderful!'

He laughed uproariously. 'That's not everything, Cecilie. Look! What do you say to this?'

As she watched in astonishment, he raised his right knee clear of the bed.

'Oh, dearest, dearest Alexander,' was all she could say, repeating the words over and over again. 'Have you been *exercising*? In secret?'

'Only for the past few days, not before – but I must tell you that ever since Tarjei removed the musket ball, I have known that I would be well again because I have had such unspeakable pains in my legs! A thousand million ants have been creeping all through them, especially when you, the spirit of torture, pressed on the sore.'

'Was that what caused you to be so fretful?' she laughed, tears rolling down her cheeks. 'Why did you say nothing? I was so unhappy, thinking you had tired of me.'

'Please know that is something I shall never do,' he said solemnly. 'Besides, I did not want to give anything away until I knew with certainty that all would be well.'

'That was wise of you.'

He took her hand and pressed it hard against his cheek. 'Thank you, thank you, dear Cecilie,' he whispered. 'You will always have my warmest thanks and heartfelt devotion – for your patience and steadfastness, and your undying optimism. Without your belief that all would be well, I should have given up completely long ago.'

Cecilie swallowed hard several times. She was so overcome that she was unable to utter a single word. When at long last she finally found her voice, she asked him: 'Can you only raise your right knee at present?'

He waited a moment before replying. 'Yes, that's right. I still cannot lift my left leg.'

'But you were able to move your left foot,' she cried. 'You wriggled *all* your toes! I saw it.'

He laughed at her eager excitement. 'Yes, I can move my left foot. But something is not yet as it should be in that leg.'

'Perhaps, with exercise …?'

'Perhaps,' he replied, still a little sceptical.

But in fact things improved rapidly in many directions for Alexander from that day on. When the morning came that he got out of bed and stood shakily on his own two feet with no help at all, Cecilie wept with joy, although she had not been there to see it herself.

'You are not allowed to watch me fall to the floor at your feet like an empty sack,' was what he had said. Wilhelmsen, however, had been thrilled to be the bearer of such good news.

'His Grace wishes me to inform you that he has just stood up unaided for the first time – but only for a moment,' he said, bowing with exaggerated formality. The smiling manservant however diplomatically omitted to add what exactly had happened afterwards.

The end-of-year celebrations were drawing near and by the time the Yuletide festivities started, Alexander was able to walk almost unaided to the well-laden dinner table. True, he was on crutches and needed some discreet help from his manservant and his wife, but that did not detract from his achievements. Every member of the household retinue cheered and applauded loudly as he took his place triumphantly at the head of the table.

As he hobbled along on the crutches, he noticeably dragged his left leg and Cecilie suspected that Alexander had possibly sustained an incurable injury to that limb. Still, she thought, men have often returned from the battlefield with much worse wounds. Overall, perhaps he had been lucky. Or had devoted care and love saved him? If the truth be told, reflected Cecilie, he had probably been blessed with a good deal of both.

Chapter 12

By the time they received an invitation to a grand ball at Frederiksborg the following February, Alexander had discarded his crutches for good. He was able by then to walk by himself unaided with a reasonable, regular rhythm. Only the faintest hint of a limp remained unless he took on too great an excursion and overdid things. On seeing the Court invitation to the ball, Alexander was reluctant at first to accept, but after some thought Cecilie insisted that they should attend.

'You need to meet other people again, Alexander,' she said. 'To remain here on the estate and see no one but Wilhelmsen, me and a few occasional houseguests, must be boring. You need to enjoy the conversation and companionship of your peers.'

She blushed suddenly, realising as soon as she had spoken that she had chosen her words badly. But he seemed not to have noticed and merely smiled.

'You are too kind, Cecilie. We shall go, but I am thinking more of you. You have toiled all this winter and now you must dress in your best gown and wear the family jewels for the first time. The tiara, Cecilie, I promise you is so dazzling that it outshines any worn by the King's ladies. And you are truly worthy of it.'

And so it was, that Cecilie, her arm resting gently on her husband's and feeling like a queen, entered the castle. The Chamberlain announced their arrival in a loud voice and they bowed and curtsied to His Majesty, now back in Denmark with dubious battle honours to his name. They walked slowly, at a pace that made Alexander's limp less noticeable, and she enjoyed feeling that all eyes in the room were gazing at her.

For Cecilie looked adorable that evening, far more beautiful than she realised. Her slightly slanted, almond shaped eyes sparkled and the tiara glittered, set off by her chestnut hair. Her complexion had always been perfect, but tonight, against the dark blue velvet of her gown with its wide lace collar, enhanced by her sapphire necklace, it was flawless. Alexander had still not quite recovered from the delight he felt when she had presented herself to him at Gabrielshus earlier, prior to their departure.

She quickly became the centre of attention and, as he was unable to dance, Alexander gladly allowed her to dance with the many men who respectfully asked him if they could have the pleasure of her company. But after each dance she returned to his side and as the evening progressed, her eyes grew brighter and the colour of her cheeks heightened.

Alexander spoke to many old friends in the royal household, some of whom had similar tendencies to his own. The conversations were largely light-hearted and superficial – devoted largely to small talk after the subject of his extraordinary recovery had been exhausted. But one acquaintance, a baron of about his own age, took him to one side, obviously intent on probing more deeply.

'How are you, Paladin?' he asked in a jocular tone. 'Have you found another favourite yet?'

Alexander shifted his gaze away from Cecilie. She was dancing the elegant slow sweep of the pavane with a young blonde youth who obviously admired her.

'No!' replied Alexander very curtly.

'Really?' said his friend staring impassively at a decorative display of sprigs in a copper urn. 'No, you have been bedridden for so long, I suppose. Come and visit me at my country seat, why don't you? Soon.'

Alexander felt a slight shiver of distaste. He deliberately chose to misinterpret the invitation.

'Thank you, we should be pleased to come.'

His friend's expression showed no change, but both men were aware that the visit would never take place.

Cecilie, meanwhile, was enjoying catching up with Court gossip. It was being said that Kirsten Munk had been showing an interest in one of Christian IV's German officers, Count Otto Ludwig of Salm who, that winter, had been engaged as Grand Marshal of the household. But these rumours, it was to turn out, were unfounded.

On the other hand, however, it was known that the King had betrothed his eldest daughter, nine-year-old Anna Catherine, to one of his up-and-coming young blades, twenty-three-year-old Count Frans Rantzau. Cecilie saw him at the ball and failed to be impressed. In her opinion he was a foolish conceited little dandy, who basked in the glow of his own self-importance. Poor dear Anna Catherine, thought Cecilie, is she always to be destined for misfortune?

It so happened that the child was at the ball and on seeing Cecilie, she approached her and spent some time talking. During their conversation, she had whispered to Cecilie, with childish delight: 'Look, that is the man to whom I am betrothed. Is he not handsome?' Cecilie could not argue with her about that! He was much too handsome. A peacock!

The two other older children, Sophie Elisabeth and Leonora Christine, were also among the guests. While they both begged Cecilie to come back and be their governess,

Leonora was especially insistent. Cecilie, however, told them she could not, explaining that her husband needed her now. While this might not have been strictly true – Alexander was now well able to look after himself – and she was still very fond of the girls, she had no desire to be part of the quarrelsome royal household again.

Kirsten Munk had given birth to two more daughters, Hedvig and Christiane, since Cecilie was last at Court. Spiteful tongues claimed that the King kept her in a permanent state of pregnancy in order to prevent any unfaithfulness on her part. She had borne him eleven children during the twelve years of their morganatic marriage, although not all of them had survived their first year.

Prince Christian, the twenty-four-year-old heir to the throne, was present at the ball, of course. During the previous two years he had, on occasion, acted as Regent while his father had been waging war in Germany, but it could not be said that his leadership had been very inspiring. His main preoccupations were the seduction of women and the consumption of ale, pursuits to which his large pot-belly already bore part witness.

The festivities were due to continue late into the night, but Cecilie did not want Alexander to tire himself too much, and they left shortly after the King had departed – rolling like a royal ship in a storm and escorted by several two-legged 'support ships'. When they were seated comfortably side by side in their carriage again, Alexander remained silent, but Cecilie laughed and chatted excitedly about the ball all the way home, commenting on the beautiful gowns the ladies had been wearing, their hairstyles and the ballroom's fine decorations.

Back at Gabrielshus, as he was helping her remove her ermine-lined velvet cape he inquired: 'What was young Höchsthofen like to talk to?'

'Who?'

'The young man that you danced with for so long.'

'Did I dance for long with anyone? Oh! You mean the blonde-haired boy? Well, he was a little shallow, but that is the way on such occasions.'

'Indeed,' said Alexander dryly.

Because of the lateness of the hour, they were served a light supper, but all the while he kept looking at her as though his thoughts were elsewhere. He was puzzling over something. His mood remained the same throughout the following day – and the next.

Finally, after five days of brooding, he exclaimed suddenly: 'So did you like him? Höchsthofen, I mean?'

Cecilie traced her mind back. 'Yes, he was very pleasant. Everyone was.'

Alexander stood fingering the ends of a broken quill pen he was holding. Had he not been writing with it just a few minutes earlier, Cecilie wondered? What had got into him?

Oh, no! She gave an anxious sigh. Höchsthofen? No, surely not. She could not accept that. But then what he said next came as a surprise.

'Cecilie,' the words were measured, 'do you ever feel lonely here?'

'Have I ever given that impression?' she replied calmly, although the question had upset her.

'No, but … you are a young, mature woman. It would be only natural if for example, you …' His words tailed off and the sentence remained unfinished.

Cecilie stood on the spot wordlessly, her mind racing for what seemed an age. Her whole body felt numb and she hardly knew what to think.

'Are you asking me to leave, Alexander? Are you thinking of Höchsthofen?'

He looked straight at her. 'Should I be?'

'What sort of an answer is that? Tell me the truth. Do you want Höchsthofen instead of me?'

Alexander appeared shocked. 'Good God, no!'

He turned and left the room as fast as his weak leg would let him. But still, day after day, he continued pondering, contemplating and brooding, until at last Cecilie could stand it no longer. One evening, after he had carried out his personal ritual of closing up and snuffing out the candles and they were ready to go to their separate beds, she asked him point blank: 'Alexander, please tell me what is wrong.'

He stared at her, obviously taken aback. 'What do you mean?'

'The grand ball was three weeks ago and ever since that time you have been behaving so *strangely*! And then all this talk about Höchsthofen?'

'Forgive me, Cecilie,' he said, 'but I am only thinking of you.'

'Of me – why?'

'Because you are living a life that is not normal, dear friend. It was not until I saw you dancing with other men that I came to understand it.'

'If my conduct was in any way unseemly, then I apologise. It was in no way intended.'

'No, no! You have misunderstood me. I thought … Bah! I cannot discuss this sort of thing!'

'Do not turn away again, Alexander! I have to know what you mean – what you want. I am at my wits' end. It is as if I have done something wrong.'

'Dear Cecilie, you have done nothing wrong. I am thinking only of what is right for you.' He regarded her searchingly. 'Don't you understand what I mean?'

'No, truly, I do not.'

'You are a vibrant, mature young woman …'

'As you have already said.'

'Yes, but for God's sake, Cecilie! Have you never felt the need to be with a man?'

So there it was, out in the open. She stood as still as a statue, crimson cheeked. Alexander tried to retrieve the situation and end the embarrassment, but with little success.

'I mean to say – when you fell into the arms of that pastor – it shows you must have certain … feelings, doesn't it?'

Cecilie could find no words to reply and stood shaking her head in a little gesture of helplessness.

Despite his discomfort, Alexander decided to continue. He was well aware that he was entering a sensitive area and that he would be walking on eggshells. It was evident to him from her manner that Cecilie was confused and he owed it to her to clarify his thinking.

'You told me that you were not in love with the pastor. You said only that "such things" are necessary.'

Deflated, she sank into the nearest chair, still unable to summon any useful words.

'I really would like to know,' he said.

'But why?'

'Because I want only what is best for you.'

They were in the common anteroom to both their bedchambers. Cecilie's head was spinning and her vision seemed to be blurred by the pounding of blood in her temples, her ears and all through her body.

'Surely, as long as I conduct myself discreetly, as your wife, and cause you no nuisance ...'

'That was not what I was speaking of. It is you, Cecilie, I am concerned for. I wish only for your complete happiness here at Gabrielshus. You have done so much that I …' Suddenly it dawned on him what she had just said and his train of thought was interrupted. '"Conduct yourself discreetly," you said? Does that mean you have already … had a lover?'

She was tired now. 'No, Alexander, how on earth could you think that?'

He waited, not taking his eyes off her. 'Well, we'll say no more about lovers, then,' he said quietly. 'But I return to my first point. A woman's needs.'

Cecilie wriggled uncomfortably in the chair, earnestly wishing she could be somewhere else. For his part Alexander stood resolutely waiting for her response.

'And if that were so? If I should sometimes have such desires,' she said finally, with taunting bitterness, 'what could you do about them?'

When he replied, his voice was low and gentle. 'I could help you.'

That was too much for her. She flew out of the chair, rushed into her own bedchamber and stood in the middle of the floor, quaking from head to toe. She failed to notice Alexander had followed her until she heard his voice behind her.

'Please understand, Cecilie, it has taken three weeks for me to pluck up the courage to ask that question.'

Cecilie nodded her head forcefully and waited for him to go on.

He ran a distracted hand across his forehead then said: 'You gave the impression ...'

'Alexander,' she interrupted, 'you have made me so ashamed!'

'My dear friend, the question was not meant to shame you.'

'But have you really believed that I – at the ball – had desires for any of those men?'

'I did not believe it, but I was *afraid* that you had.'

'Oh, Alexander, I thought you knew me better than that.'

Very quietly he said: 'I have chosen to forget what you said to me when you thought I would die.'

'Yes, I sincerely hope you have. Yet still you offer to help me? You? How can you?'

'Let us not dwell on details! I only want to know, have you had needs?'

She swallowed hard and nodded, her head bowed in shame.

'How? In what way?'

'Alexander! Are you trying to pry into my private desires?'

'No, Cecilie dearest. But if I am to help you then I must know what it is you have been missing. I know nothing of how a woman thinks, nothing of their needs and desires. Or their cravings.'

Cecilie took a deep breath, as if she were about to explain, but then changed her mind. 'No, I cannot! I cannot expose my feelings to you when you have such distaste for womankind.'

'But not for *you*, Cecilie! To me you are my friend, a companion. One should have compassion for one's friends, is that not so? Protect them from misfortune?'

'Yes,' she agreed without conviction.

He waited, watching her face expectantly. But when she did not continue he prompted: 'Well, then.'

Cecilie was wrestling with her feelings. Her hands were twisting the folds of her nightgown nervously until it seemed she must rend the garment. Eventually she cleared her throat and spoke.

'During the night – when we have … retired to our beds …' she began cautiously, then stopped.

'Yes?' his kindly voice urged her on. 'What then?'

'That is when I feel a desire … an emptiness …'

He stood silently listening, and moved slightly behind her, so that she would not have to return his gaze.

'It is then I have a fierce hunger,' she whispered softly.

'What sort of hunger?'

She clasped her hands in front of her face. 'Do not ask such foolish things! My body seems to ache. Is that so difficult to understand?'

He placed his hands gently on her shoulders.

'Come, Cecilie.'

She remained where she was, her face buried in her hands. Carefully he bent forward and scooped her up in his arms and carried her to the bed. Cecilie dared not open her eyes as he gently put her down and stretched out beside her.

'Dearest Cecilie, just tell me what you want me to do.'

'I cannot! I do not know how to.'

Very carefully he began to run his fingers along the collar of her nightdress, loosening the ribbon.

'Then say nothing, simply nod your head if what I do pleases you.'

'You must not do this, Alexander, if you find it distasteful.'

'But I do not find it distasteful – not with you, dearest. You are a very beautiful woman – and I am interested in the secrets of womanhood. They are a complete mystery to me.'

She forced herself to ask the vital question. 'But do you – feel nothing yourself?'

'No, not as you mean. But you must not think I find this unpleasant either! Let us say I am curious – no, that is not a nice word. Amiable interest is better.' Then he lowered his voice to a whisper. 'Does this feel good?' he asked as his hand slipped inside the open front of her nightdress and gently stroked her breast.

'How can I lie?' she answered breathlessly. 'Don't your fingers tell you that my skin is shivering?'

Inside her head she was thinking: 'Oh what sweet torture is this! Where is this going to lead? To heaven or to hell?'

'Yes,' he said calmly. 'And how interesting that your breasts change their shape. They get smaller and harder. What causes this?'

'Perhaps they wish to be ki … No! Stop, Alexander. I am too ashamed and embarrassed! Let us stop now, while we are still able!'

'Were you going to say, "They wish to be kissed?" I did

not know.' And with that, he pulled her nightdress away and leant across to kiss her now naked breasts, sucking gently at each nipple as he did so.

Cecilie gasped. 'No, Alexander! No more! I want you to stop now!'

'But you do feel something?'

'Alexander! Please!'

'Cecilie, I do not want you to lie awake at night and suffer because you are tied to an oddity like me. You cared for me and did so much while I was sick. Let me now do something that pleases you.'

She sniffed back a tear and the next moment, without any warning he placed his hand firmly on her loins, directly touching the most secret part of her. Through the thin cloth, Cecilie felt at once the fire of his caress and all her passion flowed to that one part of her. Unable to resist, she responded, pushing lightly against his hand.

'No! No!' she moaned loudly. 'Go, Alexander, go to your rooms, I beg you. The shame is too much. Please, go!'

He stifled a sigh and removed his hand.

'If that is what you want, my friend. Forgive me if my behaviour was improper. I meant you no harm.'

He got up and left, closing the door behind him, leaving Cecilie outraged, her emotions in turmoil. She turned slowly onto her stomach, thumping her hand into her pillow, breathing heavily and grieving inside.

'Oh, Alexander, you beast, you beast!' she wailed.

She sat up; her legs, pressed tightly together, were dangling over the edge of the bed and her fists were clenched and pressed hard against her chin.

'Oh, dear Lord,' she whispered to herself. 'I can stand it no more, no more!' holding back a sob. 'What more am I expected to do?'

She slipped down from the bed, went to his door and knocked with trembling fingers.

'Come in!'

Cecilie opened the door. One candle was burning, and by its light she could see him lying in his bed. Unsure of what to do, she remained helplessly in the doorway, staring at him. Then without a word he moved over to make room for her and held open the covers. She closed her eyes for a moment, then walked swiftly across the floor and almost threw herself into the bed, as if she was frightened he would change his mind. After a second or two, Alexander pinched out the candle to spare her further embarrassment.

The next instant his hand reached down once again, and she opened her legs for him with a tiny guarded moan. Alexander's hand explored a realm that he had never known before. Gently, so gently he moved his fingers down across her legs, before slowly bringing them back again, his fingernails rubbing lightly along the insides of her thighs. Cecilie began to feel she was drowning in her own passion as he, delving ever deeper, moved closer and closer to the centre of her desire.

Alexander could not help noticing how her body was quivering and he began to increase the urgency of his movements. 'Where?' he whispered. 'Cecilie, tell me where?'

Ashamed of the pleasure she was feeling, Cecilie turned her face away.

'My dearest one, we are still man and wife! Show me, tell me!'

Taking his hand quickly in hers, she led him to the precise place she longed for him to be. Aah! She knew beyond all doubt, now she was ready for him.

'It is not easy for me,' she whispered in his ear, tears in her eyes. 'That you are not *with* me, I mean.'

'But I am finding pleasure in this too, my friend,' he breathed. 'Otherwise I should not have asked you to let me do it. It is an experience for me as well.'

Cecilie bit her lip in near despair, struggling both to understand and say nothing at the same time.

The movement of his hand was becoming more urgent and she noticed that his breath too was beginning to quicken.

'Do not forget that I have waited three weeks for this,' he breathed. 'When I saw you with other men I realised what you must have missed. But also I realised I did not want you to fall into another man's embrace.'

Like sudden shafts of sunlight, his words brought a dazzling new warmth to her. Was he jealous? It certainly sounded as if he was and she thought she felt her heart skip a beat.

'At the grand ball, I began to find I could not bear to think of you lying in secret with someone else,' he whispered urgently. 'It started to be an agony.'

'Oh! What sweet, sweet words!' thought Cecilie, and how they brought such great joy to her soul!

'Relax, Cecilie! Surrender to what you feel – I can tell that you are somehow holding back … Yes, just like that.'

He touched her so gently and tenderly that suddenly she could resist no longer. She felt herself let go, as a wave of pleasure washed over her. She threw her arms around him and kissed his shoulder, clinging dizzily to him as he helped her through the tempest of delight.

She lay, calm and exhausted, her arms covering her hot crimson cheeks.

'You were wonderful, Cecilie.' His voice was hoarse. 'Good God, what fire you have within you! Will you sleep here with me tonight?'

'No,' she muttered, and rolled off the bed. Her knees were trembling as she lurched to her room, slammed the door and tumbled back into her own bed, where she lay shivering for a long time before finally falling asleep.

* * * *

The next morning she knew it would be awkward seeing Alexander alone in broad daylight. So she delayed the inevitable as long as she could, washing very slowly and elaborately and putting up her hair. She deliberately asked a maid to bring breakfast to her room, but she found she could eat very little of the food, having lost much of her appetite through the emotion of the night. When she could not postpone it any longer, she dressed quickly and left her bedchamber, unsure of what to say or do.

Alexander was waiting in the magnificent drawing room, where everything was still as it was before she had arrived at Gabrielshus. Cecilie had not wanted to change the style of this room by adding things that reflected her own taste, although she had made her mark discreetly but unmistakeably, in other parts of the house. But always she had sought Alexander's advice first and waited for his approval.

'Good morning,' she muttered on catching sight of him, and tried to hurry blindly past him into the next room.

But he moved with surprising speed and gripped her arm.

'Cecilie dearest, you have nothing to reproach yourself for,' he said lowering his voice on catching sight of a housemaid sweeping the hall floor. 'Do you admonish me? Are you angry with me?'

She shook her head. 'No, only with myself.'

'Why?'

'Because I behaved in an unseemly manner.'

His eyes were smiling. 'There are times when seemliness is foolish. May I ask you a favour?'

'What is it?' she said anxiously.

'Tell me when you want me again!'

She looked shamefully at him. 'You want to relive the misery?'

'It was not misery, not at all. For me it was the most wonderful experience. What do you say?'

'I shall let you know,' she mumbled, for no other reason than to end the conversation – and then hurried away to keep herself to herself for the rest of the day.

* * * *

A game of chess that evening helped to redress the balance in their relationship, and by the end of it, Cecilie was her usual smiling self once more. She had made up her mind firmly during the day to forget the whole embarrassing episode and not refer to it again.

She discovered, however, that it was not going to be that easy. Her days were busy and, as the mistress of a large estate, she had many things to think about and a wide variety of duties to perform. But her nights, when in her dreams she could sense his closeness, feel his gentle hands and touch his warm skin – that was different. And sometimes, late in the evening before she slept, she remembered how she had gone to his door, her heart pounding and she recalled the look in his eyes as he gazed across the room at her – and how it had all begun, in her room, when he first discovered that he could arouse her with his tentative kisses.

But she was still astonished when, three weeks later, she

awoke from a light sleep to find Alexander standing by her bedside. On the table a candle he had brought with him was flickering.

'You never came to me,' he said, smiling a little uncertainly. 'I have been wondering – why?'

'No, I – I didn't think you needed me.' She half turned her head, not wanting him to see the true answer in her eyes.

'May I?' He gestured towards the bed.

She nodded and started to whisper, 'Of course,' but her voice had deserted her.

'So you have not longed for a man again since I was with you?'

'You know the answer to that, Alexander!' she replied in a firm voice. 'You know very well.'

'No, I do not. Night after night I have waited for you, because I thought we had experienced something wonderful that last time we were together. I watched a dull ember burn brighter and brighter until it became an inferno of passion. But you never came, and I was disappointed. I thought you were still incensed by my behaviour.'

'I am not angered by you, Alexander,' she told him more evenly. 'On the contrary! But it is an unfair union – you are but a cold and dispassionate observer, whilst my innermost feelings are laid bare.'

'In Heaven's name, Cecilie, I am not dispassionate! How can you think that? Please give me the chance once more to bring you pleasure.'

She put her head on his chest, but said nothing.

'Dearest Cecilie, it is I who should be ashamed – because I am inadequate. You are alive, warm and beautiful in your desire. Or has that flame now died again – perhaps forever?'

She did not answer him, because those gentle tender hands were there again and her yearning to relive the wild uncontrollable passion was so strong that this time she surrendered to him at once. She gasped and moaned, pressing herself against his hand, rubbing her knee up and down against his thigh in painfully slow, nervous movements. She groaned aloud as every muscle in her body stiffened.

Alexander knew that her pleasure was almost at its peak as he provoked and tormented her urgent desire – but he was not prepared for the sudden violence that exploded as her passion reached its zenith. He had always thought her to have a cool, reserved manner even though she could be impulsive at times, but in the throes of passion's fulfilment she abandoned herself shamelessly to her own inner nature and that of her kinspeople.

Later, when her moment had passed and she was growing calmer again, he put his arms around her to try and stop her from feeling ashamed.

'Thank you my dear,' he whispered gently in her ear. 'Would you like me to stay with you tonight?'

It was a voice she hardly recognised, because of its tenderness, but with a shake of her head, she again refused him permission. But this time she lay for a while, unmoving, breathing heavily, in his arms before she indicated that it was time for him to leave her. Alexander tenderly kissed her on the forehead and eased himself out of her bed.

He cannot understand why I ask him to go, she reflected. He does not realise how hard it is not to be able to give him the small, impulsive, tender caresses that are the sign of a deep mutual trust, respect – and love. Though she could not be anything but grateful to him; after all he was giving her all he was capable of.

Two evenings later, however, she astonished him when she appeared in the doorway to his room, holding a large glowing candelabra in her hand.

'May I come in?' she asked very softly.

'Cecilie! Of course!'

When she had snuggled down beside him she whispered: 'You probably think that I am in urgent need of a man?'

He rubbed the tip of his nose against her cheek. 'Yesterday evening I had to stop myself from knocking on your door again. Tonight I was sure I would not be able to resist. But you have come to me instead! It gladdens me more than I can say.'

'It is not just any man I need, it is you,' she whispered in his ear. 'I would never allow any other man to touch me as you have done.'

He stroked her hair slowly with one hand and pulled it tenderly aside from her temple. 'So you have been longing to feel me close, have you?' he asked softly.

'My whole body is heavy with longing for you.' Her voice was so hushed that he had to strain to hear her at all. 'I have never known anything like it before in all my life.'

They realised now that there was nothing more they could say and the only sound in the bedchamber was the gentle murmur of Cecilie's excited breathing as Alexander let his tongue play slowly over her neck, across her breasts and down to her belly. She moaned with pleasure as he caressed her, and opened herself to him, waiting for his hand to reach the very centre of her being.

She caressed his scarred back with a growing urgency and gently ran her fingers around the wound that had healed so well. He in turn, eased himself forward until he was on top of her and she could feel his lips against her cheek. He had never kissed her properly, not since that first compulsory bridal kiss on the day they were wed, nor did he do so now – a kiss, reflected Cecilie, was beyond all else a gesture of true love.

Then she let out a sudden gasp of shock and surprise. The blood rushed to her loins with such fury, and yet such tenderness, that she ached. Alexander had entered her!

'Alexander?' His name was on her lips and she looked up at him, eyes wide with wonder. 'Oh, Alexander!'

'Hush!' he whispered, quivering, not daring to move. 'Say nothing!'

Cecilie realised how delicate the situation was. One unthinking word, one careless movement might destroy this moment – as easily as dropping a crystal vase.

She could see the near panic in his eyes, the fear of what he had done. He stayed very still, trembling slightly, barely breathing. Then slowly, tremulously, he began to move inside her. She held her breath, not daring to make the smallest movement. Her heart was pounding. Oh, God! It was such ecstasy – she was truly ready – she must hold back.

But Alexander could feel her need, and he had seen the passion on her face. He squeezed her shoulders and begged her to let go.

In an instant she climaxed tumultuously, the indescribable feelings arriving in a frenzied rush. Nothing else mattered. She heard herself cry out. She saw Alexander's tortured face. She felt him writhing within her. Then she lost all sense of time and place and stopped caring what happened.

They lay breathless side by side, for a few minutes before Alexander got up and reached for his nightshirt.

'Forgive me,' he muttered, his voice hardly recognisable, and left the room in a great hurry.

Cecilie was stunned and lay on the bed without moving. If he goes out to be sick now, she thought, I should never forgive him. But Alexander did nothing of the kind. Instead he stood in their anteroom and cried – a deep, heart-rending, frightful sobbing. He could not have known how well he could be heard through the closed door and Cecilie listened to him, filled with the deepest compassion. She wanted so badly to go to him, to hold him and let him know he was not alone, but he had chosen to leave her and she knew that above all else he needed to be on his own for a while.

Eventually she crept quietly back to her room, her heart still racing, listening for any further sound of Alexander, but there was none. She did not know where he had gone.

In the morning when she awoke, she found Wilhelmsen standing at the door of their rooms. From his grave face she could see that he had something of importance to impart.

'Good morning Wilhelmsen,' she said enquiringly, 'can I help you?'

'His Grace particularly said he did not wish to wake you, My Lady. He sends his compliments and says that he will be away for a time.'

Disappointment cut her like a knife. 'Away?' she asked incredulously. 'Do you mean he has already left the house?'

'Yes, My Lady.'

'When will he return?'

'He did not say, My Lady. I do not think he knew that himself.'

'And where did he go?'

'He did not tell me that either.'

'Thank you, Wilhelmsen!' She let out an agonised sigh. 'That will be all.'

'So I have finally lost him,' she thought as the manservant silently turned and left the room. At that moment the pain of a deep and sudden despair bit into the very core of her being. 'That must mean the dream is over,' she thought hopelessly. 'Last night was more than he could take.'

Chapter 13

Over the next few days no message arrived at Gabrielshus from Alexander telling of his whereabouts. Cecilie did her best not to worry. She reminded herself frequently that he had at least been considerate enough to leave the message with Wilhelmsen before his departure and that the best thing to do was remain patient and await the outcome of his sudden journey, whatever it might be. Her hopes were raised briefly one morning when a personal message was brought to the house by a special courier, but on inspecting the handwriting, she could see immediately it was from her mother, not Alexander.

Once she had got over her disappointment, Cecilie opened the letter, to find that it was quite long. Liv obviously had many things to get off her chest.

It read: 'Gråstensholm in April AD 1627. My Dearest Cecilie, Many things have been happening here, you can be sure. Are's youngest son, Brand, has really put the cat among the pigeons! He has brought shame on the daughter of Niklas Niklasson of Högtun, the owner of one of the largest estates hereabouts. Can you imagine? Brand is only just eighteen! Meta has locked herself away out of shame and refuses to speak to anyone. She has always been considered one of the most highly respected farmers' wives in the district and now her son has brought disgrace upon them.

'Are himself is calmer about it all. He is brewing beer and distilling *brännvin* for the wedding, which will take place on Walpurgis Eve, the night before 1 May. It is being held so soon because time will not wait for them, as you will no doubt understand. You must come to the wedding, you simply must, and Tarjei is back home so you can see him again. It is a great comfort for Are and Meta to have him with them. He is so relaxed and reassuring to have nearby, do you not agree?

'And your dear husband is, of course, restored to health following such misfortune, we were so glad to hear. God be praised for that! Our Lord's ways are truly wise. And what's more, he has never been here – your husband, I mean, of course.'

Cecilie crushed her handkerchief tightly. Would Alexander go to the wedding? She did not even know where he was! The letter continued:

'I cannot imagine how it happened because Brand has never shown any interest in girls. But I believe to some extent it was the fault of that stable lad, Jesper, who led him to ruin. That boy chases after girls all year round. It is said they were allowed to go to Högtun as "night-suitors", the local tradition, which you will know about, and it proved too much for Brand, unaccustomed to girls as he was.

'Nor do I know how much the two of them care for each other. It is all so distressing and the father, Niklasson, is enraged! His wife is quietly pleased, though, knowing her daughter could go to far worse homes than Linden Allée. But she is so young. Seventeen years. Her name is Matilda – you would surely have met her many years ago.

'Tomorrow I shall travel to Oslo to look for fabric for a

wedding gift, which I shall sew for them. And, oh! How awful it is that Oslo is now called "Christiania"! It has been so these past three years, but I shall never learn! I did hear a story about the dear leader of our country, King Christian IV, whom you see occasionally. He was to found the silver-mining town of Kongsberg, also three years ago as you know. But he had drunk so much that, when asked to point out where the town should be, he waved in completely the wrong direction. So Kongsberg, which should have stood at a place called Saggränden, was built instead at Numedalslågen!

'I do not know if that is a true story, but it is amusing, don't you agree? Mind you, it is a good thing that Mama Silje did not hear it, so proud was she of our Royal Family. Ah, I miss her and Father so! I cannot tell you how difficult it is to be an elder and most respected in the family. I do not feel old at all and I cannot understand how I came to be. And yet I have two wonderful grandchildren, Kolgrim and Mattias.

'But I should not speak of grandchildren when you have lost your own longed-for child. How are you, my dearest? No, I will not pry, but it has been two years since it happened and you know how a mother grows impatient to be a grandmother anew! Forgive me, Cecilie dear, if I am meddling in matters that make you feel unhappy!'

Cecilie broke off from her reading. 'Dear tactful Mama – who has said nothing for two long years,' thought Cecilie. If only her mother could imagine the scale of her other difficulties and their bizarre nature! Her thoughts started to spiral downward again at this thought, so she shook herself and continued reading.

'I spoke to Are yesterday. He is worried about Tarjei. The lad must have experienced some awful things during the war. He sometimes has nightmares and wakes everybody up, shouting and yelling. It seems in his nightmares he is afraid that the dreaded Devourer of Corpses is coming to take his dead brother Trond. It was something like that. I did not quite understand, but Are seemed to think that Tarjei believed Trond to be the Devourer himself! How tragic it is that the poor boy should have to see so much violence and death when still so young!

'Your Father liked Alexander very much, as did I. It will make us both very happy to see him here at Gråstensholm, so you must promise to come, Cecilie. Both of you, please! I am always thinking of you, dearest. Your affectionate Mama.'

Cecilie gave a sigh as she set the letter aside. A great feeling of homesickness came over her. Everything now seemed so hopeless.

More days passed and Alexander still did not return or send any message. Cecilie lay awake every night, her tangled emotions passing from desire to anxiety, to anger – and then to intense disappointment that he did not care, at the very least, to tell her where he was going or where he was now.

At long last a sign came that he was still alive. A letter arrived after he had been gone for fourteen days, by which time she had been ready to allow her anxiety to defeat her shame and begin asking friends and acquaintances if they knew of his whereabouts.

To her surprise, when she looked at it, she saw that the letter was dated the day after he had disappeared. So he had wanted to tell her after all. But the letter post could never be relied upon. In the meantime it had obviously been languishing somewhere along the way.

Although she could barely contain her eagerness to begin reading it, part of her was in fear of what the letter would say. For several minutes she stared at its exterior, trying frantically to guess what it might contain. Was it the final death knell? Would it end all her hopes beyond any shadow of doubt? Or was there a slight chance that the news might be good? The thoughts whirled in her mind and when she could bear the suspense no longer, she tore it open with her heart pounding in her ears, and started to read.

In the letter Alexander said: 'My Dearest Sweetest Girl, What can I say, what can I write that will express the chaos that rages inside me? First of all: thank you for last night! And please try to forgive my hasty departure. But believe me, there was nothing else I could do. Please understand that what happened was as great a revelation for me as when I discovered I was not like other men.'

Yes, thought Cecilie ruefully, that was something she could understand. She could only guess at the scale of the emotional impact he had felt, but it would obviously have been overwhelming.

'I could not account for what had happened, Cecilie, thinking myself to be incapable of such an act with a woman. Nor do I believe it could have happened with any woman but you. For you mean something very special to me as you know.'

Cecilie did not realise it, but as she read those words a glowing smile gradually lit up her face.

'The experience was so overpowering that I had to try and make sense of it on my own. I do not think that I am one of those who can readily switch from one sex to the other with ease. But it is as though I am now hanging in mid-air and I sense I must choose one side or the other. Do you understand me? It is for this reason that I am travelling to meet my old friends that I may decide what I feel for them. Hans Barth is in prison, and he disgusts me, so I shall avoid him. But I should like to see my friend Germund once again – he who never knew anything of my early dreams. I shall also visit a friend who tried to rekindle a relationship at the ball at Frederiksborg. There are one or two others whose company I also find agreeable. But believe me when I tell you that I intend nothing more than to pass the time and engage in conversation with them. It is my feelings of which I must be sure. I have to know!

'Try to be patient with me, dearest! This is so difficult and so fragile that I feel I am walking on a thread stretched across a bottomless pit. You must remember that it was not so long ago that I swore I could never have any feelings for a woman! Please do not be sad during this time, Cecilie. If you are prepared to wait for me at Gabrielshus, despite the knowledge that you may suffer a great disappointment, then I shall be forever grateful to you.

'I never realised that it could be so wonderful to lie in a woman's arms! Or to be more precise, in your arms! But perhaps it was something I felt unconsciously at the very beginning of our friendship. I do not know. But I do know that now it is something I must find out once and for all and come to know myself for what I really am beyond any shadow of doubt. I thank you, dearest Cecilie, for all your kindness and patience. Your difficult, but affectionate husband, Alexander.'

Cecilie remained seated, sapped of all strength, with the letter resting in her lap. He had wanted to put her mind at rest after all by writing a letter the very next day. She could not now blame him for her two weeks of hellish torment. But whether the letter had calmed her many fears was doubtful. Very doubtful!

* * * *

To Cecilie's surprise, Alexander arrived back at Gabrielshus the very next day. She saw him dismount from his horse and went out on the steps to greet him. A keen spring breeze was sweeping across the yard, as he came towards her and she could see he was watching her expression closely to see if he could detect a hint of her mood.

'Welcome home, Alexander,' she said, her voice strained. 'I am very glad to see you.'

'Thank you, Cecilie. I am very glad to be back. Did you receive my letter?'

'Yesterday.'

'Only yesterday?' he exclaimed, pausing in the act of opening the door for her. 'Then, all this time – you have not known?'

'That's true.'

She replied as calmly as she was able, but her tears were very close. A fierce anguish was also burning inside her as she tried to anticipate from his expression and manner what he had decided.

'Oh, my dear Cecilie,' he said, clearly upset. 'Have you been – concerned for my whereabouts?'

'When your letter arrived, I was about to begin a humiliating journey to seek news of you. I have been so deeply worried as you will surely understand, both for you – and for your decision.'

For the first time he noticed how pale she was. He opened the door for her to go in and they found Wilhelmsen waiting respectfully inside.

'Good day, Wilhelmsen,' he said. 'Like the prodigal son, I have returned. Fetch us a carafe of something strong and flavoursome and two glasses, please! Serve it in the small drawing room and then see that we are not disturbed, will you!'

When Alexander had poured a glass for each of them and persuaded Cecilie to take a sip, he sat back in his favourite armchair, the wheels long since removed, and she faced him from the other large armchair that had become 'Her

Ladyship's chair'. This was where they would normally while away long winter evenings playing chess and a variety of board games.

'Cecilie, I am so sorry that I have caused you two weeks of turmoil. Had I but known – well. But now I shall tell you what I have decided.'

She sat bolt upright in the chair, gathering all her powers of self-control. In his turn Alexander appeared to be doing the same. They gazed at each other in silence for a time; then he drew a long deep breath.

'I travelled first to my old friend Germund, as I said I would. I stayed with him and his wife in their beautiful home for four or five days, just to be really certain of my feelings. But I felt not the slightest pang of envy, or the desire to get closer to him. So that aberration is dead and gone, and as you know, that was the strongest I ever felt for anyone.' He gave a chuckle. 'All I felt when I saw the happiness their family shared, was a strong desire to be with you.'

Cecilie dared to let herself smile, a cautious, trembling smile because she knew there was still much more he had to tell her. After looking at her uncertainly, Alexander stood up again and began pacing back and forth.

'I am too nervous to sit still, Cecilie! However, I stood by my decision to complete my journey and visit all my old friends. I have met all three of them Cecilie, and I have been given clear signals, even intimate suggestions – careful hands on my arm or resting on my shoulder …' He fell silent.

She waited a few seconds. 'And?' she prompted.

Alexander walked over to her and took her hands, drawing her up from the chair. He grasped her shoulders and she looked up at him. He was almost a head taller than her, and again as she looked into his face, she realised anew how incredibly handsome he was.

'My dearest, will you let me stay with you?' he asked tenderly. 'In spite of all you have suffered for my sake? I know for certain that I belong with you now. But remember, I can say nothing of what the future holds. I do not believe it will happen, but a man might one day awaken other feelings in me.'

Cecilie nodded slowly, considering what he had said. 'There is no one, man or woman, who is married that can guarantee not to fall in love with another,' she said soberly. 'Sadly we are all human in that respect.'

'That is true, but in my case it would be much worse, and far more hurtful to you.'

She nodded her head again. 'And if that should happen, what would you do, then?'

'Nothing! I should quash all those feelings and stay with you, of course.'

'I would not want that. But do you think it could happen?'

'No. I am as certain in myself as I can be of anything that it will not.'

'And how can you be so sure?'

'Because I have found something new.'

'Do you mean what happened with us that last evening?'

'No,' he replied. 'It is something a lot stronger and more far-reaching.'

'What is it Alexander?'

He looked straight into her eyes, pulled her to him and kissed her. It was a long, stirring kiss that told her more than any words could ever have done. He pulled her even closer, holding her in his powerful embrace, and when his lips finally parted from hers he said, 'I love you, Cecilie,' in a voice filled with emotion. 'I suppose I have loved you for a long time, but the sensual companionship was not there – the physical side of love. But now, the love I have for you is more intense and more real than anything I have ever known before.'

Cecilie was smiling and wiping away her tears at the same time.

'And of course I do not need to tell you how I feel about you!' she said.

'Yes, tell me!'

'There was a time, only a short while ago when my love for you was almost snuffed out. It was before I had learned to accept what you were. But otherwise I have always loved you ever since – well, yes, almost since we first met.'

'Dearest Cecilie! I must have put you through so much pain!'

'I have been well cared for here with you, you know that. And I entered into this marriage with both eyes open. There have been difficulties now and again, but they were not your fault or mine.'

'Perhaps, dearest.'

She shifted herself more closely into his arms, a frown creasing her brow. 'There is only one thing I have not quite understood, Alexander,' she said softly. 'And I would like to try and understand.'

'And what would that be?'

She hesitated. 'No, it is possibly too complicated to ask.'

'Surely you are not afraid of me?'

'No, but I am self-conscious.'

'You have no need to be,' he said. 'We ought to be open with one another. It is important if we are to build a bridge across the deep rift there has been between us.'

'But this is too delicate – too private!'

'I *want* you to tell me, Cecilie, whatever it is. It would warm my heart to know that I have your trust.'

She hid her face against his shoulder. 'Well – how were you able to – enter me and couple with me, so unexpectedly?'

'It was not so unexpected, my dearest. The second time we

241

lay together I could feel myself ready. I still found it difficult to believe that it was happening. It was your passion, your beauty and your body that aroused me beyond measure, my dear. After that, everything just happened by itself. It completely overwhelmed me.'

Cecilie knew she was blushing. She said nothing and Alexander continued softly: 'It was all that I needed to bring me back to where I once was, before my life was influenced by others – before that burden became too heavy for me to bear.'

'Yes. I think it must have been like that,' she agreed gently. 'You were "normal" from the beginning. But these past years have been good for me, Alexander. They have taught me to be more tolerant. I can better understand now those who do not conform – I have seen the world through their eyes and felt the malice, the stupidity and contempt they suffer from others around them. And I know how helpless they must feel.'

'What you say is true, Cecilie, and I am an exception. There are very few who are able to change the way they are. Many are forced to live with their unusual desires and their only salvation is to accept what they are – or else they will find their lives become a hell on earth. They are condemned to shame and self reproach.'

Cecilie nodded in agreement. They stood holding each other for several minutes until Alexander asked: 'Will you move into my room, my dear friend? I have the biggest bed!'

'Gladly, My Lord,' she replied smiling ironically and dropping a small curtsey. 'But I should like to keep my bedchamber as a room for myself, where I can have things of my own. And it is such a pretty room.'

'Of course you shall! Now, let's see the look on Wilhelmsen's face!'

'Hah! I doubt there is anything that will ever make him

change that mournful professional expression! But do you know what I think?'

'What?'

'I think it will make him very happy.'

'I'm sure it will – not least because of his fondness for you.'

'For both of us. Oh, Alexander, I had almost forgotten to tell you! Mother has asked us to attend my cousin's wedding. She is very insistent.'

'Whose wedding? Tarjei's?'

'No, his younger brother, Brand.'

'Ah yes. I have met him, I believe, in the field hospital. He is but a lad and not yet of age!'

With an embarrassed grin she said: 'It is customary among the Ice People and the Meidens to enjoy the pleasures of wedlock before marriage.'

'I see,' he said with a laugh. 'And besides, if he is old enough to be sent to war, he is surely old enough to make love to a woman, which he apparently has! When is the ceremony to take place?'

'Just before the Walpurgis festival at the start of May. You will come too, won't you, Alexander? To Gråstensholm and Linden Allée to see all the wonderful places I want to show you! And to meet my brother, Tarald, and Yrja whom you have never met – or their little one, Mattias. Here is the letter. Read for yourself.'

Liv's letter was neat and clearly written. Charlotte Meiden, Liv's beloved Aunt Charlotte, later to be her mother-in-law, had taught her well. Alexander could read Norwegian effortlessly and he picked it up and scanned it quickly. When he had finished the letter, he smiled gladly at her.

'Walpurgis? That's quite soon, isn't it? We really should not waste any time.'

243

The intervening days passed quickly as they settled into their new life together and they both prepared for the journey to Linden Allée and Gråstensholm with a pleasurable sense of anticipation. When they arrived just in time for the wedding, Alexander was immediately regarded as the senior guest on account of his eminence. It was not something they had intended, but as a Marquis he was far too interesting a personality for anyone to ignore. His rank and status easily surpassed that of Tarjei, Baroness Liv and Baron Dag the Notary.

Even the bashful couple themselves were eclipsed by Alexander's stature as they stood beside this tall elegant figure with his impressive list of titles. Even Niklas Niklasson of Högtun, where the wedding ceremony was held, was in a better mood because of the presence of such a celebrated guest at his table – and one who was now a member of the family, to boot. Well, was he strictly speaking, a full member of the family, some people locally would slyly ask? Perhaps, perhaps not – and they winked and quoted the old saying that declared: 'The tree doesn't taste of poultry just because the bird nested in it!'

But, in spite of all the upset that his hasty actions had caused, Brand the perspiring crimson-faced groom, finally met with approval among his wife's relatives. Matilda was not the sort of person who would normally have been thought suited to the ranks of the unconventional Ice People. Yet, in her favour, she was splendidly rotund – not only because of her condition – and seemed ideally suited to becoming a farmer's wife.

Her upbringing had obviously equipped her well for the early role of wife, as she brought with her, in her wedding chest, eighty hand towels, eight tablecloths, six table runners and so on and so forth. All of it had been stitched and sewn very carefully by her own tender hands and in fact everything for Matilda had to be prim and proper. In that way she was the ideal match for Brand, who tended towards accepting things just as they were and a certain personal sluggishness.

It was this fact that caused Cecilie to make a fleeting, slightly unwelcome remark to the bride as they were standing in the wedding garden. In one of those coincidental moments when everybody stops talking, Cecilie's embarrassing words were the ones left ringing in the air: 'Yes, Brand is a bit slow sometimes to get his backside moving!'

But in general it was a good wedding with many fine gifts for the bride and groom – and if such things demarcated a good wedding from a bad one, a considerable number of men were still sleeping off their excesses at the roadside or in a field the following day.

Jesper, the stable lad's son, became the cause of some consternation when he was discovered by Niklas Niklasson and his good wife, lying in their large comfortable bed when they were about to retire after a long wearying day. What he was, or had been, doing there remained unknown, as he was too drunk to explain himself.

* * * *

The next morning, before everybody was awake, Cecilie and Alexander went out into the fields and pastures, meandering slowly along the hedgerows hand in hand, feeling intensely happy in each other's company. It was as if they had grown much closer here, where they both felt at home, surrounded by a throng of people – family, friends and strangers.

It was a wonderful spring day, the air was growing warmer and there was a faint green hue of young grass, sprinkled with the tiny white nameless flowers that were everywhere. After returning briefly to the house for breakfast, they soon set out again and this time they heard small padding footsteps following them as they walked away from Gråstensholm. They turned and smiled, not letting on that they would rather have been left on their own.

'Kolgrim,' said Cecilie, 'I thought I recognised those distinctive little footsteps.'

He pushed wordlessly between them and they held his hands. Now six years old, his face was truly fascinating and everyone was struck, particularly, by the amber colour of his eyes. Other than that, no one would have noticed that he was one of the Ice People's most extraordinary progenies – except for those shoulders. Just like Tengel's shoulders before him, they were high and wide, rising to a slight upward point, in the same way as a Chinese mandarin's coat collar. These were the shoulders that had taken the life of her first sister-in-law, Sunniva, and Cecilie knew very well that she risked the same fate, if she should ever give birth. It was not a pleasant thought and she dismissed it hurriedly from her mind.

They decided to walk towards Silje's avenue of linden trees and as they went, Alexander chatted with Kolgrim. They were both struck during the conversation by the boy's obvious antipathy towards his father, Tarald. He also seemed only to tolerate Yrja and talked a lot about his little brother, Mattias. But in doing this, they got the impression that he was possibly fishing for something, trying to discover what they thought of his angelic sibling.

Cecilie still felt she was the only one in the family who really understood Kolgrim and nothing that was said that morning led her to revise her decision, not to put too much trust in his apparently reformed good nature. 'If I am blessed with children of my own,' Cecilie told herself as they walked, 'I shall never allow them anywhere near their bizarre cousin.'

She reached this conclusion mainly because she felt they would be especially vulnerable, with Kolgrim openly worshipping her and wanting no rivals for her affection. Kolgrim seemed not to have anything against his grandparents, Dag and Liv, and for that she was grateful, as she adored her parents. Neither did she believe that the child who would soon be born to Brand and Matilda had anything to fear from Kolgrim. But of his attitude towards Mattias, on the other hand, she was not too sure. Thank God that all seems well at present between the two brothers, she thought, momentarily clutching Kolgrim's hand so hard that he looked surprised and hurt.

They had arrived at the allée of linden trees and were strolling along the broad avenue towards the house, with Kolgrim skipping between them. The tree-lined drive still had a majestic feel to it and Cecilie felt she understood why Silje had always dreamed as a girl of living at the end of such a splendid avenue.

'There are only three of Tengel's original enchanted lindens left here now,' she said pensively. 'One is my father Dag's, one is Mother's and the other is Are's.'

'Which ones are they?' inquired Alexander, who had long ago heard the story of the trees.

'I don't know which is which, but they are the three oldest trees, the very biggest ones,' she said gesturing, 'right there at the top of the avenue.'

They walked slowly in the direction she had pointed, enjoying the morning and the panorama of the landscape spread out around them.

'I think one of them looks weakened,' said Cecilie

anxiously as they drew nearer. 'Look at all this lying on the ground! Branches, bark and buds …'

'It's probably just the work of some very active squirrels,' said Alexander gently, trying to calm her fears.

'You think so? Yes, most likely you're right.'

They did not linger beneath the trees, but walked on more quickly. Cecilie decided that she wouldn't try to find out whose tree it was. But she could not forget the piles of natural debris strewn on the ground and the generally sad air of the sagging branches of the tree above.

As they entered the yard at the end of the avenue, Cecilie said: 'That is the old house, where Tengel and Silje once lived. Tarjei lives there now. Let's go over and see him.'

'Have your family lived here a long time?' Alexander asked.

'Not really. I was born here, up at Gråstensholm. But otherwise, I think they came in the year that Uncle Are was born. That must have been about 1586. Mother was born before they came here.'

'So where did they live before they came?'

'That is something of a mystery. It is said they lived in a valley in Tröndelag – the Valley of the Ice People, they called it. But outsiders named it "a nest of witches and warlocks", I think.'

Kolgrim was listening to every detail, his serious face indicating that he was taking it all in very carefully and storing it away in his memory.

'It was there that the first Tengel – Tengel the Evil – is said to have sworn a pact with Satan,' she continued. 'At least somewhere quite close by.'

'Aha, yes! The pot that he buried is supposed to have contained the spell he used to bring forth the Evil One, isn't that it?' asked Alexander. 'I remember you telling me about it some time ago.'

'Well, Grandmama Silje kept a journal of her years in the valley.'

'That would be very interesting to read some time,' said Alexander.

Cecilie smiled. 'You're right. But I suspect that it would be very hard work. Grandmama was a very sweet person, but without much schooling. However I shall ask Mother where the journal is. I have never seen it. Perhaps it has been thrown away.'

'That would be a pity.'

They had arrived at the house and opened the door to the empty echoing hallway of Linden Allée.

'Look at that mosaic!' Alexander exclaimed, evidently impressed. 'It must have great value.'

'Indeed, it has. Silje was given it long ago by a proper church painter. She had a great love for it and it was one of the very few things they brought here from that other time …'

While she was still speaking and they were both looking together at the mosaic, a figure came quietly into the room behind them.

'Good morning,' said Tarjei, when they turned round. 'You are all out early!'

'So you have slept off the worst of last night's revels,' jibed Cecilie, smiling. 'I hope we didn't wake you?'

He grinned back at them in response. 'I always drink very modestly. I am not a great man for parties by any means. And I have been awake for a long time. Have you been admiring our family portraits, Alexander? I'm afraid you'll find them far less impressive than yours.'

'I wouldn't say that,' Alexander replied. 'I'm fascinated by this picture.'

'That's my Grandmother,' Kolgrim announced proudly. 'She was a witch!'

'I can believe that,' Alexander shivered. 'And her name was Sol, wasn't it?'

The boy nodded joyfully.

'I can see Cecilie, that you look a lot like her,' said Alexander, still gazing thoughtfully at the portrait. After a moment he turned to look down at Kolgrim. 'Sol was truly beautiful, Kolgrim, wasn't she? Someone to be very proud of!'

Thank you, Alexander, for that indirect compliment, thought Cecilie. She looked again at the striking picture herself and found she could not take her eyes off Silje's depiction of Sol's strong sensual face. And in that same instant, Kolgrim, without giving any indication, had chosen Alexander as his favourite.

'She could make magic,' said the boy loudly.

Alexander smiled and nodded, 'Yes, I have heard about that.'

'So can I!'

Very cautiously Cecilie said: 'Don't talk foolishness, Kolgrim.'

The boy's eyes turned clear yellow as he gazed back at them in turn.

'Yes I can; *I can*!'

'I believe you,' Alexander said swiftly, 'and so does Cecilie. She only wanted to tease you a little bit.'

The glow in the boy's eyes dulled as he watched Alexander carry on along the row of portraits.

'And this must be Dag, the blond-haired one.'

Tarjei chuckled. 'There is not much left of the blond hair now.'

Cecilie's heart skipped a beat. She could not bear to think of her beloved father growing old.

'Aah! This is Liv, that's clear to see,' said Alexander. 'And this last one is Are.' He fell silent again, absorbed in thought as he continued to study and re-study the pictures. 'You know,

Cecilie,' he said at last, 'your grandmother was a really good artist.'

'You have to see her wall paintings and tapestries as well,' she replied.

'May I?' he asked, looking at Tarjei. 'I would be very honoured.'

Tarjei gladly arranged for the other rooms where they were stored and hung to be opened and at the end of his browsing, a very impressed Alexander asked most graciously if he might be allowed to take one or two back to Gabrielshus. Cecilie immediately expressed her approval of the suggestion and promised to talk to Liv and Are about it.

Responding to a discreet wink from Cecilie, Tarjei lured Kolgrim away to allow her and Alexander to continue looking over the estates on their own. The boy was unable to resist Tarjei's exciting offer to 'swap magic tricks' and at once trotted off obediently at his heels. Very quietly, Alexander and Cecilie left Linden Allée and made their way across the fields and into the trees.

Lost in thought, conversation and the pleasure of each other's company, they wandered deeper and deeper into the forest, until they chanced upon a sunlit clearing, beside a stream. Unbeknown to them it was the precise secret place where Sol often went alone with her cat to practice and cast her spells. They sat down happily together on the grass, relishing the peacefulness of the forest, the birdsong and the warm sunlight.

'I have that feeling again,' said Cecilie, as she lay back on the grass and looked up at the sky.

Alexander had plucked a blade of grass and was running it across her brow.

'What feeling is that?' he murmured.

'That I have been here before.'

'That's quite possible, isn't it?'

'No, I would have remembered if I had – because it is such a long walk through the forest. But I feel I like this place very much.'

'I do too. We are lost to the world here.'

They drew closer together and put their arms around one another. The birds continued singing sweetly, the sunshine became warmer and the leaves of the forest stirred only very gently in the spring breezes. And so it happened in this place, where Sol had once laid out her spells and potions and muttered her incantations, that Alexander's seed found its way to where it would create new life, new families, new generations.

Sol would most certainly have approved of their presence there on that lovely fresh spring day. She would have approved specially too of the intense pleasures they shared and gave each other, time after time after time. In short, she would have concluded that they had chosen a perfect and ideal spot to celebrate their newfound and passionate love for one another.

Chapter 14

Brand and Matilda were delighted at the birth of their baby boy when he arrived safely some months later. He was as splendid, normal and robust as his parents, and Linden Allée's new son was baptised Andreas. As Tarjei had, by then, felt sufficiently recovered to return to complete his studies in Tübingen, Are and Meta moved into the older part of the house to make way for the younger folk.

Beyond the boundaries of Linden Allée and Gråstensholm and the daily events in the lives of the Ice People who lived there, the conflict that would later become known as the Thirty Years War was continuing. Before it ended it would irrevocably change the boundaries of many European states, but now it had become the turn of Sweden to lead the new Protestant armies.

The Swedish King, Gustav II Adolf, whose full title was Gustavus Adolphus, was a far more able strategist than King Christian, and signs were already emerging that his efforts might be rewarded with success. King Christian's Danish expedition had by this time ended in failure – utter failure. The Danish troops had panicked when they heard that Wallenstein's mercenaries were harrying them and they fled for home, towards Jutland. As they went, they pillaged and plundered for all they were worth, because, just like their Catholic pursuers, they were also mostly mercenaries.

For the population of Jutland it was a catastrophe, made worse by the failure of the harvest in 1627 and compounded further by the arrival shortly afterwards of Wallenstein and his furious rampaging hordes. He occupied all of Jutland and countless Danes, from peasants to nobles, were forced to flee from the mainland peninsula to Zealand or Norway.

Nor did fate smile on King Christian himself. He endured constant pain from a wound in his arm, which he had received in combat, and furthermore he had nagging suspicions about his wife, Kirsten Munk, who had become somewhat cool and brusque towards him. He was already heavily weighed down by the setbacks and defeats he had suffered on the battlefield and, to add insult to injury, the Swedish King now looked set to take over and claim all the glory. This, above all else, upset him beyond measure.

The Court in Copenhagen therefore, was not the happiest of places, but Marquis Alexander Paladin and his wife Cecilie stayed well clear of its disharmonies and defeatist intrigues. They preferred to carry on with their increasingly happy lives, undisturbed by the world beyond Gabrielshus, where one of Silje's fine tapestries now adorned a wall. To Alexander's well-concealed anger, Ursula had taken charge of the household. She had arrived almost as soon as she received word that Cecilie was expecting another child. This time nothing was to be allowed to happen to the heir of the estate and family name. Ursula had firmly announced on her arrival that she would see to that.

They had successfully kept her at bay during Alexander's long period of recovery, but on this occasion they might as well have tried to whistle for the wind.

Once ensconced, she commanded the territory of Gabrielshus with a determined and wily strategy. She appeared to be kind, considerate and sweet and wanted the best for everyone – but she almost pestered them into oblivion with her thoughtfulness. As the days passed, the servants' faces all took on a look of quiet desperation.

In the end, Alexander stooped to a slight deception to entice his ever-helpful sister back to Jutland and told her that Wallenstein's soldiers were about to expropriate her estates in her absence. There had been no other way, since Cecilie could not endure such zealous care; she had not even been allowed out of bed, let alone take a walk outside to get some fresh air.

Once they had said their fond farewells to her, Alexander and Cecilie sat down in their favourite chairs and laughed out loud with relief. After their laughter subsided, Alexander ran his eyes over Cecilie's matronly form, which she was doing her best to keep concealed under the skirts of a large crinoline.

'He is certainly going to be a well-built lad, isn't he?' he said, smiling across at her with great affection.

She looked back at him very gravely. 'Don't say that, Alexander. It frightens me. The Ice People's "well-built lads" have an unfortunate habit of killing their mothers in childbirth.'

'That will not happen here! We shall send for Tarjei.'

'No, thank you!'

'And why not? He is far better skilled than people realise.'

Cecilie was adamant. 'He is my *cousin*, Alexander! And he is five years younger than I. There has to be some privacy between cousins, doesn't there?'

'But …'

'Don't try to persuade me. There are certain parts of my body that you alone may gaze upon, and nobody else.'

'What about the midwife?'

'That is a very different matter.'

'I never thought that you would be so prudish, Cecilie.'

'Nor am I! Just – not Tarjei! He is a good friend with whom I have squabbled many times, but also enjoyed scholarly conversation. Where he is concerned, I exist only above my waist. I am a lady – there are no nether regions, do you understand? And besides, would you want your sister to see you naked?'

'No, God preserve me! You have won – but I shall still have a field surgeon I know on hand.'

Cecilie nodded. 'Do so by all means. The legacy of the Ice People is not to be taken lightly.'

He looked at her with a wary expression. 'But did you not say that there was already an accursed one in this next generation?'

'Yes – Kolgrim! But many times in the past there has been more than one in a generation. It is said there was a woman in the Ice Valley who was the same age as Hanna and she was just as terrible a creature. And the clan and kin are growing again after having been reduced to so few. For a time there was only Grandpapa Tengel, my mother and Tengel's niece Sol. That was at the time when the Ice People's valley was destroyed and everybody, except for Tengel's small family, was put to death. Now our numbers are growing again, and there will be more to come.' She stopped and pondered her words carefully before continuing. 'There just is one other thing you ought to know about us, Alexander. The women of the Ice People bear few children. Uncle Are was exceptional with his three sons – nothing like that had ever happened before. I have already had one child, so in all probability this will be my last.'

Alexander could not find the words to answer her. He simply crossed to her chair and reached for her hand to squeeze it lovingly.

Cecilie sighed. 'Kin of the Ice People should never really be allowed to wed, that's the truth of the matter.'

'I beg to disagree,' he said quietly. 'I think they are to be cherished and sought after for all their wonderful qualities – their courage, compassion for others and their tolerance …'

She waved a hand and stopped him in midstream. 'Thank you, but I was not fishing for compliments.'

'I know you would not do that.'

'I know this is tempting fate,' Cecilie was thinking, 'and whatever this child may or may not be, it will be made very welcome. But dear Lord, please let it be a boy – for Alexander's sake and for the family name of Paladin!' She seethed at the weight of responsibility providence had decided to burden her with. 'But what matter if it is a girl. She shall still have all my love and never be made to feel unwelcome. She will be worth much more than …'

Alexander's voice suddenly interrupted her unruly thoughts. 'There are already three small boys in your family, so it is most likely that you will have another …'

Cecilie's cheeks reddened. 'Another?'

Alexander took a sharp breath – he could have kicked himself. 'Forgive me! I had completely forgotten that you did not know. The child you lost would have been a male. I am so sorry.'

Because of her condition, Cecilie was far more emotional than she would usually have been and she burst into floods of tears.

'Are you still really distressed at losing that child?' he asked gently.

She had begun to regain her composure. 'No, not really, but what you said just then made him seem suddenly more real. A baby boy? My distress is for him – the result of a relationship between two people who meant nothing to each

257

other. And he never lived to see a moment of sunshine, poor little thing!'

'I understand how you must feel, my dearest friend. But let us look at it another way. If we already had a son, no matter that I had accepted him as my own, and you gave birth to another now – well, we might have been faced with a dilemma over who would be the rightful heir.'

She smiled ruefully and gave a little nod. 'I understand. It wouldn't have been fair to the second son, because he would have been *your* firstborn, Alexander.'

'Indeed, and likewise if son number two had been left everything, it would have been unfair to his elder brother.'

Cecilie's voice was suddenly calmer and brighter. 'Yes, then probably it was all for the best – if this one is a boy!'

'Let us put that in God's hands,' he replied.

His piety always surprised her because, where Alexander Paladin was concerned, the Good Lord had not always been so considerate. She wondered about his faith and deepest beliefs, but as she did so, something else of a very contrary nature flashed unbidden into her mind and she chuckled.

'This might sound uncanny, even blasphemous, Alexander, but you know that I believe the seed for this child was sown when we were in the forest at Gråstensholm.'

Alexander nodded but said nothing.

'And do you remember that I also had a strange overpowering sense then that someone or something was there with us?'

Alexander gave her a questioning, slightly bemused look. 'It was not Kolgrim, my dear, that I am sure of. He was with Tarjei until late into the afternoon.'

'No, of course not. But I cannot really explain it. At the time I had such strong feelings of Sol, the witch. As if she must have been there at that exact spot a long time ago – long before us, Alexander.'

'Was it as if the place was bewitched? Is that what you sensed?'

'Or blessed, for it is there I was made with child.'

'Yes, that is true,' he answered.

Cecilie did not want say any more to him, but her unspoken thoughts were very troubling. 'What sort of a child will it be if a witch of the Ice People was watching at the moment of conception?' she asked herself. 'And even worse, a witch guided by Hanna to preserve all the evil that the Ice People possess. It does not bode well.'

She looked into Alexander's eyes and could see that his thoughts mirrored her own. With a concerned frown, he moved round to stand behind his wife's chair and leaned down to put his arms round her, as though he were protecting her from some unseen attack. But how, he reflected as he did so, would he be able to protect her from a danger that may already lie within?

* * * *

On a cold dark February night in the year of Our Lord 1628, a carriage left Gabrielshus with all the speed the driver could muster. It was on its way to fetch the midwife and surgeon and there was not a minute to waste. Infants had a habit of choosing to come into the world at night, and often as agonisingly as they could. This thought had never been far from the minds of Alexander and Cecilie, and their emotions had become numbed from the constant shift between confidence and anxiety.

The worst nightmare for any woman of the Ice People was that they should give birth to one of the accursed ones. So it was for Cecilie, and to make matters worse, she appeared to be carrying a large baby. They had talked over many things in this connection and one outcome was that she had forbidden Alexander to be present when her time came.

'Call me shy or prudish, what you will,' she had told him, 'but I definitely prefer to do this on my own – well, almost on my own!'

One of the older experienced servants waited anxiously with her until the midwife arrived. Cecilie had already caused consternation by having several false alarms, but this time there was no mistake. Several more hours, however, elapsed before the child was born, by which time the surgeon was also at her bedside – and at the outset, he did not like what he saw.

A little later, Alexander heard Cecilie's sudden scream of agony. She had not cried out at all until then – bravely enduring all the discomfort and pain through gritted teeth. But now she had become quiet again and he could hear only the sound of hurried footsteps.

'Dear God,' he prayed silently. 'Dear God!'

And then, like a rusted wheel being spun faster and faster on its axle, the sound of a pitiful squeak reached his ears. His heart started to beat harder. 'That's my child!' he thought. 'A true Paladin! How extraordinary that I – the most worthless and despised of all people – should be part of this!'

He cast his mind back to when Cecilie had confided to him her suspicion she was expecting his child – *their* child. He had almost not believed her, convincing himself that because of his earlier 'disposition', and more especially since he had been paralysed, he would never be able to father any children. But had it now happened at long last?

'Thank you, dear God, for that miracle, if this has happened,' he said inwardly. 'But ought I to go in yet? No, Cecilie forbade me. But it is all over now, isn't it? Why are they so quiet? There is seemingly no sound but the cry of the child. Lord, be merciful!'

His long wait finally ended when the door opened and the midwife came out. Very tenderly she placed a small swaddled bundle in his arms.

'Goodness, it's as light as a feather! Surely there is nothing inside?' he thought, in astonishment. Hesitating, he peered into the tightly wrapped bundle of cloth. The sight of a shock of black hair and a little dark red face rewarded his curiosity. Two incredibly tiny, perfect hands were gesturing to him.

'A baby Marquise, My Lord,' said the midwife. 'It is your daughter.'

Alexander swallowed to clear his throat. His daughter! A girl. He felt a slight sting of disappointment, but it was gone in an instant. He had already held this tiny life in his arms and felt the bond, the tenderness and the responsibility that he owed it. He was also filled with a wilder feeling of unrestrained affection and love. He laughed joyfully and his eyes were brimming with tears.

'Just think,' he said, 'how big Cecilie had grown and then there was only this little gem inside. What a lot of effort for such a tiny thing – but what a wonderful tiny thing she is! And it has all ended very well … '

He could not take his eyes off his newborn daughter. She looked utterly enchanting. Then he realised that the field surgeon had appeared in the doorway.

'Oh, no, my dear Marquis! I fear we are not finished quite yet. There is more to come!'

'What?'

'Come back in here, quickly please,' the surgeon urged the midwife. 'There is more to do.'

'Twins?' thought Alexander in amazement. 'Two baby girls!'

261

The midwife took the baby from him and hurried back to Cecilie. Alexander stood empty-handed, listening to the faint and distant whimpering of his daughter. He suddenly yearned, above all else, to hold her again. She was so quiet all the time I was holding her in my arms, he thought. Perhaps she felt safe with me, her father? He wanted so much to believe it was true.

Cecilie did not scream again, but he could hear her choking and moaning, and knew that something was happening. Then a second wailing cry joined the first. Both children were alive!

'Once again, dear God, Thank you!' Unable to wait in the anteroom another minute, he knocked on the door to their bedchamber.

'Wait just a minute, please!' ordered the midwife. Then after a while she called again: 'You may come in now!'

Alexander opened the door and entered the room. Cecilie's eyes sparkled as she saw him. The midwife and the surgeon were both smiling at him too. The birth of twins was always a special event. It was true that there were still some people who believed twins were all bewitched and would therefore kill the second-born at birth or leave it out to die, but this belief was only prevalent among the most superstitious and unenlightened of people.

'Twins?' exclaimed Alexander wonderingly. 'Are they twins? They are not at all alike! I thought twins always looked like two peas in a pod?'

'When they come from the same caul, this is indeed true,' said the surgeon. 'But that has not happened here.'

The second little sprite had shimmering, dark, reddish hair that lay in curls instead of sticking straight up like the firstborn's. The two babies did not share the same facial features either. But they were both fit and well and Alexander laughed helplessly and joyously.

'We had thought to name a daughter Gabriella, after my

unfortunate mother. But what shall we name the other one, my dearest? Lisa, after your mother Liv? Or Leonora?'

'I would imagine *he* would be most insulted, if we did,' said Cecilie with a smile. 'Leonard, perhaps, might be more appropriate.'

Alexander's chin dropped in astonishment; then a wide grin lit up his face. 'You mean – that we have a boy?'

'What else?' retorted Cecilie, as the new father of twins slumped joyously onto her bed. 'You always have to do everything with such thoroughness, Alexander! But thank you, anyway, for the sweetest of gifts!'

'It is you who deserve the greatest thanks, dearest,' he replied, and turning to the others he asked, 'We have done a fine thing, have we not?'

'Nothing could have been better, Your Grace,' answered the surgeon.

Without speaking, Cecilie and Alexander were sharing one silent thought: had Sol, the multifarious witch with her elusive laugh, been there at that enchanted woodland glade where his seed was sown? Had she played a delightful prank on them? Was it really possible she had somehow brought her influence to bear? It was no more than a passing thought, but as they confirmed to each other later, it did occur to them both simultaneously.

Now, apart from Trond, who had never had the opportunity to start a family, Tarjei was the only one of Tengel's grandchildren without an heir. And he seemed not to be in any hurry to marry.

* * * *

At Gråstensholm, a few days later, Liv called out excitedly to Kolgrim as he was playing in the front courtyard. 'Come quickly. Have you heard the news? Your beloved Aunt Cecilie has had twins – two small babies, a boy and a girl.'

'Oh, that's nice,' Kolgrim replied, panting from the exertion of running into the house. 'What are their names?'

'The girl is called Lisa Gabriella, after Alexander's mother and me. They found no suitable name with "D", after grandfather, Dag Christian, so they have named the boy Tancred Christoffer, because there are so many of the Ice People whose names begin with "T", after Tengel the Good.'

'Or Tengel the Evil,' said Kolgrim.

'Oh Kolgrim, that's not nice! Don't say that!'

'Who was I named after?'

Liv's momentary hesitation was not lost on him.

'After your Grandfather Christian. You can hear that can't you? Christian – Kolgrim. Won't it be fun when they come to visit and you can all play together?'

'Yes, Grandmama. Are they coming soon?'

'No, they are far too small.'

'Did Aunt Cecilie say hello to me?'

'Yes, of course she did! Look, here in my letter, it is written: "Say hello to my dear Kolgrim from Alexander and me!" You can see your letter "K" there, can't you? And there is Uncle Alexander's.'

'Nothing to Mattias?'

Liv didn't answer straight away. 'Uh, yes, but not in the same place.'

Kolgrim gave a curt nod. 'I am going outside again, Grandmama.'

'Yes – do not stay out too long and get cold. It isn't spring yet.'

How wonderful that those two half-brothers get on so well, she reflected, as she gave Kolgrim a quick hug. After he had gone outside again, she hurried in to see Yrja. Her eyes brightened when she saw little Mattias, now a cheery three-year-old, playing happily with his carved wooden horse. When he heard his Grandmama, he looked up with a smile so tender it would have warmed the heart of anyone alive.

Mattias is a strange little lad, she thought. Everyone always says, that no matter how difficult things are for them, they feel so much happier and brighter whenever they see the boy. Perhaps it is his personality itself that gives them back their belief in all the good that life can offer.

* * * *

Meanwhile Kolgrim had already climbed to the top of the hill behind Gråstensholm. He enjoyed going up there, to a place where he could look down on both farms from on high and feel he was master of the whole world. This was normally how it made him feel, but today his spirits were low. Other children might have said, 'Everything's gone wrong! It's all ruined!' But this was not Kolgrim's way. Instead he stood gazing out over the landscape with a faraway look in his eyes, before uttering a few words in a ritual whisper.

'The final bond is broken. There is nothing that binds me to them any more. I am free at last! Free!'

Then he turned and strode off, heading deeper into the forest. Finally he found a place where he stopped and made a fire with a flint and steel he had stolen from the kitchen wench. His eyes shimmered gold as he stared into the flames.

'So stupid,' he murmured aloud. 'They are all so stupid and easy to fool! Just look at them sweetly and they love you – and they also cease to be vigilant.'

As he spoke, Kolgrim broke a small twig into three pieces. Only he could see that they represented dolls, three child dolls – three infants. One by one, he threw them into the flames of the fire. Nobody had taught him to do this – it was instinct.

Resting on his haunches, he watched as each separate twig-child caught fire and burned. The little boy whom everybody saw as kind, mild and sensible grinned. It was a cold and hideous grin that, in an instant, changed Kolgrim's features back to the way they had been on the day he was born. Reflecting the flames, his eyes shone like the eyes of a ruthless predator, half-seen, stalking ominously at the edge of the forest on a black winter's night.

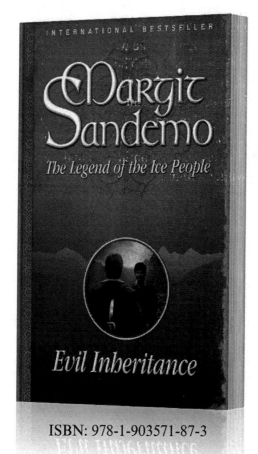

INTERNATIONAL BESTSELLER

Margit Sandemo

The Legend of the Ice People

Evil Inheritance

ISBN: 978-1-903571-87-3

Book 6 of The Legend of the Ice People series, Evil Inheritance, *is to be published on 4th December 2008*

Further Information

Publication for the first time in the English language of the novels of Margit Sandemo began with *Spellbound*. The first six novels of *The Legend of the Ice People* are being published monthly up to Christmas 2008 and further editions will appear throughout the following year.

The latest information about the new writing of Margit Sandemo and worldwide publication and other media plans are posted and updated on her new English-language website at www.margitsandemo.co.uk along with details of her public appearances and special reader offers and forums.

All current Tagman fiction titles are listed on our website www.tagmanpress.co.uk and can be ordered online. Tagman publications are also available direct by post from: The Tagman Press, Media House, Burrel Road, St Ives, Huntingdon, Cambridgeshire, United Kingdom PE27 3LE.

For details of prices and special discounts for multiple orders, phone 0845 644 4186, fax 0845 644 4187 or e-mail sales@tagmanpress.co.uk